THE CAST

ARETHUSA MONK—The reigning queen of regency romance has three admirers at her feet . . . will one of them die for love?

ANDREW McNASTER—They used to call him Andy McNasty. Now he's a virtuous innkeeper playing the part of a villain. Or is it the other way around?

CAROLUS BLEDSOE—He's the hero of the play but a devil with the ladies. Is it his vengeful ex-wife—or a jealous rival—who's trying to give the devil his due?

WILHEDRA THORBISHER-FREEP—She was the other woman in Bledsoe *vs.* Bledsoe—but she wonders who's kissing him now!

LEANDER HELLESPONT—Leader of the Scottsbeck Players, he has a show-stopper of a motive to want his rival dead.

Charlotte Macleod
WRITING AS
Alisa Craig

THE GRUB-AND-STAKERS PINCH A POKE

AVON BOOKS ◆ NEW YORK

THE GRUB-AND-STAKERS PINCH A POKE is an original publication of Avon Books. This work has never before appeared in book form. This work is a novel. Any similarity to actual persons or events is purely coincidental.

AVON BOOKS
A division of
The Hearst Corporation
105 Madison Avenue
New York, New York 10016

Copyright © 1988 by Alisa Craig
Published by arrangement with the author
Library of Congress Catalog Card Number: 88-91505
ISBN: 0-380-75538-6

First Avon Books Printing: August 1988

AVON TRADEMARK REG. U.S. PAT. OFF. AND IN OTHER COUNTRIES, MARCA REGISTRADA. HECHO EN U.S.A.

Printed in the U.S.A.

K–R 10 9 8 7 6 5 4 3 2 1

For the incomparable trio:
Barbara Mertz, Elizabeth Peters,
and the Sitt Hakim

THE SHOOTING OF DAN McGREW

A bunch of the boys were whooping it up in the Malamute
　　saloon;
The kid that handles the music-box was hitting a jag-time
　　tune;
Back of the bar, in a solo game, sat Dangerous Dan
　　McGrew,
And watching his luck was his light-o'-love, the lady
　　that's known as Lou.

When out of the night, which was fifty below, and into the
　　din and the glare,
There stumbled a miner fresh from the creeks, dog-dirty,
　　and loaded for bear.
He looked like a man with a foot in the grave and scarcely
　　the strength of a louse,
Yet he tilted a poke of dust on the bar, and he called for
　　drinks for the house.
There was none could place the stranger's face, though we
　　searched ourselves for a clue;
But we drank his health, and the last to drink was Dangerous
　　Dan McGrew.

There's men that somehow just grip your eyes, and hold
　　them hard like a spell;
And such was he, and he looked to me like a man who
　　had lived in hell;
With a face most hair, and the dreary stare of a dog whose
　　day is done,
As he watered the green stuff in his glass, and the drops
　　fell one by one.

Then I got to figgering who he was, and wondering what
he'd do,
And I turned my head—and there watching him was the
lady that's known as Lou.

His eyes went rubbering round the room, and he seemed in
a kind of daze.
Till at last that old piano fell in the way of his wandering
gaze.
The rag-time kid was having a drink; there was no one else
on the stool,
So the stranger stumbles across the room, and flops down
there like a fool.
In a buckskin shirt that was glazed with dirt he sat, and I
saw him sway;
Then he clutched the keys with his talon hands—my God!
but that man could play.

Were you ever out in the Great Alone, when the moon was
awful clear,
And the icy mountains hemmed you in with a silence you
most could *hear*;
With only the howl of a timber wolf, and you camped
there in the cold,
A half-dead thing in a stark, dead world, clean mad for the
muck called gold;
While high overhead, green, yellow and red, the North
Lights swept in bars?—
Then you've a hunch what the music meant . . . hunger
and night and the stars.
And hunger not of the belly kind, that's banished with
bacon and beans,
But the gnawing hunger of lonely men for a home and all
that it means;
For a fireside far from the cares that are, four walls and a
roof above;
But oh! so cramful of cosy joy, and crowned with a
woman's love—
A woman dearer than all the world, and true as Heaven is
true—
(God! how ghastly she looks through her rouge,—the lady
that's known as Lou.)

Then on a sudden the music changed, so soft that you
    scarce could hear;
But you felt that your life had been looted clean of all that
    it once held dear;
That someone had stolen the woman you loved; that her
    love was a devil's lie;
That your guts were gone, and the best for you was to
    crawl away and die.
'Twas the crowning cry of a heart's despair, and it thrilled
    you through and through—
"I guess I'll make it a spread misere," said Dangerous
    Dan McGrew.

The music almost died away . . . then it burst like a
    pent-up flood;
And it seemed to say, "Repay, repay," and my eyes were
    blind with blood.
The thought came back of an ancient wrong, and it stung
    like a frozen lash,
And the lust awoke to kill, to kill . . . then the music
    stopped with a crash,
And the stranger turned, and his eyes they burned in a
    most peculiar way;
In a buckskin shirt that was glazed with dirt he sat, and I
    saw him sway;
Then his lips went in in a kind of grin, and he spoke, and
    his voice was calm,
And "Boys," says he, "you don't know me, and none of
    you care a damn;
But I want to state, and my words are straight, and I'll bet
    my poke they're true,
That one of you is a hound of hell . . . and that one is Dan
    McGrew."

Then I ducked my head, and the lights went out, and two
    guns blazed in the dark,
And a woman screamed, and the lights went up, and two
    men lay stiff and stark.
Pitched on his head, and pumped full of lead, was Dangerous
    Dan McGrew,
While the man from the creeks lay clutched to the breast of
    the lady that's known as Lou.

These are the simple facts of the case, and I guess I ought
  to know.
They say that the stranger was crazed with "hooch," and
  I'm not denying it's so.
I'm not so wise as the lawyer guys, but strictly between us
  two—
The woman that kissed him and—pinched his poke—was
  the lady that's known as Lou.

Robert W. Service

Chapter 1

"What the heck do we need Sarah Bernhardt's Sunday bustle for?" demanded Zilla Trott.

"There's nothing here about Sarah Bernhardt's bustle," said Dittany Henbit Monk. As secretary to the trustees of the Aralia Polyphema Architrave Museum and also to the Grub-and-Stake Gardening and Roving Club into whose collective hands had fallen the task of managing the museum, Dittany had dealt with a wide range of correspondence. This letter opened up a new vista. "It just says theatrical memorabilia."

"Huh! Signed photographs of Ivor Novello and a lock of Rudy Vallee's hair, I'll bet." Hazel Munson was on a diet, therefore inclined to take the darker view.

"Oh, for Pete's sake have a cookie and quit grumping," said Minerva Oakes. "Rudy Vallee had gorgeous hair. Come on, Dittany. Let's hear the rest of the letter before we get down to the wrangling."

"Well, as I said, it's from Desdemona Portley on behalf of the Traveling Thespians. You know how hard she's worked to keep the troupe together, but things haven't been the same with them since Mum married Bert and went into the fashion eyewear business."

"I'll bet the fashion eyewear business hasn't been the same, either," said Dot Coskoff, who'd once played the former Mrs. Henbit's bosom friend in a souped-up production of *Anne of Green Gables*. "Skip Dessie's maunderings, she always did go on and on. What's the gist?"

1

"The gist is that Jenson Thorbisher-Freep and his daughter Wilhedra are trying to get up a drama festival over at Scottsbeck. They want to restore the old opera house and make it a center of cultural vibration for the citizens of Scottsbeck and surrounding communities of which, as Dessie points out in some detail, Lobelia Falls is one."

"As if we didn't know," sniffed Dot. "Cultural vibration sounds like a pretty shaky proposition to me. Is she trying to hit us up for a donation?"

"I expect she means vibrancy and not exactly a donation," Dittany replied. "She wants us to participate."

"Participate how?" Zilla shook her head till her thick, short gray hair stood out like a Sioux war bonnet, though in fact she was mostly Cree. "Are we supposed to dance in the chorus?"

"Why not?" chirped Minerva. "My varicose veins are no worse than Dessie's."

"And your teeth are a darn sight better," Zilla conceded loyally.

"Look," snarled Dittany. "Do you want to hear this or don't you?"

"Offhand I'd say no," snapped Hazel Munson, "but go ahead and get it over with. Desdemona Portley wants us to be in some play she's getting up for the Thorbisher-Freeps, is that it?"

"Not precisely, eh. The thing of it is, the Thorbisher-Freeps expect the different groups to produce their own plays. Dessie's asking us to write the play, paint the scenery, provide costumes and props, fill whatever parts the Traveling Thespians don't have enough actors for, and sell lemonade and cookies between the acts on behalf of the Opera House Fund."

"Anything else?"

"Nope, that seems to be it. The plum in the pudding is that whichever group puts on the best performance wins the Jenson Thorbisher-Freep collection of theatrical memorabilia."

"You already said that, and what's so plummy?" Zilla argued. "What would we do with a bunch of false whiskers and old theater programs?"

"We'd be expected to keep the collection intact and on permanent display either at the opera house or in some appropriate public building," Dittany explained. "Like for instance the Architrave."

"We do still have that little back bedroom over the kitchen to fill up," Minerva pointed out.

"Yes, but would that be the right kind of stuff to fill it with?" asked Hazel. "The Architrave's supposed to represent a typical Canadian house of the post-prairie settling period, you know."

"Couldn't it be the typical home of some Canadian who collected theatrical memorabilia?" Dittany argued. "Anyway, if we decide we don't want the collection, we can always let the opera house keep it."

"What do you mean we?" yelped Hazel. "You're not proposing we stick our necks out again?"

"We always do, don't we?" Dot Coskoff pointed out. "We did use to have a lot of fun at the Traveling Thespians, I must say."

"I didn't," said Dittany. "I always got stuck with the tiny toddler parts."

"That's because you were a tiny toddler at the time," Dot reminded her. Dittany was still roughly a quarter of a century younger than any of her fellow trustees, and indeed always would be unless one of them resigned from the board and somebody's daughter stepped in. Dot didn't go into all that, but merely added, "I suppose Dessie expects Arethusa to write the play."

Arethusa Monk, the one absent trustee, was renowned far and wide as a well-nigh indefatigable author of roguish regency romances. She'd been off queening it at the Moonlight and Roses convention in New York all the past week, but would be back tomorrow.

"Why can't Arethusa and Osbert write it together?" Minerva suggested amiably.

Dittany blanched at the mere thought. At this very moment, as she entertained her colleagues on tea and molasses cookies with crinkly edges around the kitchen table where they always tended to collect regardless of any previous alternative plans, she could hear her husband's typewriter galloping merrily down some far-off arroyo.

Osbert Reginald Monk, better known to his legions of clear-eyed, clean-cut readers as Lex Laramie, was by nature the mildest and sunniest young man any woman could want to be married to. Dittany herself, who was surely in a position to know, had often declared him a woolly baa-lamb with fur-lined booties on. She could think of only one thing that might turn her loving husband into a howling, ravening berserker; and that one thing would be to collaborate with his Aunt Arethusa on anything at all. The thought of having to ride herd on the pair of them while they turned out a full-length play gave Dittany the kind of feeling that Sergeant MacVicar, Lobelia Falls's dauntless defender of law and order, would describe as a cauld grue. She spoke her mind in no uncertain terms. Minerva only shrugged.

"Then Osbert had better hurry up and write the play himself before Arethusa gets back. I personally don't see why we shouldn't give Desdemona Portley a helping hand. She'll never get anywhere with that gang of deadheads she's working with now, and heaven knows they could use a little culture over at Scottsbeck. Besides, Mr. Glunck was saying only yesterday that it mightn't be a bad idea to get more variety into our exhibits."

After having made the spectacular mistake of hiring a curator with a wife,* the trustees had selected Mr. Glunck as his successor primarily because Mr. Glunck was a widower. Fortunately, he'd also turned out to be an able and likeable curator. The funding problem they'd faced in trying to run the Architrave had been solved by their selling one artifact so valuable that they could never have put it on exhibition without hopelessly expensive round-the-clock security. An expert replica kept its memory green, and a pamphlet describing the romantic way in which the museum had acquired the original was now on sale and bringing in a pleasant amount of added revenue.

What with one thing and another, the Architrave was

The Grub-and-Stakers Quilt a Bee.

gaining a reputation as one of Ontario's finer small museums and being mentioned in some of the more recent tourist guides. On the strength of what the Grub-and-Stakers had already accomplished, it wasn't too surprising that once the initial "Oh gosh, not again" feeling had abated, their chosen representatives had begun to think seriously about acquiring the Jenson Thorbisher-Freep collection, whatever it might consist of. That brought up an interesting question.

"I know the Thorbisher-Freeps live over in Scottsbeck, in that big green house with the chartreuse and canary trimmings between the bandstand and the burying ground, but who are they?" Dittany asked. "I mean, how come Jenson's collection is so important?"

Everybody looked at everybody else. Then Minerva exclaimed, "Wait a minute, eh. Wasn't there a piece about him in the *Scottsbeck Sunday Semaphore* a while back?"

"That's right," Zilla confirmed. "My lifelong love affair with the stage, he called it. Jenson wanted to be an actor, but he was too rich to tread the boards professionally because his family owned all those copper mines. So he built a private theater and put on amateur performances. When he got sick of that, he went to New York to be an angel."

Dot Coskoff sniffed. "I suppose he figured they could use a few down there."

"I don't mean the harp-and-halo kind. Freep was one of those angels who cough up money to put on big shows because they're sweet on the leading lady. He married an actress or two or three, then I expect he got smart and realized they were just playing him for a sucker. Anyway, he quit angeling and just traveled around going to different theaters. But he never went overseas because he's scared of flying and gets seasick on a ship. Anyway, Freep claimed to know all the big stars from 'way back, so maybe this collection amounts to something, after all. I wish I'd kept that paper, but how was I to know?"

"We could go over to the Scottsbeck library and look it up," said Hazel. "They keep them all on file."

"Or I could phone Dessie and try to get a little sense out of her," Dot offered.

"Why don't we just call up this Freep man and ask him?" Minerva suggested.

Dittany sighed. "Why don't you all button up and let me finish this letter? Where was I? Oh yes the play has to be about some aspect of Canadian life in an earlier time. What does he mean by an earlier time, I wonder?"

"When they were putting the railroad through?" Hazel's great-grandfather had run the first 4-4-0 engine through Kicking Horse Pass.

"And slaughtering the buffalo," snorted Zilla, her Indian blood beginning to simmer as it often did. "There's a plot for you."

"We can't slaughter a stageful of buffalo," Dittany objected, "even if we could get hold of any."

"We might tie horns and a hump on that so-called dog of yours. Ethel's probably part buffalo anyway, from the look of her."

She might well be, but Dittany was not going to stand for any rude levity about the quasi-canine partner of her youthful joys and sorrows. "Ethel is not going to be a buffalo, and that's final. Let's see if Osbert has any ideas."

No real necromancy was involved in Osbert's appearing as she uttered his name. The psychic bond between the Monks was strong and besides, he'd quit pounding his typewriter a moment ago. Osbert's cowlick was sticking straight up and his shirttail hung half out of his trousers. It must have been a rough afternoon around the old corral.

"Howdy, ladies," was his greeting. "Any tea left in the pot, pardner?"

"Haul up an' set, Old Paint." Dittany couldn't resist putting out a loving hand to smooth down his cowlick. "We were just talking about you."

"Oh?" Baa-lamb though he might be, Osbert had learned to be wary of such casual wifely remarks. "Dittany, if it's about moving those fifty-seven folding chairs back to the library meeting room—"

"No, dear." That had been the time the Boy Scouts were supposed to help out and their leader, who was in love with a sergeant in the Salvation Army, had gone off with her to prayer meeting and forgotten to let the troop know they had a good deed to do.

"Or running the slide projector—"

That had been when somebody stacked the slide holders wrong side up before the lecture and Osbert hadn't noticed quite soon enough. Before he could add to his litany of objections, Dittany intervened.

"Darling, you know I promised never to ask you to do any of those things again. We simply want you to write a play."

"Oh. Then I suppose I—"

Osbert had picked up one of the few remaining molasses cookies and begun to bite the crinkles off its edges. Now he reared back and glared at the cookie as if it had retaliated by taking a snap at him. "Did you say write a play?"

"It's either you or Arethusa, dear. Unless you'd prefer to work as a team?"

Osbert quit glaring at the cookie and glared at his wife instead. "Dittany, are you trying to be funny?"

"No, precious. I'm simply trying to lead up gently to the fact that we need a play written rather quickly so that we can win the Jenson Thorbisher-Freep collection for the Architrave."

Osbert turned his attention back to the cookie. "What kind of play?"

"A play about earlier times in Canada."

"Which earlier times?"

"Any earlier times, I guess. It's supposed to capture the dauntless spirit of our hardy forebears. At least that's what she's got written here."

"Who has?"

"Desdemona Portley, an old friend of my mother's. She's trying to revive the Traveling Thespians."

"Why?"

"So they can compete in a drama festival over at Scottsbeck. Mr. Thorbisher-Freep's offering his collection as bait so he can use the ticket money to renovate the old opera house into a center of culture."

"What makes him think Scottsbeck wants culture? They've already got six barrooms and a high-class cocktail lounge."

"That's why they need culture, darling, so everybody won't just sit around guzzling beer."

"They don't just sit around guzzling beer. They also guzzle whiskey, gin, vodka, rum, or peppermint schnapps, as the case may be. And they carry on profound intellectual discussions."

"About what?"

"Hockey, mostly. Were you planning to pour me some tea?"

"Osbert Monk, answer me. Are you planing to write us a play? Or are you going to let Arethusa write it, and find yourself being forced to act the role of a snuff-sniffing, garter-stapping regency buck from Saskatoon?"

"Dittany, you jest!"

"Here's your tea, sweetheart. Finish your cookie and mull it over."

Since Minerva, Zilla, Dot, Hazel, and the wife of his bosom were all eyeing him with the breathless expectancy of spectators at a balloon ascension, Osbert did not enjoy his tea. Rather he started out not enjoying it. Then the dreamy expression Dittany had come to know and respect stole over his comely features. His hazel eyes gazed not upon her, not upon the cookie, but toward some far horizon. The cowlick so recently smoothed down popped up again. He finished his cookie, helped himself to another, and began biting off the crinkles with confidence and determination.

"'A bunch of the boys were whooping it up in the Malamute saloon,'" he murmured somewhat crumbily.

"Hasn't something along those lines already been done?" Dot Coskoff ventured.

"That's exactly the point." Osbert's eyes were now alight, his blondish cowlick rampant. "We know what happened to Dan McGrew, but why? Who was that miner fresh from the creeks, dog-dirty and loaded for bear? How did he know Dan McGrew was a hound of hell, when they hadn't even been introduced? Why did the lady known as Lou kiss him as he died?"

"And pinch his poke," cried Dittany, all agog at this fresh insight into the stirring annals of Canadian literature. "More tea, darling?"

"Please, darling. Yes, ladies, the shooting of Dan McGrew is one of the great unsolved mysteries of the Yukon Territory. And we, by gum, are going to solve it."

Chapter 2

Now that he'd got the bit between his teeth, Osbert took off like a one-man stampede. By feminine wiles, Dittany succeeded in getting him to stop for a bite of supper, but he was back to his typewriter at a brisk canter as soon as his plate was empty. He accepted a cup of cocoa at bedtime, but went on typing with one hand even as he quaffed the sustaining beverage.

"Go ahead up, darling," he said, giving his wife a cocoa-flavored kiss. "I'll be along."

But he wasn't. Dittany fell asleep to the clicking of the keys. Come morning, she was relieved to awaken with the head she loved to pat on the pillow beside her. Two heads, in fact. Ethel had sauntered in to drop a hint about breakfast. Dittany strove to quell the whining and tail-thumping on humanitarian grounds.

"Shh," she whispered. "Daddy needs his rest."

But Daddy was in no resting mood. Dittany had barely got the dog food into the basin and the tea into the pot when Osbert came leaping and bounding down the stairs like a particularly sprightly young mountain goat, grabbed a bundle of semi-legible pages off his typewriter stand, and hurtled into the kitchen.

"What do you think of my play, dear?"

"I'll know better when I've read it," Dittany replied. "You don't mean to tell me you've finished the whole thing?"

"Well, not exactly finished, but the rough draft will give you a general idea. Shall I pour the tea?"

"Do. And you might butter the muffins while you're about it."

Dittany could see she wouldn't be allowed to do anything else until she'd dealt with the latest flare-up of Osbert's inspirational fires. She was a fast reader, but not quick enough to suit Osbert.

"Notice how I build up suspense about the miner, dear?" he urged. "I never call him by name."

"Not even in front of his loving wife and tiny golden-haired daughter? I never knew he had a family."

"I don't suppose anybody did until now, except maybe Robert W. Service; and he never said. You understand, darling, we've got to probe deep into the background to grasp the complexity of the characterizations. Besides," Osbert admitted, "the poem as it stands wouldn't stretch to more than a five-minute skit. So anyway, I'm starting back in the halcyon days when he's head feedbag man on the horsecars."

"What's so halcyon about feedbags?"

"Oh, his is actually a sort of junior executive position. He has to make sure all the feedbags are kept in perfect munching order, he's responsible for oat procurement, and a lot of important stuff. He also makes sure every horse on the line gets a carrot with its breakfast, for the vitamins."

"Darling, I'm not sure they had vitamins in those days," Dittany objected. "I mean I don't know whether they knew they did."

"Ah, but the miner—I mean the feedbag man who becomes the miner—is a man ahead of his time. He hypothesizes vitamins. Anyway, all is serene on page one in the cozy flat where he lives with his loving wife and tiny tot, whom he's teaching to play the piano. He's a gifted pianist himself, though of course his heart is in the feedbags. I'm calling the daughter Evangeline. The wife, of course, is Louisa."

"Darling, you don't mean—"

Osbert nodded his head sadly. "I'm afraid that's the way it has to be, dear. Louisa is more to be pitied than censured, though. We make that plain as the gripping drama unfolds.''

"That's a load off my mind." Dittany took a bite of her muffin. "So how do you manage the unfoldment?"

"I start by revealing that the feedbag man has a hated rival who's after his job. The rival stages an oat robbery and lays the blame on the feedbag man."

"How dastardly!"

"Oh, it's all that and then some," Osbert agreed. "The boss, who's none other than Dan McGrew, fires the feedbag man and blackens his reputation so that nobody else will hire him. This is before unemployment insurance, remember, so the family's financial situation soon becomes desperate. One dark and stormy night, the ex-feedbag man scrapes together what money he has and leaves it in a pathetic little heap on the washstand, along with a note explaining that he's going to the Yukon to seek his fortune in the gold fields and will return to his loved ones as soon as he's panned out his pile.''

"How brave, and how sad," sighed Dittany.

"Cheer up, darling, it gets worse. McGrew, who has long lusted in his black heart after the beauteous Louisa, starts putting the moves on. Needless to say, Louisa spurns his caddish advances, so he has to resort to sinister wiles."

"He would." Dittany fluttered a few more pages. "He sounds to me like just the type."

"Oh, McGrew's a Grade A rotter, no question about that. Do you know what he does next?"

Dittany might have taken a shrewd guess, but she wasn't about to stem the flow of Osbert's creative juices. "No dear, what?"

"He sells his horsecar business to the hated rival, who has by now repented of his wickedness and vows henceforth to make sure the horses get their daily carrots, which he had quit giving them under McGrew's evil influence. Then McGrew promises Louisa he'll take her to the Yukon to find her beloved husband.''

"And she falls for this fiendish ruse?"

"Consider her position, darling. She's spent her pittance to buy bread and milk for her sweet little daughter. They've had to sell Evangeline's piano and the landlady's threaten-

ing to turn them out in the snow. I thought Zilla Trott
might be good as the landlady. It's a cameo role but one
Zilla could really sink her teeth into. So anyway, Louisa
unravels her best flannel petticoat to knit Evangeline a
warm cap and mittens, and off they go to the Yukon.''

"Osbert," cried Dittany, "I never fully realized the
depth of your creative genius. This positively tears at the
heartstrings.''

"Do you really think so, darling?" Osbert's self-satisfied
smirk indicated that he thought so, too. "So that's the first
scene. Or maybe the first and second. Don't you think it
might be a fine dramatic touch to drop the curtain after the
feedbag man writes his pathetic note, kisses his fair wife
and winsome wee one as they sleep, and staggers off,
grief-stricken but resolute, into the night?''

"Terrific, darling. And you could begin the second
scene with the as yet unrepentant rival taunting the poor,
tired horses by eating a carrot in front of them and not
giving them any.''

"I'm not quite sure we ought to bring in the horses,
precious. I've got to shove in all that attempted seduction
business, remember, and the landlady giving Louisa and
Evangeline the heave-ho and McGrew twirling his big
black mustache in a villainous and lustful manner while he
promises to take them to the Yukon. Then there's the
gripping moment while they're packing up their few remaining bits and pieces and saying good-bye to the landlady's cat.''

"Why the landlady's cat? Couldn't they have a faithful
dog who's their one stay and comfort throughout their
tragic ordeal?''

"You mean Ethel?" Osbert pondered. "I was sort of
planning to powder her fur and use her for a polar bear
when we get to the Yukon. But your idea's better, darling.
The feedbag man can shake Ethel's paw in the parting
scene and have a wrenching little chat with her about
guarding his loved ones while he slogs through the frozen
wastes in quest of the precious metal that will restore their
ruined fortunes. Only mightn't Ethel bite Dan McGrew
while he's striving to force his unwelcome attentions on
Louisa?''

"She won't realize what Dan's up to because she has such a guileless, trusting nature. Ethel's not terribly b-r-i-g-h-t about some things, you have to admit."

Dittany spelled out the word because Ethel happened to be taking a postprandial snooze under their feet at this very moment, and she wouldn't for anything have hurt the stay and comfort's feelings.

"That's true enough," Osbert conceded. "Any dog that could manage to fall in love with a—"

"Shh. Don't reopen old wounds."

They'd gone through a painful month or so last summer when Ethel had formed an ill-conceived and unreciprocated *tendresse* for a woodchuck. That was all behind her now and best forgotten.

"So what happens next to Lousia and Evangeline?" Dittany went on briskly. "Do you show them riding in the train or the oxcart or whatever?"

"No, we flash directly to the Malamute saloon, of which Dan McGrew is now the proprietor. He's seated stage left, rear, cheating himself at solitaire. Watching him is the feedbag man's wife, still chaste and loyal but gaudily painted and bedizened and contemptuously referred to as Lou by the roistering miners clustered about the bar. And dear little Evangeline, the erstwhile darling of her vanished father's heart, whom he may even now be envisioning in their once happy home playing 'I'll Be With You When the Roses Bloom Again' is perched at the tinpanny old piano, hitting a jag-time tune."

"She's the kid that handles the music box!" cried Dittany. "Osbert dearest, is there no limit to your powers of invention?"

"There hadn't better be, pardner," Osbert replied soberly, "or you may wind up rattling the music box over at Andy McNaster's inn."

Dittany started, and looked up at the big old schoolhouse clock that hung since long before she could remember over the black iron stove. "Speaking of that moderately unpleasant subject, dearest, what time are we supposed to pick up your Aunt Arethusa?"

Dittany's question was less irrelevant than might appear. Ever since the previous August, and it was now the succeeding December, the once most hated man in Lobelia Falls had been laying siege to Arethusa Monk's affections. So far McNaster had made little headway and that little only because Arethusa, after her long steeping in the field of roguish regency romance, was a sucker for a reformed rake.

Andrew McNaster did seem to be sincere in his efforts to clean up his act, as Desdemona Portley might have expressed it. He was still showering endless benefactions in the way of free carpentry and plumbing repairs on the Aralia Polyphema Architrave Museum. According to informed sources like Roger Munson, who always knew everything, Andy had quit cutting corners in both his contracting business and his innkeeping and was running both enterprises in strict conformity with every code and regulation he could find to conform to.

Whether anybody in Lobelia Falls believed McNaster had actually turned over a new leaf or was merely laying down a smoke screen to cover some piece of chicanery even more devious and dire than his previous coups depended on how seriously the townsfolk took their personal commitments to peace on earth and goodwill toward men. Osbert at this juncture was not disposed to pass judgment on his aunt's unlikely swain one way or the other. He was merely looking stricken.

"Dittany, did you have to bring up Aunt Arethusa just when I'm in the midst of writing my first play?"

"But you have the plot all worked out, dearest. All you have to do now is get the feedbag man into the saloon and hold the shootout."

"You talk as if it were a mere bagatelle. Don't you realize creative writing is the hardest work there is?"

"Yes, love," said Dittany, "you've told me lots of times. That's why I think you ought to take a break. Would you mind looking in your little notebook and seeing what flight Arethusa's coming in on? You wrote it down when we took her to the airport, remember?"

"But if I tell you when she's coming, you'll start agitating to meet the plane," Osbert protested.

"You did promise we'd pick her up," his wife reminded him.

"That was when I was temporarily dazzled by the prospect of being rid of her for a week. Promises made in a state of euphoric delirium don't count."

"All right, dear," she said. "If you really don't want to, I'll go myself."

"Drive alone for hours and hours along a lonely road on a dark and gloomy night with a blizzard coming on?" he howled. "Not by a jugful you won't."

"Darling, it's ten o'clock in the morning and clear as a bell. The highway's dry, the airport's precisely two hours and three minutes away, and we haven't seen a snowflake for a week."

"Then the weather's due for a change and you're not going without me. That's final."

"But we can't leave Arethusa stranded."

"In my opinion, it's the only sensible thing to do."

Of course Osbert didn't mean that. After a certain amount of searching for his notebook, which turned up at last in the pocket of his beaded buckskin vest, he found the page where he'd written down that his aunt's plane was due in at thirteen minutes past one o'clock, and even squandered a long distance call to make sure the flight was on time. It probably wouldn't be, but there wasn't much he could do about that.

There wasn't all that much time to get ready, either. Dittany put on her new blue-green suit that matched her blue-green eyes, her camel-hair coat and beret that went so well with her blond-brown hair, and the high-heeled boots she never got to wear much around Lobelia Falls because Lobelia Falls wasn't that kind of place. Osbert would have liked to wear the Stetson hat and cowboy boots Arethusa hated; but they weren't comfortable to drive in so he settled for his clomping-around boots, his buckskin jacket with the six-inch thrums, and a multicolored Laplander hat that came up to little horns fore and aft.

"I wish I had time to grow a beard," he said fretfully.

"You can grow a beard tomorrow." Dittany straightened his horns for him. "There, you look just lovely. We really ought to get started. Have you any money in case Arethusa wants lunch? She'll be starved after that long flight, don't you think? Or will they have fed her on the plane?''

"She'll be hungry anyway," snarled Osbert. "She's always hungry. Come on, Ethel, let's find something smelly for you to roll in. Then you can sit next to dear old Auntie.''

"Ethel, you know better even if Daddy doesn't," Dittany chided. "Wipe your paws before you get into the car, that's a good girl. Do you want to drive, Osbert, or would you rather curl up in the back seat and have a good cry?''

"Oh, I'll do it. I don't know why people go around saying it's always the woman who suffers.'' He flung himself into the driver's seat, untangled his car keys from his thrums, and started the motor.

The Monks had a brand-new ranch wagon, purchased less than two weeks ago to celebrate Osbert's having sold a book to the movies. *Maverick Malamute* (to be released as *Pulsing Passion*) was a gripping tale of the frozen north in which Ethel, thinly disguised as a dauntless sled dog, rounded up a gang of yak rustlers virtually single-pawed after her temporarily snowblind master fell into a seal hole and froze his mukluks.

She'd rescued him and nursed him through the crisis, of course, but he was still convalescing on ptarmigan soup when the rustlers happened along and took advantage of his weakened condition, little recking what sort of dog they were up against. The movie producer was planning to replace the malamute with a trick poodle, turn the hero into a heroine, switch the setting to Palm Springs, and substitute alpacas for the yaks, but Osbert had been solemnly assured that the basic thrust of his story would be meticulously retained.

Anyway, they hadn't chosen the ranch wagon out of any illusion that the Henbit-Monk homestead on Applewood Avenue resembled the old Bar-None, but simply because the wagon had plenty of room in back for Ethel to stretch out and be comfortable. She probably enjoyed her ride to the airport more than either of her companions did. Osbert chafed to be back at his typewriter shooting it out with Dan McGrew, and Dittany was filled with a dire foreboding as to what Arethusa was going to think of having been committed in absentia to the Scottsbeck drama festival. Since neither of them felt like talking, they turned on the car radio to a station that played mostly bagpipe music and skirled into the airport to the poignant strains of "Macrimmon's Lament," which seemed appropriate enough.

After a fair amount of sorting out, they located the gate where Arethusa's plane was alleged to be coming in, and stood around. Other people were standing around, too. Lost in their own thoughts, Dittany and Osbert didn't pay much attention to their co-standees, but Ethel did. She checked them over one by one, then she growled. This was unlike Ethel, who usually had a wag and a whoofle for just about anybody. Startled, Dittany took a firmer grip on her leash and glanced around to ascertain what ill-bred child had taken a notion to swing on the nice doggie's tail.

Chapter 3

There was no child. There was, however, a large, red-cheeked man running a little to flesh. His black hair was slicked down, no doubt with some expensive he-man slickum. His blue overcoat was brushed to a fare-thee-well, his boots positively glittered. His arms were fully occupied with a huge bouquet of white chrysanthemums and what could only be a two-kilogram box of expensive chocolates. The box was covered in gold paper and had a multi-looped red bow on it that he was trying hard not to squash. When he caught Dittany's eye, he gave her a nervous smile.

She smiled nervously back and gave Osbert a surreptitious nudge. "Don't look now, darling, but guess who's here."

"Why shouldn't I look if I choose to?" Osbert was still cherishing his snit.

"Because your jaw would drop."

"I could pick it up." Suddenly Osbert's lips twitched upward in a knowing little grin. "Darling, you don't mean it's the lovesick swain?"

"Don't I, though? Andy's got a bunch of flowers with him that would choke a horse."

"He must have stopped on his way and robbed a cemetery."

"And a big box of fancy chocolates."

"Snatched from an infant in its pram, no doubt. I wish

19

Andy McNaster would quit chasing Aunt Arethusa. Or else catch her and take her far, far away," Osbert amended.

"He wouldn't," Dittany pointed out. "He'd move into her house and inveigle her into deeding it over to him."

"And they'd both invite themselves to supper at our house five nights a week." Osbert clenched his jaw, perhaps to keep it from dropping. "I'd better mosey on over and tell him we've just got word Aunt Arethusa's developed a virulent case of measles on the plane and will be oozing germs from every pore by the time she gets off. No, dad-drat it, that wouldn't do any good. Andy's so besotted he'd insist on catching them and sharing her tragic fate. Like what's-her-name being walled up in the tomb with that soldier she'd been going around with. Would you let yourself be walled up with me, darling?"

"They don't wall you up for measles," Dittany objected. "They just make you keep the blinds down and not read Peter Rabbit for fear you'll strain your eyes. At least that's what Gram Henbit did when I had them. It was right after my fourth birthday. Look, people are starting to come off the plane. Can you spot Arethusa?"

Osbert, being so much the taller of the two, always handled the family neck-craning. He stood with his chin up, his mouth set in a thin, resolute line, and his eyes bravely fixed on the living stream of incomers. Dittany in turn gazed up at him, and was pleasantly surprised to see his lips return to their upward curve. Darling Osbert! For all his snapping and snarling, he did after all cherish a soft spot for his celebrated though often exasperating aunt.

But that wouldn't be why Osbert was now grinning like a catfish. As Arethusa broke out of the pack and surged up the ramp, Dittany could see that she had an orchid corsage about the size of a sofa pillow pinned to the front of her billowing purple cloak and her arm linked to that of a personable gray-haired man almost as tall as she. Andrew McNaster, who'd spied her and begun to strain forward like a greyhound after a rabbit, froze. His lips formed a syllable that might have been "You!" or "Oo!" but was more likely "Who?"

That was what both Dittany and Osbert wanted to know and indeed could easily step forward and find out. At the moment, though, they were riveted by the tableau before them.

"He's suffering," Dittany murmured, surprised by the wave of compassion that swept over her. Even Ethel had stopped growling at McNaster and was whining in sympathy. She knew how Andy felt. She'd been through it with the woodchuck.

Arethusa Monk was not the reigning queen of regency romance without knowing how to handle her beaux. She disengaged herself from the stranger and held out both purple-gloved hands, causing the large leather handbag she was carrying to swing dangerously close to the red bow Andy had been striving to preserve in its pristine splendor.

"Zounds, Mr. McNaster, do mine eyes see aright? Prithee, what brings you here?"

McNaster stammered something to the effect that he'd thought she might need a ride home. Then he remembered his tributes and thrust them forward. "I brought you a little remembrance, Miss Monk."

Arethusa accepted the armload with a swooping curtsey and a smile that caused McNaster's knees visibly to wobble. "La, sir, you are a veritable *preux chevalier*. Actually, my mannerless lout of a nephew was supposed to—oh, there you are, Osbert. Come here, you caitiff knave."

"Go ahead," hissed Dittany. "We'll support you."

For once her urging was redundant. Osbert was just as curious as she to meet his aunt's new acquaintance. He greeted her cheerily.

"Hi, Aunt Arethusa, how's the rheumatics? Had any trouble with that spavined hock this trip?"

"Oafish jocosity, i' faith. You should have been exposed on a barren hillside at birth. Hello, Dittany. In case you were planning to file for divorce, I've brought you a lawyer. At least I had one a moment ago."

She peered from under her vast lilac velvet hat with the artificial bird of paradise on it and located her recent escort standing a modest two paces rear right. "My unfortunate niece-in-law, Dittany Henbit Monk, may I present Carolus Bledsoe, Esquire?"

"How do you do, Mr. Bledsoe?" Dittany replied politely. "And this is my beloved husband, Osbert, whom I have no intention of divorcing, and our dog, Ethel. And our local innkeeper, Mr. Andrew McNaster," she added, remembering Ethel and the woodchuck.

Osbert held out his hand, Ethel her paw. Andrew McNaster clenched his now disburdened fists. Carolus Bledsoe, Esquire, shook the hand and the paw and ignored the fist, acknowledging his introduction to the innkeeper with a decidedly stiff nod. McNaster's nod was even stiffer. This was the kind of moment when everybody wishes he were somewhere else except Arethusa Monk, who was loving it.

"Ecod, Mr. McNaster, since you've driven all this way to accord me welcome, I am right fain to ride back with you. Mr. Bledsoe has his own conveyance, he informed me."

"I was hoping I could persuade your aunt to share it," Bledsoe told Dittany with a rueful smile.

He had a voice like a well-brandied fruitcake, she thought. Where had she heard it before? Maybe he'd been on the news. Lawyers were always giving interviews about why their clients ought to be pardoned for having done whatever they did.

Osbert had no thought for Carolus Bledsoe's shattered hope. "Where are your luggage checks, Aunt Arethusa?" he demanded.

"Here. Somewhere." Arethusa gave McNaster back his candy and flowers to hold while she explored the dark caverns of her handbag and emerged at last triumphant. "There you are, churl. You can pick up my cases and follow along behind. We'll meet at suppertime."

"Where, for instance?" Osbert snarled.

"At the inn." Andrew McNaster had somehow come out on top in this encounter and was clearly eager to consolidate his position.

"I regret," Carolus Bledsoe was beginning when the sudden change of expression on his handsome middle-aged face made it plain he was only warming up for some real in-depth regretting.

An older man with glistening white hair, a black homburg, a silver-headed cane, and a cape much like Arethusa's, only black and without orchids, was bearing down on the party. Accompanying him was a less handsome, less elderly woman who looked enough like him to be his daughter and, as events transpired, was. They were smiling and waving.

"Ah, Carolus." The old man's voice was even fruitier than Bledsoe's. "We were afraid we might have missed you. We got held up."

"We wanted to surprise you," the not so elderly woman added with a baleful glance at Arethusa's hat.

She herself was wearing an uninspired though no doubt costly brown mink beret to match her brown mink coat and the brown mink tops of the brown suede boots that went with her brown suede gloves and brown suede bag. Her eyes were brown, too. But Arethusa's were much browner, and it was into Arethusa's that Carolus Bledsoe was gazing even as he bestowed the obviously expected salute on the other woman's frost-nipped cheek.

"This is indeed a surprise," he replied, and nobody questioned his sincerity. "Ah—Miss Wilhedra Thorbisher-Freep and Mr. Jenson Thorbisher-Freep, may I present Miss Arethusa Monk and Mr. and Mrs. Osbert Monk and their dog, Ethel?"

"And Mr. Andrew McNaster, our local innkeeper," Dittany added briskly. "We're glad to meet you, Mr. Thorbisher-Freep, because the trustees want to know what's in your collection."

"The trustees?" Jenson Thorbisher-Freep appeared taken aback by Dittany's direct approach, as people often tended to be.

"Of the Aralia Polyphema Architrave Museum in Lobelia Falls," she amplified, amazed that so well-traveled a man wouldn't know. "Will it do for us, or won't it?"

Wilhedra Thorbisher-Freep emitted an amused little titter. "I can't imagine my father's collection of theatrical memorabilia wouldn't do, as you so quaintly put it, for any museum in the civilized world. But I'm afraid it isn't for sale, Mrs. Monk, assuming there'd be money enough in Lobelia Falls to buy it."

Now it was Andrew McNaster's turn to emit an amused little titter. "I guess maybe you don't know who you're talking to, Miss Freep. Miss Arethusa Monk, if I may make so free as to allude to her by her given name, no offense intended, is reigning queen of the roguish regency romance. And her nephew here is Lex Laramie.''

''I thought you said his name was Osbert Monk, Carolus,'' said Wilhedra, not deigning to address the innkeeper directly.

Dittany thought she might as well try an amused little titter, too. ''He did and it is. Lex Laramie is my husband's nom de lariat. If you should ever happen to go into a bookstore, you'd find both his and Arethusa's books among the current best-sellers.''

''What books are those?'' Wilhedra demanded.

Dittany shrugged. ''Whichever ones they've most recently published. They're always best-sellers. By the way, Arethusa, Osbert got the advance for that movie contract and we've bought Ethel a ranch wagon.''

''You've bought your dog her own car?'' Tittering now seemed the last thing from Wilhedra's mind.

Dittany arched her light brown eyebrows. ''Doesn't everyone? The Architrave has such an enormous endowment now that it doesn't need our support, so we thought we'd give Ethel a little indulgence. After all, if Arethusa can order a custom-made lead crystal bowl on a solid gold base for her pet goldfish—but I mustn't bore you with our silly family jokes. I expect you're champing to be on the road.''

''No, no,'' boomed Jenson Thorbisher-Freep. ''I'm wholly intrigued. We must get to know such enchanting new acquaintances better, Wilhedra. We'll be delighted to show you the entire collection any time you care to visit our unostentatious mansion, Mrs. Monk. And Miss Monk, too, I hasten to say. Among its incomparable exhibits you'll find the sword carried by Dame Sybil Thorndike in her first performance as Shaw's *St. Joan,* Erich von Stroheim's prompt book from the Berlin Staatstheater, the scarf Jeanne Eagles flaunted when she played Sadie Thompson in *Rain,* the pantaloons Claude Rains wore as a tiny tot in his Drury Lane portrayal of Little Nell, and the wood and enamel hand mirror used by Sarah Bernhardt in her last performance of *Phedre.*''

Not her bustle. That would be a load off Zilla Trott's

mind. "My stars and garters," Dittany replied politely, "I can see you've been a busy man, Mr. Thorbisher-Freep. How many artifacts does it contain in all?"

"A total of one hundred and fourteen, not counting the used theater tickets. Some more valuable than others, of course. The total valuation is around six hundred thousand dollars."

"Very impressive," Dittany said, trying not to look impressed. "You must have had a lot of fun getting it together."

"It has been the labor of a lifetime. A labor of love, I hasten to add. But now the flame burns low. It's time for me to think of sharing my great responsibility with the vast theater-loving public. To that end, my daughter and I have decided upon a plan of which I gather you may be aware."

"Oh, yes, the drama contest. We're going to win it. But we really mustn't keep you here any longer," Dittany added, for she could see Osbert was champing at the bit and she herself was getting a bit sick of being smarmed over.

"*A bientôt*, then."

Jenson Thorbisher-Freep was ready to leave, but Wilhedra wasn't. As he took her by the arm to lead her away, she looked back at Carolus. "Aren't you—my God, what's that on your back?"

Wrenching free of her father, she swung her brown suede handbag and dealt Bledsoe a mighty thump. Something black, fuzzy, and many-legged tumbled to the concrete floor.

"Holy dogies, it's a tarantula!" cried Osbert.

"A deadly giant spider!" Wilhedra breathed hard through distended nostrils. Like a winded mustang, Dittany thought unkindly. "Carolus, you could have died from its bite."

"But I didn't, you see."

The lawyer was putting up a good front, but he was distinctly white around the gills, as who wouldn't have been? The tarantula must have measured fully six inches across, though it was hard to tell because Wilhedra had swung with verve and purpose.

The elder Thorbisher-Freep stirred the carcase with the

tip of his silver-headed cane. "Where do you suppose it could have come from?"

"Out of that—er—floral tribute Miss Monk is wearing, I should think," his daughter answered spitefully. "They're exotic tropical creatures, aren't they?"

"Not necessarily," said Osbert. "The *lycosidae* are quite widely distributed, and they're not really all that venomous. Some people keep tarantulas as pets. It would have suited you just fine, Aunt Arethusa."

"Poor bug." The reigning queen of regency romance stooped and picked up the mangled remains by the tip of one furry leg. She laid it gently in a nearby ash receiver, detached one of her many orchids, and placed it on top of the corpse. "I would have made a home for it," she murmured brokenly. "Well, Osbert, stir your stumps. I'm starving."

The Thorbisher-Freeps swanned off, dragging the still wobbly Bledsoe with them.

"Whoopee," said Andrew McNaster jocosely. "Those Freeps saved me the trouble of poisoning Bledsoe's soup. You two are coming to the inn, though, I hope?"

"We can't, I'm afraid," said Dittany, who in truth wasn't afraid at all but pleased to have an excuse. "Osbert's writing a play."

"A play, forsooth?" exclaimed Arethusa. "You mean an oater? One of those claptrap and balderdash horse operas where the cayuse lynches the maverick?"

"Surely you jest, Aunt Arethusa."

Because if you don't, you can darn well go and collect your own suitcases, eh. Osbert didn't come straight out and say so because strong men of the west don't go around threatening their aunts with retribution in front of shady contractors who run ill-gotten inns. However, the steely glint in his eye made the implication plain. Arethusa didn't miss it.

"La, the creature's in a bait," she cried. "Fetch the luggage like a good nephew, Osbert, and I won't cut you out of my will."

"A fat lot I care whether you do or not," Osbert replied with immense dignity. "Come on, Ethel, it's a good dog's duty to assist the aged and infirm. You'd better be careful

Aunt Arethusa doesn't slip on the ice getting out to the car, McNaster. She probably forgot to put her arch supports in. Her memory's not what it used to be."

"Stinker," Dittany said fondly as they walked away to the luggage pickup. "What did you think of Carolus Bledsoe, Esquire? Do you suppose he's the one who bought her all those orchids?"

"If he did, he needs to get his head examined," was Osbert's considered opinion. "I expect what happened was that some editor who's trying to persuade her to switch publishers gave her a bunch, and then her own editor gave her another bunch not to go. They put them on their expense accounts."

"Did anybody ever give you any?"

"They wouldn't dare. What do you think we Western writers are, a bunch of sissies? I've never even been offered a tarantula. By the way, when did Aunt Arethusa order a custom-made crystal bowl for her goldfish? I didn't know she had a goldfish. How come she didn't expect us to fish-sit while she was away? Don't tell me she's given McNaster the run of her house?"

"Darling, don't bug your eyes out like that. Of course she hasn't. Arethusa may be a trifle absentminded, but she's not plumb loco. I only made up that story about the goldfish bowl to take Wilhedra Thorbisher-Freep down a peg or two. She had no business being so snippy about Lobelia Falls."

"Was Wilhedra snippy?"

"Certainly Wilhedra was snippy. She talked as if we were all a bunch of starving church mice."

"Now that you mention it, I am starving. Want to stop on the way home for a nibble of cheese?"

"If we can find a place," Dittany agreed.

What she meant was a place that didn't object to large doglike creatures with less than perfect table manners. Stopping at a restaurant was apt to mean either take-out hamburgers or hurt looks from Ethel for having been left alone while they ate.

They settled for hamburgers and ate in the car, Dittany having first spread a large plastic tablecloth so they wouldn't get meat juice all over the new upholstery. Back in Lobelia

Falls, they put Arethusa's two pink tapestry suitcases inside her front door, to which they had a key, and went home half expecting to see her and Andrew McNaster seated at their kitchen table with napkins in their laps and knives and forks at the ready.

But Arethusa never came, not even at suppertime. The evening was peaceful, pleasant, yet somehow a trifle unsettling.

Chapter 4

Working at fever heat, stoked by Dittany with cups of tea, stacks of cinnamon toast, bowls of stew, and molasses cookies which he wolfed down without taking time to bite off the crinkles one by one as was his wont, Osbert finished his play late Tuesday night. On Wednesday, he held a reading for the board of trustees and Desdemona Portley to tumultuous applause, even from Arethusa.

Nobody doubted *Dangerous Dan McGrew* would win the competition hands-down. Mr. Glunck thought the theatrical collection would be just the ticket for the upstairs back bedroom provided the Thorbisher-Freeps threw in the display cases. Everybody was agog to get rolling.

And roll they must. One thing Desdemona hadn't happened to mention until she'd got the Grub-and-Stakers safely hooked was that they had only about a month left to put on their play. She'd already wasted most of the time allotted for the contest in vain efforts to get her old company back together. The new group understood her difficulties as soon as they started trying to assemble a cast.

Specifically, the problem lay in the ingrained reluctance of the average Canadian male to make a fool of himself in public. Nobody's husband had any particular objection to being one of the boys whooping it up in the Malamute saloon, as long as the rest of the boys would be right there whooping it up with him. Persuading any one of them to accept a role where he'd have to stand up on his hind legs all by himself and spout off a lot of high-flown guff was a

far, far different matter. Yet the characters of the miner
and Dan McGrew were absolutely central to the play.

Osbert refused to take either part. He was proud to have
written the play, as well he might be. He was not only
willing but eager to direct his play the way it ought to be
directed. But he was dad-blanged if he was going to act in
it, and who could blame him? Anyway, he couldn't possibly look dangerous enough to be Dan McGrew, and he just
wasn't the type to be a head feedbag man, much less a
gold miner. Besides, there were enough members of the
Monk family in the cast already.

Ethel was to be the faithful dog, needless to say, since
the role had been written for her and nobody else's dog
wanted to do it anyway. Dittany, inevitably, would be
Evangeline.

"But I don't want to be Evangeline," she wailed when
she got hit with the casting committee's verdict. "I'm too
old to be a tiny tot. I'm a grown woman with a husband
and a dog, for Pete's sake."

"Dittany, the show must go on," pleaded Desdemona
Portley. "You've got to play the tiny tot. Your mother
would play the tiny tot if she were here."

That was no argument. Dittany knew perfectly well, and
Desdemona Portley ought to know she knew, that the
former Mrs. Henbit would also have played Dan McGrew,
the miner, and the man who wouldn't give the horsecar
horses any carrots if she'd been given the chance.

"You're not a bit too old," Desdemona insisted. "I've
still got your old baby-blond wig with the corkscrew curls.
With that and a big pink hair ribbon, you could easily pass
for ten years old. Twelve, anyway. Evangeline can't be all
that tiny a tot, eh, if she winds up tickling the ivories in
the Malamute saloon. Besides, we have nobody else in the
company who can look winsome while playing ragtime
without a music book."

"Why shouldn't Evangeline have a music book?" Dittany demanded.

"Nobody carried a music book to the Yukon during the
gold rush. For goodness' sake, Dittany, even if we let the
piano player use a music book she'd still have to act
Evangeline convincingly, and that narrows it right down to

you. You've played more tiny tots than anybody else in Lobelia Falls, you know all the old songs your grand-mother taught you, and I never thought I'd live to see the day when a Henbit would let a personal whim stand in the way of her civic duty.''

''Well, you're seeing one now,'' Dittany grumbled.

But she gave in, of course. Osbert's debut as a dramatic writer and director couldn't be allowed to fall flat for lack of a kid to handle the music box. But Dittany would be dad-blanged if Desdemona Portley was going to stick her with another big pink hair ribbon. She'd wear a sober, matronly blue this time even if she could pass for twelve in her old baby-blond wig.

Desdemona herself would fain have played the lady who came so regrettably to be known as Lou. Even in the former Mrs. Henbit's day, however, Dessie Portley had got cast as the heroine's dear old mother just as inevitably as Dittany had been dragooned into portraying the corkscrew-curled infant daughter. Trouper that she was, Desdemona put on a brave smile and accepted the unsympathetic role of landlady. Zilla Trott didn't want it anyway; she was learning to make her own tofu and the effort was taking a lot out of her.

As for Louisa, there was really no contest. All the former heroines of the Traveling Thespians had been snapped up by other companies or graduated, like Desdemona, to character parts. Only one member of the Grub-and-Stakers had the looks, the carriage, the dramatic intensity, and the black lace Merry Widow corset to essay the leading lady. Even Osbert had to admit Arethusa Monk would be a smash hit as the miner's ill-fated wife.

Casting Arethusa in the female lead brought a fringe benefit nobody could have anticipated. As a lawyer, Caro-lus Bledsoe must perforce have had a streak of the thespian in him already. Impressive in appearance, affable in man-ner, he was the very type to have experienced a meteoric rise from lowly groom to head feedbag man at the horsecar barns. As soon as Arethusa happened to mention that the role of her cruelly misused husband was still uncast, Bledsoe leaped for it as though it had been a twenty-thousand-dollar fee. And once Andrew McNaster got wind that

Carolus Bledsoe was going to be in the play, he employed his well-known skill at connivance to obtain for himself the swashbuckling role of Dangerous Dan McGrew.

That took care of the leads. A bit of rewriting on Osbert's part eliminated the rival feedbag man from the first act, where he hadn't had all that much to do anyway. The gap was easily filled by having the true feedbag man, as he'd then still be, pour out his heart to Louisa about the rival's machinations while Evangeline strummed sentimental melodies in the background, little recking the woeful disruption in store for her family.

Then Dot Coskoff's husband, Bill, said he guessed he wouldn't much mind playing the bartender at the Malamute saloon as long as he didn't have to do anything but pour cold tea out of whiskey bottles and spread a couple of reasonably clean bar cloths over the faces of the demised as the final curtain was about to descend; and the show was on.

It is perhaps worthy of note that the first hint about Andrew McNaster's availability as Dan McGrew was channeled via none other than Jenson Thorbisher-Freep. This came about because while McNaster's interests were in Lobelia Falls, he still maintained bachelor quarters in Scottsbeck near the Thorbisher-Freeps, of whom the Monks had been seeing a fair amount since that first meeting at the airport.

Dittany, Osbert, and Arethusa had paid their call at the unpretentious mansion, which it certainly wasn't, to check out the memorabilia. They'd had Mr. Glunck in tow that day. The curator had been impressed and Wilhedra had been gracious, not only to him but to Dittany and Osbert. She hadn't had to be gracious to Arethusa. Her father handled that end of the operation with zeal and enthusiasm that Osbert thought might better have been applied to a loftier purpose.

Nor had the old actor's zeal abated. Jenson, as he insisted the Monks call him, had made it plain to all entrants that because he knew so much more than they did, he was willing to act as consultant on any general problem where theatrical expertise was needed. Naturally, Jenson explained, he could not become personally involved with any one of the six productions that were by now formally entered in his competition. This led a good many people to wonder what general problems were causing the theatrical expert to turn up so often in the immediate vicinity of Miss Arethusa Monk.

I' faith, as Arethusa herself might say, the reigning queen of regency romance who for years had asked only to be left alone with her typewriter and her fantasies when she wasn't practicing her archery, attending a club meeting, or inviting herself to one meal or another with Dittany and Osbert, had suddenly become the eye of a veritable social hurricane.

Neighbors who'd started patronizing the inn now that Andy was running his Bargain Buffets (all you could eat for six dollars a head) and his Family Specials (kids at half price and free cocktails for the grown-ups) reported seeing Arethusa at the best table, being plied with filet mignon and imported champagne by the infatuated innkeeper. Andy had even taken to wearing a dinner jacket that Hazel Munson said made him look like the bouncer in a gambling casino. It wasn't as though she'd ever been to one herself, but Hazel, normally the most down-to-earth of women, could sometimes startle her intimates with amazing flights of imagination.

As for Carolus Bledsoe, who could have dreamed a man trained to wade through a writ of attainder or a habeas corpus without batting an eyelid would have so much trouble mastering his part that he required private rehearsals with his leading lady twice and sometimes thrice a week? Jane and Henry Binkle, close friends of the Monks who kept the bookshop over at Scottsbeck and were kept *au courant* on town gossip by customers who used the shop as a sort of clubhouse, reported that Wilhedra Thorbisher-Freep was having an awful time lately remembering to be gracious.

"She lives in the mansion of aching hearts," remarked Dittany.

Young Mrs. Monk, alias Evangeline, had been boning up on her tearjerkers in preparation for the opening scene at the Malamute saloon. The dance hall girls and the miners were to have a merry fling which should heighten the tragic impact when the miner entered fresh from the creeks, dog-dirty and loaded for bear. Hazel Munson was to be one of the dancers, as were Dot Coskoff, Therese Boulanger, Ellie Despard, and several more of the Grub-and-Stakers. They were planning to wear red skirts, black stockings, and a good many ruffled petticoats. This super-abundance of undergarments would be the reverse of slimming, but Osbert assured the complainers that in the eyes of a gold rush miner, the fattest had shone the brightest.

Getting back to Wilhedra, however: "I shouldn't be surprised if she does," said Jane Binkle, who'd dropped over to bring Ethel a box of dog biscuits for auld lang syne. "Wilhedra's been after Carolus Bledsoe ever since he got divorced. She thought she had him all thrown and hog-tied, if I've phrased the expression correctly, until Arethusa happened along."

"I rather think it's roped and hog-tied," said Osbert, gallantly passing Jane the cookies. "I can look it up in Louis L'Amour if you like. When did Bledsoe get divorced, Jane?"

"Not too awfully long ago because some question about jointly held property still hasn't been resolved, from what we're hearing around the shop. According to the terms of the divorce, there's a building that's supposed to be sold and the profits divided between Carolus and his former wife, but he's using some kind of legal maneuvers to hold up the sale and contest the ruling in the hope of getting it all to himself. I gather she's not taking his shenanigans any too calmly."

"What's she like?" Dittany asked.

"Excitable, I'd say offhand. They say she used to throw things at him."

"What things?" Osbert wanted to know.

"Books, slippers, dishes, assorted produce, whatever came handy. She alleges the judge showed unfair prejudice in the defendant's favor because Bledsoe carried the scars of a ham and macaroni casserole into the witness box with him. Otherwise, she claims, she'd have been awarded the property free and clear, so Bledsoe has no right to hold up the sale."

Jane paused to hold out her teacup for a proffered refill.

"Thanks, Dittany. The crux of the matter seems to be that the property was left to them jointly by the terms of an aunt's will. However, the aunt was hers, not his. Bledsoe had been handling the old lady's legal affairs while she was alive and Mrs. Bledsoe, as she's still calling herself because her maiden name was Whiffenpoof or something in that general vicinity, maintains her husband exerted undue influence. She says the aunt had told her several times in the past that everything would be left to her. Bledsoe, on the other hand, insists the aunt wanted him to have the property because she didn't approve of the way her niece was carrying on with the postman."

"Was she really?" asked Dittany.

"Mrs. Bledsoe says not and the postman says not, but he's got quite a reputation as a roving Romeo. The consensus at the bookshop appears to be that there's no smoke without fire. Anyway, Mrs. Bledsoe moved to Toronto after the divorce and Wilhedra moved in for the kill. Now Mrs. Bledsoe's back raising the dust and goodness knows what will happen, especially with Arethusa in the picture. Wilhedra Thorbisher-Freep's love life is none of my business, of course, but a person can't help being interested in the ever-changing kaleidoscope of human relationships." Being around so many books sometimes lent a literary tinge to the Binkles' conversation.

The ever-changing kaleidoscope of human relationships was a never-ending source of interest around Lobelia Falls, too. Dittany got pretty sick of being backed into corners and being asked, "Which of them do you think she's going to take?"

"She who?" Dittany said to Margery Streph, who'd got her pinned behind the greeting card rack at Mr. Gumpert's stationery shop while she was trying to pick out a birthday card for her mother-in-law. Margery was the seventeenth pinner so far, and Dittany didn't care much for her anyway.

"Your Aunt Arethusa, of course," Margery replied with a little laugh.

"She's not my aunt. She's Osbert's aunt."

"Well, it's all in the family, isn't it? Come on, Dittany, who's leading the pack? Jim says Andy's so wound up he doesn't know which end he's standing on."

Jim Streph was an architect who designed the houses McNaster Construction built. He'd also not got to design a few that Andy had been prevented from building in the wrong places as a result of a public outcry spearheaded by the Grub-and-Stake Gardening and Roving Club. Dittany didn't have a good deal of use for Jim, either.

"As far as I know," she replied shortly, "Arethusa's still wedded to her art and intends to remain so. The reigning queen of regency romance has a responsibility to her vast reading public, you know."

Margery had the bad judgment to snicker. "Where did that reigning queen stuff come from? Her press agent?"

"Arethusa has no press agent. She's never needed one. The title came out of a worldwide poll held by the International Moonlight and Roses Writers' Organization. She was crowned last month at their convention in New York."

"What do you mean she was crowned?"

"Really, Margery, I should have thought you'd know the meaning of a common transitive verb. She had a coronation. Sort of like when they crowned Elizabeth the Second only a good deal flossier, Arethusa says."

"How could it be, for heaven's sake?"

"Well, for instance, they didn't release two hundred snow-white doves wearing frilly pink pantalettes in Westminister Abbey, did they?"

"Not to the best of my recollection," Margery had to concede.

"And Elizabeth wasn't borne to her throne on a palanquin draped in purple velvet, balanced on the shoulders of eight Nubian slaves wearing leopard skins, was she?"

"Of course not. Prince Philip would never have stood for having eight leopards killed to make work shirts for Nubians. He's a big gun in the World Wildlife Fund, you know. A big anti-gun, I suppose I should have said. Arethusa should have known better."

"It was only fake fur made to look like leopard, for Pete's sake," Dittany said crossly. "I doubt every much they were real Nubian slaves either, if it comes to that. One had red hair and freckles as big as the leopard spots. Arethusa says it's the symbolism that counts with the

Moonlight and Roses crowd. She had a rose-colored velvet coronation robe with a train about five metres long, all trimmed with ermine.''

Margery sneered. ''For ermine, read rabbit, I suppose.''

''If you find rabbit easier to read, certainly. Her crown was of golden filigree in the fairy princess style, not one of those big bulbous affairs, and her scepter a slender gold rod with a big pink glass heart that lit up and had diamonds all around the edge.''

''Symbolic diamonds, no doubt.''

''No doubt whatsoever. There were also symbolic pink cupids circling above the throne wearing baby-blue satin diapers. They had golden curls and cute little white wings. Arethusa says they were too utterly precious for words.''

''The whole affair sounds too utterly precious for words, if you ask me,'' Margery scoffed. ''You'd never catch me at that kind of circus.''

''No, I'm sure I wouldn't,'' Dittany replied sweetly. She'd been told in confidence by Hazel Munson that Margery Streph couldn't even write a thank-you note without boring its reader to tears. ''Good-bye, Margery. I'll tell Arethusa you were asking for her.''

Chapter 5

Pleasantly conscious of having pinned Margery Streph's ears back, Dittany took her birthday card home to be addressed and signed. She'd already arranged by telephone for the senior Mrs. Monk to receive an elegant basket of assorted fruits, Mother Monk being on a diet even grimmer than Hazel Munson's and fruit being the one gastronomic pleasure the doctor was allowing her to enjoy. All the right things had been done. Yet as she walked up Applewood Avenue and entered to dump her bag on the kitchen table, Dittany's inner voice kept nagging at her, "Something's wrong."

It must be all this flak she was getting about Arethusa, she thought. But Arethusa wasn't doing anything wrong. Was it Arethusa's fault she couldn't turn around without tripping over three besotted males? She wasn't favoring one over another as far as Dittany could see. She was addressing herself to keeping peace among them as best she might; and she was doing her utmost to make a triumph of her nephew's play even if Arethusa did keep insisting she wasn't doing it for Osbert but for the Architrave.

Yet Dittany's mind was still in a state of perturbation as she hung up her coat, dumped her purchases on the kitchen table, and took out the magenta-colored pen she kept for special occasions. She fretted inwardly as she signed her name to the birthday card and added an affectionate message. She'd grown fond of her mother-in-law, and her father-in-law, too, for that matter, even though both were still groping audibly for an explanation to the riddle of Osbert's choosing to live in a poky backwater like Lobelia Falls and write silly cowboy yarns when he could have carried his bride to a cozy high-rise apartment in Toronto and become a high-powered executive like his dear old dad.

They weren't blaming Dittany for their son's aberrant ways. They blamed his Aunt Arethusa, which was really unfair of them because Arethusa disapproved of Osbert's writing career even more vociferously than his parents did. That wasn't jealousy, it was just Arethusa's way. She'd have disapproved of any nephew who'd never fought a duel, pledged his vast estates at the gaming table, or swashbuckled around town in a velvet suit and a satin waistcoat.

Osbert couldn't have worn a velvet suit even if he'd wanted to, which he most emphatically dad-blanged didn't, because Ethel shed quite a lot. He had quit wearing tight Levis because he and Dittany hoped to raise a family some day, but he stuck to his flannel shirts and his buckskin vest, and had even been known to flaunt a red bandana when the call of the range was strong upon him.

A little chat with Osbert might be just the nerve tonic she needed. Dittany peeked into the alcove off the dining room that they called the office. Osbert was hunched over his faithful typewriter, lashing it on to full gallop. The machine was a big old Remington manual that he preferred to a newer model because it presented more of a challenge. Besides, the letters didn't fly off the bars during his bursts of inspiration as had those of an electric portable his mother had bought him once in a well-meant effort to accept what she could not understand.

He must be heading the outlaws off at the pass, Dittany thought. This was clearly not the moment to shatter his concentration over a vague feeling of unease. Osbert had been feeling uneasy about his Aunt Arethusa all his life anyway, and would feel quite reasonably, from his point of view, that his wife might have chosen a more opportune time to unload her qualms. Dittany left the birthday card on the dining room table where he'd see it when he emerged from his rustler-rife ruminations, and went back to the kitchen.

There were more immediate crises to be dealt with, the main one at the moment being that they were almost out of molasses cookies. Dittany got Gram Henbit's old yellow crockery mixing bowl out of the pantry and began assembling ingredients. It was soothing work measuring out flour and sugar and shortening, spooning in fragrant spices, cracking an egg on the side of the bowl, pouring molasses by the glug as her forebears had done. She stirred the batter to optimum consistency with confidence born of much practice, and parked it in the fridge to rest its gluten while she found the rolling pin and the time-darkened tin cookie cutter with crinkles around the edges, and floured the ancestral breadboard.

Dittany had lit the black iron wood stove for company even though she preferred to bake in the less picturesque but more predictable electric oven. The kettle on the stove was simmering, reminding her gently that a restorative cup of tea mightn't be a bad idea before she tackled the agreeable but exacting task of rolling and cutting. Dittany hauled up the rocking chair and was sitting there with her cup in her hand and her feet in the oven when it hit her.

All at once, she knew why Carolus Bledsoe's voice sounded so familiar, and wherefore she'd been having these worrisome forebodings. There was that of which she might well be foreboded.

The struggle which the Grub-and-Stake Gardening and Roving Club had been forced to wage against Andrew McNaster and his myrmidons back when Dittany was still Miss Henbit* was fresh in her memory, as why wouldn't it have been? Dark, dire, and dirty had been the dealing and derring had been the do. Dittany's personal epiphany had come when, disguised in molting false eyelashes and Gramp Henbit's holey sweatshirt, she'd eavesdropped on a conversation between McNaster and a lawyer from Scottsbeck.

Dittany had not been able to get a look at the lawyer,

The Grub-and-Stakers Move a Mountain.

but she'd heard his voice frighteningly loud and all too clear. She'd heard Andy call him Charlie and assumed his name was Charles. The name Charles was derived, although that detail had slipped her mind until just now, from the Latin Carolus. Naturally a man named Carolus would rather be called Charlie than Carrie. She took a deep breath and reached to steady the teacup that was jittering dangerously in its saucer.

So it wasn't only their rivalry for Arethusa Monk's grace and favor which had provoked that instant show of enmity at the airport. Those outbursts of mutual antipathy that had been electrifying the cast at rehearsals weren't prompted by histrionic urges but by simple hatred of each other's guts.

Andy and Charlie had been at odds during that overheard meeting. They must have had later differences of an even more serious nature. If Andrew McNaster's reformation was sincere, he must have struggled to tear himself loose from his former disreputable association. Carolus Bledsoe might be losing his erstwhile eagerness to affiliate himself with Wilhedra Thorbisher-Freep's social position and Jenson Thorbisher-Freep's money, but he still wanted to win that lawsuit against his ex-wife.

Evidently his case rested on how successfully he was able to present himself as a man incapable of chicanery, malfeasance, buttering up old ladies for personal gain, or associating with rogues like the then still unreformed Andrew McNaster. Yet here the pair of them were, inexorably bound by their joint record of past skulduggeries and their present infatuation with the reigning queen of regency romance. She must tell Osbert!

Dittany took her feet out of the oven and was looking for a safe place to park her teacup when she froze. She must not tell Osbert! If she so much as breathed a word about Charlie, even in her sleep, the story would get around. Osbert wouldn't utter a yip to a living soul, of course, but that wouldn't make any difference. Dittany hadn't lived in Lobelia Falls all her life without coming to realize that walls do in fact have ears and every little bird is a stool pigeon at heart.

Only this morning, Osbert had had a long distance telephone call from his agent. Archie was planning to fly up for the premiere with a well-known theatrical producer in tow. Yet it wasn't the possibility of blowing another big sale that rooted Dittany to the linoleum. She and Osbert were not lavish in their tastes. They already had a well-stocked pantry to feed them and a freshly reshingled roof to shelter them, plus a nice, fat cushion of cash in the bank to fall back on. Osbert wouldn't mind so much if he didn't make any money on *Dangerous Dan*, but what if the play never got performed?

He'd been working like a sheepdog, developing his scraped-together bunch of amateurs into a pretty slick cast. Fired by his enthusiasm and by their complex emotional tensions, the cast had not only memorized everything they were supposed to learn but vied with each other in performing their roles to perfection. Everyone came on when he should, did his part without a flaw, and left on cue without tripping over his own or anybody else's feet en route.

Even Jenson Thorbisher-Freep, who was still dropping in on rehearsals to see whether any technicality might have popped up that required his expertise, had done some audible marveling at how well the Traveling Thespians were shaping. He hadn't come right out and said they were a shoo-in to carry off the prize at the competition, but he certainly hadn't dashed any hopes.

And now they were galloping down the home stretch. Tomorrow night was the dress rehearsal. Minerva had made Dittany a really delightful little girl's frock of sprigged blue calico with a ruffled white pinafore. The flat-heeled Mary Janes, the white socks and pantalettes, the corkscrew curls, the blue hair ribbon Dittany would wear in the first act and the red one she'd coerced Desdemona into letting her flaunt in the Malamute saloon were all packed and ready to travel. She was rather proud of that red ribbon. It would send the signal that Dittany Henbit Monk had at last outgrown tiny tot roles.

She also had the woolly cap and mittens she was to put on before she, her sorrowing mother, and their faithful canine friend forsook their once-happy home and headed for the Yukon with false-hearted Dan McGrew. Dan, in the person of Andrew McNaster, would be wearing the traditional villain suit: a black frock coat, a fancy waistcoat, and a high silk hat. Andy had even grown a black mustache, so great was his dedication to his role, and learned how to wax the ends into despicable little spit curls.

That was the marvelous thing about the casting. Zilla Trott had remarked on it only yesterday. Andrew McNaster was totally convincing as the bad guy because everybody knew he had a heart as black as his mustache even though the rogue was putting on a show of repentance to impress Arethusa Monk. Carolus Bledsoe, on the other hand, made the perfect hero because he was such an honorable, upstanding gentleman in real life.

Suppose word leaked out that the honorable Charlie was not only every bit as roguish as Andy ever was but also a former accomplice to Andy's roguery? Suppose Jenson Thorbisher-Freep found out the man on whom he'd been prepared to bestow his daughter's hand was a double-dyed dastard? Suppose Wilhedra found out? More to the point, suppose they all found out and then Charlie found out it was Dittany Monk who'd scraped the scales from their eyes?

Being a closet rotter didn't appear to bother Carolus Bledsoe much. The possibility that people like the Thorbisher-Freeps and Arethusa Monk, not to mention the audience who'd be watching him act the hero and the judge who'd be trying that lawsuit might find out must cause him the odd moment's perturbation now and then, though. It wouldn't perturb Dittany a bit, provided he could keep the lid on until after Saturday night's performance was safely past. She could see all too clearly what would happen if the story popped.

To begin with, the play would flop. Even if Carolus Bledsoe had the face to go on (and who could replace him at this late date?) the dramatic tension that had been working so magnificently up to now would be shattered. Arethusa was no trained actress. Once she realized who her stage husband really was, she'd be able to work up about as much semblance of wifely affection for him as she had for that reviewer who referred to her books as lowgrade tripe.

Nor would Arethusa be the only one affected. Exposed, Carolus could act the hero in front of a Lobelia Falls audience till his eyes bugged out and his toes fell off, and nobody would swallow one word he said. As for Andy McNaster, he'd be so anxious to show how reformed he'd become in contrast to his unrepentant former henchman that he'd turn Dan McGrew into a cross between Santa Claus and Mother Teresa.

If the play flopped, what of the Architrave? Dittany reminded herself that it was she who'd goaded the Grub-and-Stakers into helping the Traveling Thespians so that they could acquire the Thorbisher-Freep Collection for their museum. She'd got Mr. Glunck all charged up about filling that back bedroom, though she still wasn't sure whether it was the memorabilia or the display cases he coveted.

What it boiled down to was that she had nobody but herself to blame for this dilemma. She'd talked Osbert into writing the play. She'd lined up the Girl Guides to sell cookies and lemonade during the intermission. She'd strong-armed Minerva Oakes into being wardrobe mistress.

Minerva had in turn organized a posse to sew all those red skirts and foaming petticoats for the dance hall girls. The foamy effect was achieved by yards and yards and yards of ruffles, every inch of them stitched by Therese Boulanger, the club president. Therese was the only member who not only possessed a ruffling attachment for her sewing machine but was also able to make it ruffle. All that flouncing had set Therese back at least a week on the crib quilt she was piecing for her new granddaughter. Her sacrifice must not be in vain.

There was also the matter of how actively vengeful Carolus might become toward the woman who blew the whistle on him if he found out who she was. Dittany thrust speculation from her mind and began rolling out cookies.

It was as well she did. The pressure was building. Osbert and the many cast members and backstage helpers who kept dropping in to pour out their anxieties about one thing and another turned to compulsive cookie gobbling as a temporary palliative. Dittany had been through so many dress rehearsals as a tiny tot that she herself wasn't nervous, or wouldn't have been if panic weren't so catching. At least she had her piano to bang on when the atmosphere got too tense.

Since Carolus Bledsoe didn't know one note from another, that heart-wrenching music the miner was required to play just before the shootout could have posed a problem. Osbert had coped easily enough by having Dittany play a medley of appropriate selections and recording them on tape. Carolus had only to sit down on the rickety-looking but actually quite sturdy piano stool Dittany would by then have vacated, and twiddle his fingers over the keyboard while the prop crew played the tape.

Dittany's personal worry was that her music might not be quite what Robert W. Service had had in mind when he wrote the poem. "I don't know, dear," she fretted. "Do you really think 'There Is a Tavern in the Town' fills the bills as the crowning cry of a heart's despair?"

"It's appropriate to the setting, darling," Osbert consoled her. "And that snatch of 'Just Before the Battle, Mother' at the end ought to rock their socks all right, eh. How about a cup of tea and a cookie?"

One way and another, they got through the time. About half past five Friday afternoon, because they couldn't stand it any longer, Dittany and Osbert bundled their properties into the ranch wagon, stowed Ethel—or Fido, a Faithful Dog, as she would appear on the programs—in the back seat, and headed for Scottsbeck. They didn't stop for Arethusa because Andy McNaster, Carolus Bledsoe, and Jenson Thorbisher-Freep had all offered her rides.

How the leading lady had settled the matter they didn't know, nor did they care. Osbert was running through his many checklists while Dittany tried to concentrate on driving. She wasn't too concerned about forgetting her lines, but she did wonder a bit about the elastic in her pantalettes. Well, she'd know by the end of the evening and there'd still be time to fix it tomorrow if necessary. This was only the dress rehearsal, after all. And everybody knew a bad rehearsal meant a fine performance. Softly, so as not to distract Osbert from his lists, she began to sing ''Just before the battle, Mother.''

Chapter 6

When they reached the opera house, they were surprised to find Arethusa there ahead of them. "I decided to come with Jenson," she explained, "because he has a key to the stage door."

For one who most often had her feet planted firmly on a rose-pink cloud, Arethusa was showing an unexpected grasp of practicalities these days. At least Dittany was thinking so until her aunt-in-law demanded, "What have you done with my costumes?"

"I haven't done anything with your costumes," Dittany retorted. "Why should I? I'm not the wardrobe mistress."

"Nonsense, of course you are."

"I am not. I'm the kid that handles the music box. Arethusa, try to think. Did Minerva Oakes bring anything to your house during the past week?"

Dutifully, Arethusa thought. At last she nodded. "Yes, she did."

"What did you do with it?"

"I ate it."

"Arethusa, you can't have!"

"Why not, forsooth? What else does one do with a plate of fudge?"

Dittany persevered with such patience as she could muster. "Arethusa, did Minerva bring anything else besides the plate of fudge? Anything of a textile nature, for instance?"

"Gadzooks, yes, she'd covered the fudge with a linen

tea towel. It had birds on it. Whooping cranes, I believe, or robins. Some endangered species.''

''Robins aren't an endangered species.''

''They are when Minerva gets after them with a sling-shot for pecking her cherries.''

This unrewarding discussion might have gone on for some time if Minerva herself hadn't arrived with a huge armload of costumes, followed by Zilla and a couple more, all afoam with petticoats. ''Oh, Arethusa,'' panted Minerva, ''I was hoping you'd be here. We've sewn the red skirt to that black lace corset so you won't bunch up around the waist, but I'm not sure about the hem. You'd better try this on, just in case. And the housedress for the first act, too.''

Both costumes were fine. Everything was fine. Every-body could smell success from the moment when the curtain went up and Carolus, lugging a feedbag as the badge of his calling, burst into the cozy flat where Are-thusa, in a long rose-print cotton gown and a frilly pink apron, was pretending to stir something in a bowl. Ethel lay under the table, the picture of canine contentment. Dittany, in her tiny tot garb and blue hair ribbon, tinkled, ''Call me pet names, dearest, call me a bird'' on the piano, which was placed on a slant at the rear of the stage.

Positioning the piano had been a tricky business. Osbert was too devoted a husband to make Dittany sit with her back to the audience all evening. However, she had to be out where people could see her. Minerva had sacrificed one of her late Aunt Bessie's hand-crocheted pillowcases to make those lace-trimmed pantalettes and it would be wicked to hide them.

After a good deal of shoving and panting, the stage crew had got the piano just right. Everybody could see as much of Dittany as was proper but not too much; since hers was, after all, only a supporting role. Better still, Dittany could see everybody. She didn't get to move around a lot but had to be onstage throughout the play, so sitting at the piano could otherwise have become a bore.

She hadn't expected there'd be any sort of audience tonight. As things turned out, though, she had quite a decent gathering to observe. The stagehands, the makeup and costume teams, the scene painters, the ushers and ticket takers, and even the Girl Guide mistress were all out front, along with miscellaneous spouses and offspring who'd come along to help carry things. The miners and dance hall girls, already in costume, had sat down to watch the first act in comfort since they wouldn't be going onstage themselves until after the intermission.

Wilhedra Thorbisher-Freep, wearing all her minks because the old opera house was none too warm this time of year, had joined her father in the front row. Two rows back, directly behind them, sat an even more lavishly minked woman who Dittany had never laid eyes on before. Who could she be, and what was she doing here? Furthermore, what was she looking so cross about? Maybe she was some connection of the Thorbisher-Freeps whom they'd dragged along against her will. Then why wasn't she sitting with them?

Halfway through "Home Sweet Home," Dittany had a better idea. The woman must be a spy from one of the rival companies. Performances were being given according to the order in which entries had been filed. Because Desdemona Portley had taken so long to get her act together, the Traveling Thespians would be the last to perform, and because they'd been pressed for time, they'd had to rehearse instead of attending the other plays. Dessie had sent her husband to scout them all, though. He'd reported that none was anything much to write home about and their competitors were all worried sick over what the Lobelia Falls company was going to come up with. Mr. Portley, of course, was not without prejudice.

Obviously that woman in the third row was prejudiced, too. She must be looking so sour because she already sensed the Traveling Thespians had the competition in the bag. Her scowl only grew blacker as the rest of the onlookers sat rapt and breathless, absorbing every move, every word, every gesture. Dittany could see a number of the more tender-hearted ones dabbing at their eyes while the deposed feedbag man emptied his pockets of their meager store and delivered his farewell soliloquy to the mournfully attentive Fido before going forth into the night on his ill-starred adventure.

By the time the SOLD sign had been hung on the piano and the cruel landlady had delivered her ultimatum to the impoverished mother and daughter, there was hardly a dry eye in the house. Even Wilhedra looked a trifle blurred around the mascara. Dittany watched eagerly to see whether she was going to haul out a mink-bordered handkerchief. However, Wilhedra appeared to brighten up when Arethusa yielded at last to the lascivious importunings of Dan McGrew. At that point, Dittany had to put on her cap and mittens and go to the Yukon, so she never did get to find out about the handkerchief.

The curtain went down in a puff of dust. Osbert made a clever little speech about how well it was going and would all the miners and dance hall girls please go fix their makeup, eh, and get onstage for the second act. Dittany changed to her red hair ribbon, rearranged her curls, and went back to the piano. As the curtain went up again, she was thumping out "Whoa, Emma!" for the miners to roar forth while they pounded their whiskey tumblers on the bar, on the tables, and occasionally on each other's heads to demonstrate what an uncouth lot they were.

After that she played a cancan so the dance hall girls could show off their petticoats and black net stockings, then a hoedown so they and the miners could all stamp around together amid raucous laughter and a certain amount of rude horseplay. Then she played a medley of sentimental airs to quiet them down and let them arrange themselves for the dénouement. Finally she swung into "The Maple Leaf Rag."

This was the signal for the miner's entrance. Samantha Burberry's husband, Joshua, who knew all sorts of scientific tricks, had contrived a wonderful howling gust of wind to herald the stranger's arrival. Joshua had also powdered him with some stuff that looked for all the world like snow but would conveniently disappear without leaving a mess on the stage for somebody to slip in while he tilted his poke of dust on the bar and called for drinks for the house.

The bartender began setting them up. Dan McGrew went on playing solitaire. Standing behind him, the lady now known as Lou eyed the newcomer with an artistic mixture of perturbation and puzzlement. He'd changed a lot from his feedbag days, of course. As the miner watered the green stuff in his glass and the drops fell one by one, Dittany tripped over to the bar, corkscrew curls aswing, and lisped her request for a tharthaparilla. This move left the piano stool free for the miner to take her place, which he stumblingly did.

And now his fingers flew over the keys. The tape recording tugged at the listeners' heartstrings. The miners were plainly thinking of home and mother, the dance hall girls of a cleaner, purer time when they'd been somebody's daughters.

Now that he'd got them properly spellbound, the forspent wreck who'd once been a rising young feedbag man staggered to his feet and began to speak, fumbling in his dirt-glazed poke as he did so. At last, his voice rising in a passion of hatred, he hauled out his six-shooter and delivered his final words:

"One of you is a hound of hell, eh, and that one is—"

"Carolus Bledsoe!"

It was the woman in mink, on her feet, her face contorted in rage and hatred. As she shrieked out the name, her arm flew up. Something smallish and round hurtled straight at the object of her loathing. Carolus Bledsoe recoiled slightly from the impact, put up a hand to his unkempt crepe beard, and drew it away tinged with sickly pink.

"He's bleeding!" cried Arethusa.

"He's anemic," snarled Andrew McNaster.

"You can't get a decent ripe tomato this time of year for love nor money." Even in a bright red skirt and three flounced petticoats, Hazel Munson was keeping her usual firm grasp on the facts.

Bill Coskoff leaned across the bar, waving the bar cloths he'd been holding ready to spread over the two anticipated casualties. "Wow!" he shouted, forgetting he wasn't supposed to have any lines. "Right on the button. It's a walk." Bill was a Blue Jays fan.

There weren't many left in the audience now that the miners and dance halls girls were all onstage. Those left, notably Wilhedra and Jenson Thorbisher-Freep, were crowding forward with exclamations of surprise and concern. Dittany was the only one of the lot keeping her eyes on the woman who'd thrown the tomato, hence the only one who saw her sweep her minks about her with a smirk of self-satisfaction and scoot from the theater under cover of the confusion.

There was no sense trying to stop her. Anyway, Dittany was on her side. She was pretty sure who the woman was, and so was Carolus Bledsoe.

"My ex-wife's idea of a joke, no doubt," he explained. "She has a deadly aim. Sorry everyone. Shall we take it again from where I speak that last line?"

"We'll need another bar cloth," said Hazel. "I used one of Bill's to wipe up the tomato. It didn't splash much. They're hard as bullets this time of year."

"As I know to my sorrow." Carolus Bledsoe gave the company a rueful smile through his seed-strewn beard. "You could use my bandana."

"That's okay," said Bill Coskoff, "I brought an extra, just in case."

So the show went on, though there wasn't much left to go. After the pyrotechnics of a moment ago, the actual shooting lost a little bit of its impact, but they got through with no further hitch and everybody assured everybody else that it would be all right on the night.

There was no earthly reason why it shouldn't be, provided the former Mrs. Bledsoe could be prevented from bringing in another tomato. Nevertheless, everybody in the cast, along with everybody else from the director to the youngest lemonade peddler, was affected with a certain unease the following morning.

"Something else will go wrong, I can feel it in my bones. There is a dark fatality which pursues me."

That was Arethusa Monk, speaking rather indistinctly because she was eating the last molasses cookie. Dittany wished, considering how little they'd had of Arethusa's company at the table lately, that she could have held off for another twenty-four hours and kept her forebodings to herself.

"That dark fatality is obesity," said her nephew with some heat. He'd been all set to eat that last cookie himself, although he'd planned to offer Dittany a bite, for his was a love that was greater than love. "One of these days all that free food you've been wolfing off us will go straight to your hips and you'll blow up like a hot air balloon. You know what happened to Aunt Obelia."

Arethusa licked her fingers in defiance. "Figo for Aunt Obelia. Figo for you, too. Speaking of which, Dittany, what happened to all those Fig Newtons you used to keep around the house?"

"Osbert doesn't care much for Fig Newtons."

"And prithee is Osbert the only star in your firmament?"

"Need you ask? I don't go in for polymorphism like some people I could mention."

Arethusa's jetty eyebrows went up. "Are you quite sure you mean polymorphism?"

"Certainly. I mean those three morphs you've had fluttering around your flame for the past month. Have you decided yet which one's whiskers you're going to singe?"

"I see my scurvy nephew has infected you with what he is pleased to call his sense of humor," Miss Monk replied coldly. "What a pity there isn't a vaccine against him. Ecod, is that Jenson Thorbisher-Freep's car I just saw turning in your driveway?"

Osbert sneered. "Just can't keep the morphs from swarming, eh? What the blazing heck would old Jense be doing here?"

It was in fact Jenson Thorbisher-Freep and what he was doing, they soon discovered, was dithering. "Arethusa—Osbert—Dittany. My dears, you must prepare yourselves."

"We're prepared," Dittany assured him. "Even Arethusa was a Girl Guide once, though she still can't tie a square knot. What's happened?"

"The opera house has been bombed."

"What? When? How?"

Which of them said which is immaterial; their desire for the facts was unanimous. Jenson held up a hand that had probably never done a day's work in its life.

"Let me explain. When I said bombed, I didn't mean bombed. Not in terms of an explosive or incendiary device, that is to say. What took place was more in the nature of an olfactory bombing."

Arethusa's dark eyes turned vast pools of wonderment. "Olfactory, Jenson?"

"He means a stink bomb," Dittany told her impatiently, "and he's too refined to say so. Right, Jenson?"

"Well, yes," he admitted. "Since you put it that way, I—well, yes. It's quite dreadful, I assure you. Rather as if someone had stampeded a herd of skunks down the center aisle, if I may be permitted so rude a simile."

"Have you opened the windows?" Osbert asked him.

"Oh, yes. That is to say, I had the fire brigade put on their gas masks and go in to do what they could as soon as I discovered the dreadful situation. They hold out no hope that the building will be usable this evening. Or any evening in the foreseeable future," he added despairingly.

"Then what are we to do, egad?" cried Arethusa.

"I can only see two alternatives, dear lady. One is for the Traveling Thespians to cancel tonight's performance, which I'm afraid means they'd forfeit their place in the competition. The other would be to rise to the occasion and find another space in which to perform."

"Where, for instance?"

"Aye, there's the rub. There's nothing available in Scottsbeck, I'm afraid. I took the liberty of making some inquiries before coming to you, though in doing so I may have overstepped the bounds a trifle. Under the circumstances I trust I may be forgiven, and I trust you won't bruit it about that I did so."

"Heck, no," said Osbert. "Did you happen to inquire about the Scottsbeck High School gymnasium?"

"That was my first and almost only hope. By an unhappy coincidence the school is playing a home game there tonight with Lobelia Falls."

"Then that means our gym's free." Dittany was already reaching for her cap and mittens. "I'll go talk to Desdemona Portley."

"Excuse me," said Thorbisher-Freep, "but wouldn't it be advisable to check with the school principal first?"

"Nope, I'm going straight to the top. The principal's Dessie's husband, he wouldn't dare say no to her. Darn good thing Minerva took all our costumes home last night.

What about the scenery, eh? Can we get it out of the opera
house?''

"The firemen seem to be of the opinion that you wouldn't
want to. Can you possibly make do without it?''

"No problem. The Traveling Thespians always used to
perform in the gym, so a lot of their old scenery's still
stored in the basement. We're bound to find something we
can cobble together.''

"Then you truly believe you can rise to the occasion?''

"Rising to occasions is what we do best in Lobelia
Falls. Osbert, you'd better phone the radio stations right
away and get them to announce the change, then start
rounding up the troops. Get Ellie Despard to make a big
poster for the front of the opera house, and have somebody
run it over there. Tell them not to forget the thumbtacks.
Oh, and alert Sergeant MacVicar to be sure and come
tonight so he can keep an eye out for that nutty wife of
Ch— I mean Carolus Bledsoe's.''

"And what shall I do?'' said Jenson Thorbisher-Freep.

"Why don't you take Arethusa out for a ride and buy
her a nice lunch somewhere to calm her nerves? Think you
can handle that?''

"She and I will handle it together,'' Jenson replied
gallantly. "Until this evening, then.''

Dittany didn't hear him. She was already out the door.

Chapter 7

Having to make such a drastic last-minute change turned out to be a blessing in disguise. Nobody had time to work up a serious case of stage fright because everybody was too busy doing what needed to be done.

Principal Portley had not only said yes to the gym but helped the stagehands put away the tumbling mats and set up the chairs. Luckily, Minerva had indeed taken all the costumes home for a final pressing after the dress rehearsal, so they were fresh and ready for use, or would be once the pressing crew finished their tea and got on with the job. The infallible Roger Munson, in charge of props, had tested the opera house locks and found them wanting; so he and the stagehands had lugged everything stealable back to the safe haven of the Munson garage, whence it was easily lugged over to the gym.

The piano could have been a sticker, but Roger solved that one by causing Miss Pickley's ancient instrument to be moved down from the kindergarten. Dittany knew that piano well; she'd made her public debut as a musician by playing "I know a little pussy, his coat is silver gray" on it when she was five.

The school basement had yielded up a few scroungy old flats. With hasty repainting and some changing of props these could be converted to a basic set that would serve well enough for both acts. While the scene painters labored, a squad of dance hall girls stood beside them with hair dryers set on high to make sure nobody was going to back into wet paint during the performance.

Osbert was everywhere except the one place he'd intended to be. His agent and the big theatrical producer were due into the airport at half past three, but there was no way he could go to pick them up when his very play was at stake. Andrew McNaster, of all people, volunteered as fairy godfather.

"Say, eh, how about if I send my head clerk over to the airport in the limousine? Lemuel can bring them here to the inn and get them settled in the Premiere Suite free of charge. That way Dittany won't have to change the pillowcases at your place. My housekeeper can have tea and little bitty sandwiches and some what you'd call liquid refreshment ready for them when they come. She knows all that V.I.P. stuff. They can rest their feet awhile, go down to the restaurant when they get hungry and have a steak or whatever they want on the house, then Lemuel or somebody will chauffeur them over here in time for the show. I'd go myself, only I expect likely you want me to hang around here so's I can be on hand to jump if there's any villainy you want perpetrated."

"You're no villain, Andy, you're an angel." That was the last thing on earth Dittany had ever thought to hear herself saying, but it was the least she could say in the circumstances.

They did need Andy and all the rest of the cast to walk through the entire play one more time because the gym stage was about half the size of the one they'd rehearsed on last night. The first act, which didn't have a great deal of moving around in it, worked all right except for Ethel.

"Too bad she's not a Pekingese," Osbert lamented. "You'll just have to scrooch up as much as you can, old pard, and try not to wag your tail." He gave her an encouraging pat and called places for act two.

Right off the bat, it was obvious that Ethel would have to sit this one out and come on again only to take her curtain call, for which she was going to wear Dittany's blue hair ribbon as a symbolic gesture. There were greater dilemmas to be dealt with. They could crowd all the miners around the bar, but the tables and chairs would have to go. They could manage the cancan by having the dance hall girls come right up to the front of the stage and kick out over the footlights. However, there was no way to stage the hoedown without risking a massive pileup over the footlights and down on the basketball court.

"What we'll have to do," Osbert decided, "is bring the hoedown to the audience. Stagehands, you'd better move this first row of chairs back so there'll be a little extra space to maneuver in. Girls, when you finish your cancan, you each turn around and grab yourselves a partner."

"Who takes which?" Hazel Munson wanted to know.

"It doesn't matter, you all know the dance. Take who-ever's nearest. Mr. Portley, could we have those two little sets of steps over here that the kids march up for gradua-tion? That's right, one on each side of the stage."

Osbert pranced up and down them himself a couple of times to make sure they were safe. "Okay, now as you pair off, go down whichever steps are handiest and begin jigging around the floor in front of the stage. Don't crowd and don't march off like wooden soldiers. Keep it casual. The last couple or two can stay onstage if you want. If any of the audience want to get up and join in, let them. Switch partners, dance up the aisle, do whatever you feel like. Whoop it up in grand style."

"How long should I play?" asked Dittany.

"That depends on how well it's going. I'll stand in the wings and signal. When you see me raise my hand, play a few bars of 'Abide with Me' or something so the cast will know it's quitting time and come back onstage."

"How about 'I'm Heading for the Last Roundup'?"

"Great, just the ticket. Then gradually you slow down into the sentimental stuff while they come onstage and settle down for the climax. All right, let's try it. Line up and do the last few bars of the cancan, girls. Then take your partners and sort of spill down the stairs one after the other."

"And afterward we spill up again?" Dot Coskoff liked to get her directions straight.

"Yep. Ready, Dittany?"

They tried the routine once or twice. Choosing partners and dancing in the aisles worked just fine once everybody'd got the knack of negotiating the none too adequate steps. The trouble started when they all crowded back onstage. There simply wasn't room enough left for the stranger and Dan McGrew to shoot it out the way it ought to be shot. Osbert Monk remained undaunted.

"Never mind. What we'll do is this. Dittany still plays the signal but nobody comes back onstage except Samantha and Ellie. Then three or four of you, whoever's closest, climb up and sit on the steps, as if you're worn out from the dancing."

"Which we are," said Therese Boulanger, suiting the action to the word.

"Good. Go ahead, a few more sit down. The rest of you cluster around in front of the stage and look up. Bill, you start pouring drinks. Ellie and Samantha, take the drinks as Bill pours them out and hand them down to the men. You fellows reach out and try to attract their attention, as if you're grabbing for the drinks. Don't shove or anything, but horse around a bit if you want. Tickle the girls in a playful sort of way."

"Not my wife you don't tickle," shouted Roger Munson.

"Oh, shush up, Roger," Hazel snapped back.

It took them a while to get the bugs out, but the scene worked beautifully. The girls in their bright red skirts and the miners in their blue shirts made a living frame for the stranger's entrance. They held the tableau, some pretending to sip their drinks, others listening quietly as the kid at the piano strummed her sentimental melodies.

Then Dittany wiggled her fingers, took a final swig of her sarsaparilla, and thundered into "The Maple Leaf Rag." The stranger blew in with his poke. The lady known as Lou started exercising her perplexity. Dangerous Dan McGrew put a red deuce on a black trey, got excited because his solitaire was working out, remembered he was supposed to be acting, and went back to looking mean. The stranger ordered his drink, then played his solo; or rather pretended to since Roger hadn't yet rigged up the tape recorder.

Roger had brought the guns, but he only had one blank cartridge left for the gun Dan was going to fire which they had to save for the actual performance. Yelling "Bang,

bang" didn't have the same dramatic impact, but that didn't matter. Both victims had plenty of room to expire in a convincing and reasonably dignified manner. The lady known as Lou didn't have to fight her way across the stage to clasp the miner to her bosom with one hand and pinch his poke with the other. That was all Osbert needed to know. Shortly after half past five, he dismissed his company.

"That wraps it up for now. Thanks, everybody. Go home and get your suppers. I'd like you back here by a quarter to seven, please."

He hadn't left them much time, but nobody grumbled. Nor did they dawdle. The gym was soon empty except for the three Monks, Andrew McNaster, and Carolus Bledsoe. Jenson Thorbisher-Freep had brought Arethusa to the school at about half past one and hung around for a while in case they might be looking for some technical expertise of a general nature. At last he'd said he might as well make himself scarce as he obviously wasn't needed here, and several people had assured him he wasn't. Jenson hadn't been seen since but no doubt he'd show up for the performance.

Dittany was gripped by a sudden awful thought. "Carolus"— they'd all been on first-name terms for quite a while by now— "not to bring up an unpleasant subject, but had we better rig up the volleyball net in front of the stage to ward off flying objects?"

The lawyer flushed, but didn't evade her question. "I understand your concern, Dittany, and I share it. I took the precaution this morning of having my attorney warn my ex-wife's attorney that she'll be under close surveillance if she attends tonight's performance and that if she causes any disruption, she'll be instantly apprehended and charged with a disturbance of the peace."

"Whom were you planning to have apprehend her?"

"I've arranged with an off-duty Lobelia Falls policeman to stand at the entrance and track her if she comes in. He'll be on the *qui vive* all evening, so don't worry your pretty little head for one moment. Now let's see what we can do about getting you ladies fed."

"Leaping lariats," Osbert broke in, "I plumb forgot

about Archie and the producer. Come on, darling, we'd better stop at the inn and see how they're making out.''

"Yeah, sure," said Andrew McNaster. "You'll want to eat with them, naturally, so be my guests. You too, Miss Monk, of course." Andy still couldn't bring himself to say Arethusa right out in front of everybody though she'd confided to Dittany that he sometimes managed it during their tête-à-têtes. "And I guess we can find a spare pot roast or something for the faithful friend here. What do you say, Ethel?''

That clinched it for Dittany. "Ethel says thanks and so do we. Only you'll have to put up with us in our rehearsal clothes.''

"I can't stop to change, either," Andy replied gaily. "Not till I get into my villain suit. We're all in the same boat, eh?''

He thought he had hold of the oars, but Carolus Bledsoe committed an act of piracy. "We'll all come to the inn. Only you must be my guest, Arethusa darling.''

Darling, forsooth! Dittany and Osbert exchanged covert glances. Andrew McNaster came right out and glared, but there wasn't a thing he could do. His was a public hostelry; Carolus Bledsoe had as much right as anybody else to walk in there and order two of his Cordon Bleu dinners. When one of these was being served to the woman of the innkeeper's dreams, however, and another man was sitting across from her as she prepared to eat it, that innkeeper's uncontrollable urge to gnash his teeth as he passed their table a little while after this scene in the gymnasium could well be understood.

Arethusa at least appeared to understand. She reached out and grabbed him by his coattails. "Stand, sirrah! Methought you were going to eat with us. Have your minions bring another knife and fork.''

"Sorry, I have urgent business in the kitchen," Andy snarled.

It was the snarl of a soul in torment, and Dittany, now seated at the next table, felt sorry for him. She had no chance to express her sympathy, however. She was having to make polite conversation with the big-shot producer, whose name turned out to be Daniel something, while

Osbert and Archie thrashed out a few details relating to the movie contract.

Daniel didn't look much like a big shot, Dittany thought. He looked pretty much like anybody else except for his eyes. These were dark and small and never still, like a hawk's; and they didn't appear to miss much. He'd noticed that small incident across the way and been fully as interested as Dittany.

"Magnificent," he murmured when Andy had disappeared behind the swinging door to the kitchen. "Who is he?"

"That's Andrew McNaster, the innkeeper," Dittany explained. "He's also a building contractor."

"Too bad he's not an actor in your husband's play."

"Oh, but he is. You'll see him tonight as Dan McGrew."

"You don't say! With a beard, I suppose?"

"No, just that nasty little mustache. Andy grew it specially. It's how he interprets the role."

"By George." Those relentless black eyes flickered back to Dittany. "Any of the other principals here?"

"All of us, except the landlady and the bartender. That's Osbert's Aunt Arethusa over there eating olives. She's the lady known as Lou. Andy's stuck on her, that's why he's so mad. And the man with her is the miner fresh from the creeks, dog-dirty and loaded for bear."

"He looks clean enough to me," said Daniel.

"He has to be clean for the first act," Dittany explained. "We dirty him up during the intermission."

"I see. But you said we. What's your role?"

"Oh, I'm the tiny tot."

Regrettably, Daniel had just taken a spoonful of his onion soup. Archie looked at him in some alarm.

"Are you all right, Dan?"

"Osbert's wife just told me she's the tiny tot."

"Well, yes," said Osbert. "Dittany's always been the tiny tot. It's a tradition among the Traveling Thespians."

Daniel, who had by now stopped choking, nodded his unimpressive head. "I see. That explains it, of course. I must say I'm beginning to look forward to this evening. And that's your aunt over there, eh? Striking woman. I suppose she always plays the tragedienne."

"Right now she's playing the field," Osbert replied gloomily. "Oh, gosh, here comes another morph to the flame. Who the heck is he, I wonder?"

"The second gravedigger, I should say," Daniel replied with mild distaste.

The man making a beeline for the table where Arethusa and Carolus sat was tall, dark, and almost but not quite handsome in a cadaverous sort of way. He had on a black suit of exaggerated cut, a floppy black tie, a flowing black cape like Jenson Thorbisher-Freep's, and a silky white shirt that made Dittany wonder for a moment whether he might perhaps be a flamenco dancer wanting to borrow Arethusa's Spanish shawl.

No, he wasn't. She recognized him now, he always played the leading male roles in the Scottsbeck Salute to Shakespeare. Her mother had dragged her along a few times when she was a teenager, to broaden her cultural horizons. She'd sat through *Macbeth* in an agony of suppressed giggles, she recalled, because he'd looked so darn silly in the kilt. He had a silly name, too, Leander something.

"Leander Hellespont," she said aloud. "He's with the Scottsbeck Players. How did Arethusa—"

She stopped. Leander wasn't paying any attention to Arethusa. It was at Carolus Bledsoe that he was pointing the finger of accusation; Carolus Bledsoe whom he addressed in words of scorn and vituperation.

"So, false one! You rive me of my beloved, then you cast her aside like a faded rose and turn to a gaudier blossom. You shall pay for this, Carolus Bledsoe!"

"Bravo," murmured Daniel. Dittany was beginning to like the big-shot producer.

Carolus Bledsoe laid down his knife and fork and gave his accuser a cool and haughty glance. "Oh, dry up and blow away, Hellespont. You're making a jackass of yourself."

"You defy me, ruffian? My adored Wilhedra shall learn that she has a dauntless champion. Stand and face me, Bledsoe!"

"Not here he won't." Andy McNaster was back in the room with blood in his eye. "This is a respectable inn, mister. Either sit down and order or get the hell—I mean, betake yourself elsewhere.''

"And refrain from bandying the name of a lady in public, you mannerless jackanapes,'' added Arethusa. "Aroint. Shoo. Scat.''

"Poltroon!'' Leander really did have a lovely sneer, Dittany thought. ''Go ahead, summon your henchman. Hide behind a woman's skirts. But beware, Carolus Bledsoe. You cannot escape the wrath of Leander Hellespont!''

"Bravissimo!''

Daniel was on his feet, applauding. However towering his wrath, Leander Hellespont was too seasoned a trouper to spoil such a glorious exit line. He flung his cloak about his lanky frame, distributed sneers all around, and stalked from the inn. Andrew McNaster went back to the kitchen. Carolus Bledsoe picked up his fork. Arethusa ate another olive.

Chapter 8

"I'll bet he's the one who stink-bombed the opera house."

Dittany hadn't expected such a reaction from what she herself had considered a rather commonplace remark. Osbert, Archie, and Daniel all gaped at her as though she'd produced a live panther from inside her cream puff.

"Well, it's obvious enough, isn't it?" She scooped up the last of her fudge sauce but refrained from licking her fork because she was out in company. "The Scottsbeck Players got first crack at the competition. Desdemona Portley says they put on a thing about Lord Selkirk and the Hudson's Bay Company that their leading man wrote, directed, and acted the part of Selkirk in. She must have meant Hellespont because she said all His Lordship did was stalk around in one fancy suit after another, ranting about the massacre at Seven Oaks and the high cost of beaver skins. Dessie said the best part of the whole show was when one of the trappers pretending to make a portage got his head caught inside a birchbark canoe."

"Too bad I missed it," said Daniel.

"Doesn't sound to me as if you missed much," Archie grunted. "I see Dittany's point, though. That gink's a sore loser if ever I saw one. So your theory, Dittany, is that Hellespont bombed the opera house to keep you from putting on Osbert's play and winning the competition. That didn't work so he decided to pick a fight with your leading man and put him out of business. He must be a bit strange."

"All actors are strange," said Daniel. "I ought to know, I used to be one myself."

"I'm not so sure Hellespont was really out to disable Carolus," Osbert demurred. "I'd say he was trying to make up some lost ground with Wilhedra Thorbisher-Freep. I wish Aunt Arethusa would quit this Cleopatra stuff."

"I wish we'd gone ahead and rigged that volleyball net in front of the stage," Dittany fretted.

Generally speaking, people who spend their days trying to wring bigger authors' royalty percentages out of publishers are optimists but not visionaries. Archie was therefore nonplussed by Dittany's remark.

"I don't see how a volleyball net would fit in with the concept of Osbert's play."

"It wouldn't," Dittany replied, "but it might save Carolus Bledsoe's beard. Last night at dress rehearsal, his ex-wife beaned him with a semi-ripe tomato. Tonight, Leander Hellespont will probably sic a beaver on him."

"I hardly think Hellespont would be able to locate a trained attack beaver on such short notice, darling," Osbert assured her. "Come on, it's almost a quarter to seven. We've got to get cracking. Archie, why don't you and Daniel stay here and finish your coffee? We'll save you two front-row seats. Andy McNaster said he'd get somebody to drive you over to the gym before curtain time."

"Osbert, let's ask Andy to ride back with us," said Dittany. "He's been so nice, it's the least we can do."

But Mr. McNaster, their waitress informed them, had already gone on ahead. They left Archie and Daniel aiding digestion with a brandy apiece, spoke to the receptionist about transporation for their guests, were told Mr. McNaster had it all arranged, and left the inn.

It was as well they did. The troops were already beginning to gather and Roger Munson was in a most uncharacteristic tizzy.

"I can't find the poke!"

"Well, that's no major crisis," said Dittany. "It's only a dirty little old bag. We can easily rig up another."

"But it's got the .38 blank cartridge in it."

"Well, for Pete's sake, your own son works at the

sporting goods store in Scottsbeck. Why can't he nip over and buy some more?''

"Because the store doesn't have blanks. That is"—Roger couldn't help being precise even in a crisis—"they do have .32 caliber blanks because customers use those in starting pistols for races, but there's no real demand for .38's so the store has to send away for them on order. That's why we decided to make do with the few Jenson gave us instead of having to order to whole box and get stuck with the leftovers.''

Roger's decision might not have made much sense to some people, but it did to Dittany. Guns of any kind were rare in Lobelia Falls because everybody used bows and arrows instead. Roger had experienced difficulty trying to scare up two authentic-looking revolvers for Dan McGrew and the stranger to shoot each other with. Carolus Bledsoe had finally managed to supply himself with a Colt .32 and some blanks that he claimed to have borrowed from a friend. Dittany didn't believe him, of course, but couldn't very well say so.

Andrew McNaster was either more sneaky, more reformed, or more committed to the Male Archers' Target and Game Shooting Association than Dittany had given him credit for being. In any event, he'd professed total ignorance of firearms big or little. Roger had wound up having to wangle the short-term loan of a .38 Smith & Wesson from the Thorbisher-Freep collection for Andy to use.

In fact, Roger hadn't had to wangle hard, even though the .38 had allegedly been carried in Buffalo Bill Cody's Wild West show and had certainly been used by Jenson himself when he'd made his big hit as Jack Rance in *The Girl of the Golden West* during his little theater days. Jenson was only too pleased, he'd assured Roger, to put another notch in the six-shooter's barrel by letting the man in the title role tote it during the premiere of *Dangerous Dan McGrew*.

There'd been four blank cartridges left in the gun when Roger got hold of it. Jenson Thorbisher-Freep had not only donated these to the Traveling Thespians but volunteered his technical expertise in teaching Andy how to shoot them. They'd used three of the four getting the range and making sure Andy and Carolus could shoot each other with no risk to themselves or anybody else.

That was easy enough. The only conceivable danger might be from the thin cardboard wads that covered the powder, and these wouldn't do any damage unless one happened to strike somebody in the eye. The simple solution was for the men to stand only about five feet apart, aim point-blank at the adversary's chest, and fire with their eyes shut. Dot Coskoff's grandfather's second wife had made them pads of quilt batting to wear under their shirts. These had proved in dress rehearsal to be a needless precaution but Andy and Carolus were going to wear them anyway so Mrs. Coskoff's feelings wouldn't be hurt.

The first three blank cartridges in the .38 had gone off with satisfactory bangs. If the last one didn't, that was the working of fate and no fault of Roger Munson's. If some smart aleck got hold of the loaded revolver and wasted that sole remaining bang by an unauthorized pull of the trigger, that would be a far, far different matter.

Carolus Bledsoe had so far assumed full responsibility for the .32 Colt; Roger hadn't had to worry about that. Until today, Jenson Thorbisher-Freep had likewise kept the Smith & Wesson in his possession. He'd meant to drop it off at the Scottsbeck opera house an hour or so before curtain time, then go home and gargle to prime his throat for the curtain speech he expected to make later on. But the opera house was five minutes from his home, and Lobelia Falls a good half hour away. He couldn't be expected to make that run twice in one evening, so he'd brought the gun with him on his earlier visit and given it then into Roger's keeping.

Jenson might as well have slung an albatross around Roger's neck and been done with it. Roger could probably have coped better with an albatross.

He did know better than to leave a loaded gun around unguarded, especially one loaded with the only blank .38 cartridge in Lobelia Falls. Roger's first impulse was to take it home with him when he went to supper. However, Canada has a strict and firmly enforced firearms control law. Should Roger Munson, hitherto a model citizen, get caught in possession of a handgun not licensed to him, Sergeant MacVicar, the law in Lobelia Falls, would have no alternative but to exact the due penalty.

Roger had almost decided not to go home at all, but Hazel put a damper on that notion. He'd been working hard all day, she'd pointed out. He must be hungrier than a she-bear in cubbing time, and he'd be a darn sight hungrier, eh, if he had to stay here till eleven o'clock or maybe even midnight with nothing but lemonade and Girl Guide cookies to sustain him.

After much soul-searching and some frantic thought, Roger had unscrewed the cover to one of the gym's ventilating ducts. He'd unloaded the gun, laid it inside the duct, and screwed the cover back on. He'd wrapped the blank .38 cartridge in tissues, opened the stranger's poke, and pushed the cartridge down into the rock salt that was supposed to be gold dust. And he'd laid the poke right here on the prop table next to the feedbag, and where the heck was it now?

That was the trouble with having an organized mind. While Roger stood there clutching the gun, which he'd retrieved from the ventilator duct with little effort, Dittany picked up the feedbag and shook out the poke, complete with unexploded blank cartridge.

"There you are, Roger. You just hid the poke better than you thought you did."

"Ungh," was Roger's ungrateful reply. "I wonder if I ought to load the gun now or wait till during the intermission? Of course I'll have to help set up the barroom scene then and make sure Bill has his bar rags, but if I got the gun ready now, somebody might get to playing with it and then where'd we be?"

"You do know how to load it, I suppose?" Dittany asked him.

"Oh yes, I think so. You push this little thing here. Or do you spin that other thing first? Or—"

Carolus Bledsoe had been standing near, looking a bit strained, as well he might, but taking no part in the discussion. Now he reached over and grabbed the gun.

"Do me a favor, Roger. Since I'm the one this gun's

going to be pointed at, let me load it myself, will you? I'd just as soon not have the damned thing blow up in my face."

Seeing the force of Carolus's argument, Roger handed him the blank cartridge. Carolus slapped it into the chamber, made sure the safety catch was on, and laid the Smith & Wesson on the prop table.

"Now for the love of heaven leave it alone, will you? Nobody's going to mess around with the props at this stage of the game. Here's my .32, all loaded and ready to use, if it makes you feel any better."

He dragged the smaller gun from his pocket with a hand that shook slightly, laid it on the table beside the larger, and went to get dressed as the feedbag man. It was high time Dittany got dressed, too. Being a tiny tot took longer to achieve these days than when she'd been six years old.

At the opera house, they'd had proper dressing rooms. Here in the high school gym, arrangements were communal, to use no more pejorative term. Women changed in the girls' locker room, men in the boys'. Folding tables to hold the greasepaint, benches dragged up to them, and a few illuminated mirrors borrowed under protest from teenage daughters were the amenities. There was one full-length mirror for the women, unscrewed by Zilla Trott from the back of her own bathroom door and transported in the Monks' new ranch wagon. Privacy was obtainable only in the lavatory stalls.

The whole setup was a nuisance. Nobody had anywhere to put anything. Early arrivers who had nothing whatever to do with the play kept wandering backstage out of curiosity. There was no way to keep them out; nothing separated the stage and wings from the part of the gym where the audience would sit except a row of green curtains hung clothesline fashion across the room. Anybody who wasn't limber enough or insouciant enough to duck under the curtains could easily find an opening to slip through, or else walk down the corridor and in the back way.

Most of the interlopers were locals who felt that the school was as much theirs as anybody's anyway. Everybody had a relative or a neighbor in the cast. That the relative or neighbor might not care much for being burst in on while clad in half a costume and a basic coat of greasepaint had not occurred to them. Nor did most of the uninvited visitors realize that the relative or neighbor could only be found in a locker room full of other people's relatives and neighbors in similar states of undress. There were a lot of "Oops, excuse me's" floating around.

One such stammered apology came from a tallish woman in a padded storm coat who claimed to be looking for the ladies' room. She had her hood drawn down over her forehead, which might have meant that she preferred not to show her hair in public before she'd had a chance to comb it in private. The dark glasses could have indicated an eye ailment and the scarf pulled up around her chin a toothache. Taken all together, they presented a small puzzle to the inquiring mind, particularly as Desdemona Portley's husband, in his zeal to cooperate, had jacked up the gym thermostat to a degree where most people were shedding their outer wraps as fast as they could find places to park them.

Dittany, who happened to be sitting at one of the makeup mirrors, caught the woman's reflection in the glass and paused in the act of tying her blue hair ribbon. There was something familiar in the woman's gait as she walked quickly away. Dittany gave a final tweak to her bow, slipped out of the locker room, and watched the intruder go not toward the ladies' room but out through the curtain into the audience. If that wasn't Carolus Bledsoe's ex-wife, she'd be a ring-tailed monkey with the chicken pox. What had happened to that policeman who was supposed to be standing guard?

Dittany tiptoed over to the curtains and peeked through a slit. The Thespians were well on the way to a full house, she noted with momentary elation. Sergeant MacVicar was there, eighth row center, out of uniform and looking even more Presbyterian than usual in his Sunday suit. Mrs. MacVicar had on that lovely cherry-colored wool dress she'd bought a year ago at the January sales. Mrs. MacVicar always dressed well, though never extravagantly. She knew what was due her husband's position.

It couldn't possibly have been Sergeant MacVicar who'd accepted an off-duty assignment. It probably wasn't Bob or Ray, they'd be minding the station. That left only—yes, there he was. A rotund, elderly man also in mufti—blue trousers, green shirt, and yellow cardigan—was standing up by the main entrance with a cup of lemonade, a handful of Girl Guide cookies, and an expression of gentle bemusement. She might have known.

One of the volunteer stagehands happened to wander by, bent on nothing in particular that Dittany could think of. She beckoned him over.

"Sammy, see that woman with the hood and scarf over her face, and the sunglasses? She's just sitting down, third row from the front on the left, beside the fire exit."

"In the brown coat?"

Dittany would have called the coat burgundy, but she let it pass. There wasn't another woman in the audience wearing a hood, a scarf, and sunglasses anyway. "Yes, that's the one. And do you see Ormerod Burlson up by the back door? With the yellow sweater."

"Yup."

"Could you go very quietly and casually up to Ormerod and tell him that's the woman he's supposed to be keeping an eye on?"

"Huh? What for?"

"Because she's the one who threw the tomato at Carolus Bledsoe last night. Ormerod's been hired to keep her from pulling any tricks tonight and he's asleep at the switch as usual. Tell him to come down front and sit in that empty seat just behind her."

"Too late. Some other woman's taking it."

"Wouldn't you know! Then tell Ormerod to lurk just outside the exit door."

"He won't be able to see the stage from there."

"Who cares? He's not getting paid to watch the show. Go ahead, Sammy, quick. I have to start the overture in a minute."

She probably ought to be at the piano already, waiting for Osbert to give her the signal. Still, Dittany lingered at the slit in the curtain. She saw Sammy approach Ormerod. She saw Ormerod look annoyed and make a gesture toward the lemonade stand. She saw Sammy grab Ormerod by the sweater and speak in a forceful manner. She saw Sammy walk Ormerod down the side aisle and park him at the fire exit. There was more to that kid than met the eye, by gum.

She absolutely must get to her post. Still, Dittany turned back for one more peek. The ex-Mrs. Bledsoe was unbuttoning her storm coat. The person who'd taken that seat behind her was leaning forward, perhaps asking her to drop her hood and quit blocking the view.

It was not a woman, it was a man, almost handsome in a cadaverous sort of way. Sammy must have been deceived by the flowing black cloak and the silky white shirt. What role was Leander Hellespont playing now?

Chapter 9

Almost before the curtain went up, the Traveling Thespians had the audience in their collective pocket. The people out front, and particularly those in the bleachers, applauded Dittany's overture. They applauded the makeshift set, they applauded the feedbag man, they went crazy over Dan McGrew in his top hat and waxed mustache. They even applauded the somewhat long-winded speech Jenson Thorbisher-Freep insisted on making during the intermission, though it might have been better for the gym floor if they'd all put down their lemonade before they started to clap.

If the first act was a triumph, the second was what Joshua Burberry's father the distinguished scientist would unhesitatingly have classified as a lalapalooza. The miners' singing started the spectators whistling, the cancan girls set them stamping their feet, and the hoedown snatched them out into the aisles. Dittany had to play "Sit Down, You're Rocking the Boat" twice to get them back to their seats so the play could go on.

With so much audience participation, it wasn't easy for her to keep an eye on the two potential saboteurs sitting next to the fire exit. Dittany had no faith whatever in Ormerod Burlson. Nobody from Lobelia Falls would have trusted him to guard a jam jar full of pollywogs, but of course an outlander like Carolus Bledsoe would have had no way of knowing. All Dittany could do was pin her hopes on Sammy and keep playing. She finished her sentimental medley, cutting it short because they'd already spent too much time on the hoedown, and swung into "The Maple Leaf Rag."

The miner made his entrance. The audience applauded Joshua's blizzard, but not for long. The suspense was building, the atmosphere growing tense enough to cut with a knife. People strained forward in their seats as the miner tilted his poke of dust on the bar and the lady known as Lou registered perplexed perturbation. Dittany went to get her sarsaparilla, the miner took her seat, the tape began to play. It was all going like clockwork. The Architrave had the Thorbisher-Freep collection sewn up tighter than a shrunk sock.

Now the miner was staggering to his feet. Dittany parked her sarsaparilla on the piano and stepped behind it to be out of the way. By the dim red glow of the exit light she could see Sammy nudging Ormerod over to where Leander Hellespont and the ex-Mrs. Bledsoe were sitting. For the first time that day, she relaxed. It was all over but the shooting.

Now the miner was delivering his bitter taunt, drawing his .32 Colt. Dangerous Dan McGrew was hurling his cards to the floor, reaching for his .38 Smith & Wesson. Face to face the rivals stood, guns pointed straight at each other's chest. For a second or two they held the pose while not one member of the audience either inhaled or exhaled. Then two shots tore the air apart and two men dropped.

It was a truly horrendous moment. The cartridges exploding together made far more noise than they had in the high-ceilinged old opera house. Stunned and deafened, few except Dittany could have noticed that at the moment of truth, Andy McNaster had dropped the muzzle of his gun and shot at the floor instead of at Carolus.

Now the lady known as Lou was clasping Carolus to her bosom. It was more a clutch than a clasp, actually. Dittany could hear Arethusa hiss, "Quit squirming, varlet," as with perfect sangfroid she pinched the poke, flourished it around a bit so nobody could mistake what she was up to, and stowed it away among the ruffles in her decolletage.

The curtain closed. The applause went on. Under its cover, the actors scrambled to assemble for curtain calls.

Tradition among the Traveling Thespians decreed that the entire cast must appear together so that nobody's feelings would be hurt. It was a job packing them in and Carolus Bledsoe wasn't making things any easier by remaining prone where Arethusa had dumped him.

"All right, Carolus," said Osbert, who was shoving actors into place like toy soldiers, "the curtain's closed. You can get up now."

"The hell I can," groaned Bledsoe. "That bastard shot me!"

"The hell I did!" Andy retorted in a kind of whispered roar. "I shot at the floor. And it was only a blank anyway."

"The hell it was! You shot off my foot."

"The hell I—oh, my God!"

The hole in the toe of Carolus Bledsoe's boot offered no room for further argument.

"Curtain calls, Carolus," Arethusa commanded. "You can bleed later."

"Here." Roger Munson had rushed onstage to kneel beside the wounded man with an ampule of ammonia and a flask of brandy. "Sniff this. Drink this. I'll get the stretcher ready offstage. The show must go on."

And on it went. Carolus was helped into a straight chair center stage. Arethusa sat beside him, holding his hand to give him courage. Ethel the faithful friend was brought to flop at his feet, hiding the bullet-torn boot and the blood that was beginning to ooze out of it. Andrew McNaster stood behind Arethusa and Desdemona Portley behind Carolus, ready to prop him up if he fainted. Bill Coskoff, with a bar rag at the ready, squeezed in back of Dessie, who wasn't very tall. The rest of the cast clustered around as best they could without hiding anybody.

The curtain parted again. Dittany tripped in from the wings, handed Carolus back his feedbag with a pretty curtsey, and sat down on the stage floor beside Ethel. The applause went on and on. The stagehands had to draw the curtain and open it again ten times in rapid succession. The cast could easily have taken ten more calls, but Carolus was beginning to look white around the beard. Osbert murmured, "Thanks, everybody. Go get dressed. Roger, take Carolus to the hospital, quick. I'll try to keep the hordes away from backstage.''

He stepped out in front of the curtain and raised his hands for silence.

"That's it, folks. Thank you all, you've been the greatest audience any company could ask for. We also want Mr. Portley to know how grateful we are to him for letting us take over the gym on such short notice, and to thank the Girl Guides and Mr. Thorbisher-Freep and the scene painters and the stagehands and the wardrobe crew and if I've left anybody out it's not because I don't appreciate what you've done, it's just that I'm too dad-blanged beat to think straight. And now I'd like to ask you all for one more really important favor. Would everybody here, with the single exception of Sergeant MacVicar, please not try to come backstage?''

There were a few indignant murmurs, but Osbert explained them away. "You all know why we couldn't use the opera house as we'd planned. We couldn't even get our scenery out. We've been breaking our backs ever since we got the word this morning so that we wouldn't have to disappoint you of tonight's performance and forfeit our chance to win the Thorbisher-Freep collection for the Architrave Museum. So now it's late and the whole gang back there's plumb tuckered out. There's not much room for them to change in even without a lot of extra people milling around. We also have to dismantle our set and lug all our stuff out of here tonight. That bargain varnish the painter used on those pews over at the Presbyterian Church still hasn't dried and doesn't look as if it will, so the minister wants to hold services here tomorrow morning and I'm sure none of you want to stand in his way. Your folks will come out here as soon as they're ready. If you'll all cooperate by leaving through the main exit as quickly as possible, the Traveling Thespians will sponsor a full evening of reels and hoedowns as soon as Mr. Portley will let us use the gym again.''

"Next Saturday night,'' the principal called out, good sport that he was.

"You heard him, folks.'' Osbert was hoarse now but still in there punching. "Everybody's invited. A buck a head for the Senior Class Outing Fund and the lemonade's on the house. So I guess that's it for now. Good night and thanks for coming. See you next Saturday night, seven-thirty sharp, and wear your dancing shoes.''

The audience laughed and clapped, except for one cheeky young sprout in the back row of the bleachers. ''Hey, how come Sergeant MacVicar gets to go backstage if the rest of us can't?''

''They need him to arrest creeps like you if you don't do like the director says,'' yelled back the invaluable Sammy.

Osbert stayed out front shaking hands, accepting congratulations, and wondering what to do about Archie and Daniel. Jenson Thorbisher-Freep and his daughter Wilhedra went around shaking hands, too, though some people wondered why. Pretty soon Desdemona Portley and some of the other Thespians came out from behind the curtains and helped to cope with the lingerers.

Not many of the audience were hanging around. The gym clock showed how late the show had run. Sounds of pounding emphasized that the wrecking crew was on the job. More cast members emerged, more patrons left. Somewhere along the line, Leander Hellespont and the ex-Mrs. Bledsoe trickled away unnoticed.

The exodus was proceeding as Osbert had hoped. Nobody out front could have caught on that the Monks' new ranch wagon, with Roger Munson at the wheel and Carolus Bledsoe stretched out on Ethel's blanket in the back, was speeding toward Scottsbeck Hospital. None of them could see Sergeant MacVicar shaking his head over a splinter-edged hole in the stage or overhear the bizarre story he was getting from a badly shaken Andrew McNaster.

''I was supposed to fire straight at his chest,'' Andy blurted. Then he shook.

''Yet you fired into the floor,'' Sergeant MacVicar prompted. ''Why, Mr. McNaster?''

Andy was still wearing his villain suit, although it now had a red bandana at the throat. He untied the bandana and mopped his forehead with it, swallowed hard, and searched for the words he needed.

''Well, eh, I was the bad guy. You know that, I knew it all along. But all of a sudden here I am with a shooting iron in my hand and it's like what they call the moment of truth. It hits me all of a sudden what a lowdown ornery rotter I've been right straight through from the beginning of act one, scene one. I've ruined the feedbag man's career. I've brought his wife and kiddie to the brink of starvation. I've lured a chaste and noble woman way the heck and gone up here to the Yukon with false promises I never meant to keep.''

"Hence the falsity. Go on, Mr. McNaster."

"So anyway, here's his wife having to flaunt her shapely limbs in a black lace corset for rude men to leer at and make remarks. And here's his kiddie sitting up late and knocking back the sarsaparilla, sullying her pink ears with a bunch of cheap talk from a class of customer no innocent maid of tender years ought to be hanging out with. And it's me that drug 'em here. You follow me so far?''

"Aye, Mr. McNaster, I'm with you every step."

"Thanks, Sergeant. So now here comes this poor bugger out of the night that was fifty below, so beat and bedraggled they can't even tell it's him. He calls me a hound of hell and like I said it hits me right between the eyes, the bugger's right. He's going to shoot me and it's no more than I deserve. But the hitch is, I'm supposed to shoot him back, which means leaving his grieving widow and her little chickabiddy alone and unprotected in this den of iniquity to which I in my wickedness and vainglory enticed them. You get my drift, Sergeant?''

"Aye." Sergeant MacVicar was rubbing his jaw, his ice-blue eyes still fixed on the perspiring McNaster. "You found yoursel' confronted by a moral dilemma."

"That's the situation in a nutshell, Sergeant. Some forgotten vestige of a nobler nature rises up and stays my hand. I'm standing there with my gun aimed at his gizzard and the stern voice of conscience is chewing me out. 'Dan McGrew,' it's saying, 'you ruined that poor bugger's life. You can't shoot him now.' But I've got to fire or louse up Osbert's big scene, so what I did, see, I waited till Charlie pulled his trigger, then I quick dropped my hand and fired at the floor. Only I guess I didn't drop it quite far enough. So that's my story, Sergeant, and I can't tell you any different.''

"Indeed, Mr. McNaster. And now will you kindly show me your license for yon ugly great firearm?"

"That's not my gun! It belongs to Jenson Thorbisher-Freep. He just lent it for the play."

"And how long have you had it in your possession?"

"I never had it in my possession. Ask anybody. Jenson brought the gun to rehearsal and took it away again afterward. I suppose he did the same thing tonight. All I know is, Roger put it on the prop table when he was getting the stuff ready, and handed it to me when I went on for the second act. Jenson couldn't come backstage during the performance, see, because the other companies in the contest might think he was playing favorites."

"Nae doot. During rehearsals did you shoot the gun at Mr. Bledsoe's chest?"

"Sure, but that was different."

"How, Mr. McNaster?"

"Well, see, at the rehearsal I knew I was rehearsing, if you get what I mean. I was just Andy McNaster making believe I was Dan McGrew. I knew that was a blank cartridge in the gun and Bledsoe wasn't going to get hurt when I pulled the trigger, so it didn't matter. But tonight" —Andy mopped his face again then shook his head as if to rattle his thoughts together—"I wasn't me, I was Dan McGrew. What I'm trying to say is, I knew I was me but I was Dan and Dan was shooting a real bullet even if Andy only had a blank in the gun. I guess that sounds pretty crazy, eh."

"Dinna fash yoursel' about craziness, Mr. McNaster. It's for you to talk and me to sort out what you say. What happened to the gun after you shot it off?"

"It dropped from my nerveless hand and I fell on top of it. Dan McGrew got killed, too, you have to remember. I stayed dead till the lady known as Lou finished pinching the stranger's poke and I heard the curtain close and people start to clap. Then I got up and put the gun back in my holster and went to my place for curtain calls, like we practiced in rehearsal. I was me by then. My mind was functioning like a steel trap. Only I guess you think the trap could of stood some oiling, eh."

"You didn't notice you'd shot yon Bledsoe?"

"Nope."

"None of us noticed," Arethusa Monk put in. "I didn't myself, forsooth, not even while I was pinching his poke."

"Mr. Bledsoe said nothing to you?"

"No, but he thrashed around a bit. Meseemed the churl was simulating death throes to pad out his part, egad. I wrestled him into a seemly posture and hissed at him to lie still, little wotting he was actually writhing in pain. Then I felt him go limp. Perchance he swooned, but that didn't occur to me at the time. I simply went through my business with the poke, then unbosomed myself of Carolus and got set for the curtain call, like Andrew."

"Leaving Mr. Bledsoe lying on the stage?"

"I' faith, yes."

"You have to remember this all happened faster than it takes to tell," Dittany put in. "You may recall, Sergeant MacVicar, that I was standing right behind the piano, so I could see exactly what happened. Carolus did shoot first, and Andy did deliberately tilt his gun down before he shot. I couldn't think why. I didn't realize Carolus was hurt and I don't think anybody else did at the time. He fell forward on his face, as he was supposed to, and that hid the toe of his boot, you see. He did squirm around a bit and I heard Arethusa tell him to keep still. I do think Arethusa's right about his fainting. He lay there so long that Osbert finally went over to him and said something like, 'You're not dead any longer, Carolus.' Then Carolus said he was, too, because Andy had shot him."

"Were those his words?"

"That was the general thrust. His actual phrasing was a bit more pungent," Dittany replied primly. "Then Andy said he didn't, and Carolus rolled over and we could see where the toe of his boot had a hole in it. So Roger Munson gave him first aid and we shoved him into a chair and took our curtain calls as fast as we could. Roger's driving Carolus to the hospital now. We knew you'd understand. Osbert wasn't sure how fast he could get you back here without starting a stampede in the audience, and we couldn't very well leave Carolus lying around wondering how many toes he had left."

"You didna remove the damaged boot?"

"Oh no, we didn't dare. It was a great, clunky thing. Roger said we'd better leave it for the doctors to cut off with a laser beam or something. We didn't want to lose any bits and pieces that might have to be sewn back on, you know."

Sergeant MacVicar nodded in understanding. "Now, can you tell me who loaded yon gun? Was it Jenson Thorbisher-Freep?"

"No, it was Carolus himself. Jenson had brought the gun already loaded, but Roger'd got nervous about leaving it that way, so he'd taken out the cartridge and hidden it in the poke."

"Assuming the cartridge was a blank, eh?"

"Yes, of course. You see, it was the only one we had left. Jenson had brought four to start with, but we'd used up three of them rehearsing. We couldn't get any more because the .38 ones have to be ordered specially and Roger didn't see any sense in spending the money for a whole box when we only needed one bang. So anyway, Roger'd got the cartridge out all right but he didn't seem quite sure how to get it back in. Carolus was standing there watching Roger fuss around and getting edgier by the second. Finally he took the gun and said he'd as soon load it himself since he was the one getting shot at, so Roger let him."

"Carolus Bledsoe also being under the impression he was loading a blank cartridge?"

"Well, naturally. That is, he must have, mustn't he? Unless he was planning to commit suicide and pin the rap on Andy."

Chapter 10

Sergeant MacVicar rubbed his chin again. "And why should he want to do that, Dittany?"

"I don't know," she admitted. "It was just a passing thought. I might alternatively have suggested that Carolus had meant to switch guns in order to kill Andy without being too obvious and it slipped his mind at the last minute, but that's only because I've typed so many of Arethusa's manuscripts. What I really think is that Carolus mistook a real bullet for a blank cartridge, just as Roger and I and Jenson Thorbisher-Freep did."

"Dittany lass, not even you could mistake a real bullet for a blank cartridge."

"I could try."

"The effort would avail you naething. A blank cartridge is flat on top and has but a wee disc of cardboard inserted to compress a light charge of gunpowder. Yon disc is referred to as a wad, nae doot frae the time when a wad of tow was inserted to tamp down the powder in a muzzle-loader. A bullet projects noticeably from the cartridge case and comes to what might be described as a rounded point. It is most often of a silver color in contrast to the brass cartridge."

"Then how could Carolus have made such an awful mistake?" she demanded. "He knows about guns. At least he knows more than the rest of us."

"More than Deputy Monk?" Sergeant MacVicar had a

special regard for Osbert, who often served as his unpaid deputy.

"Certainly more than Osbert. Osbert doesn't shoot guns, he just writes about them. Anyway, Osbert didn't know about the unloading and reloading because he was out front checking the set. But I saw the cartridge myself, Sergeant. I helped Roger find it."

"Oh aye? Find it where?"

"It was in the poke, and the poke was inside the feedbag. Roger was so sure he'd left the poke on the table by itself that he never thought to look. That's the trouble with being organized. But anyway, the cartridge I saw was flat on both ends and had a little red dot on top just like the three we used at rehearsal. So how could it hurt anybody? Unless someone took it out and put in a bullet," Dittany added in a rather scared tone.

"Or unless what you took for a blank cartridge was in fact what is known as a wad-cutting bullet," Sergeant MacVicar amplified. "These are normally used for target shooting, but one of .38 caliber could certainly be lethal at close range. The bullet is pushed down inside the cartridge and covered by the wad, which it cuts as it emerges."

"Hence the name, no doubt. But then it's perfectly easy to mistake a live bullet for a blank cartridge so why did you say it wasn't?"

"Because I wasna thinking straight," Sergeant MacVicar admitted handsomely. "A wad-cutter weighs more than a blank, I needna say, and is distinguished by a wad of a different color, as red for a blank and green for a wad-cutter."

"But if you didn't know what a .38 blank was supposed to weigh, you mightn't notice the cartridge was too heavy," said Dittany, "and you could always paint a green dot red."

"Or if you loaded your ain cartridges, you could substitute the wrong wad for the right one, either by accident or on purpose. Is Mr. Thorbisher-Freep still here, lass?"

"I'll go and see."

Dittany ran out into the auditorium. Yes, Jenson was still there, and so was Wilhedra, looking as if she might be coming up to the boil. The lid hadn't popped yet, but it was jittering a little. She was talking to Daniel, but not listening when he talked back. It was the long, green curtain that she kept glancing toward, and anybody with half an eye could have seen she was pretty steamed because Carolus Bledsoe hadn't yet come through it to meet her. Before Dittany could get to the elder Thorbisher-Freep, Wilhedra tackled her.

"Why, you're still in costume. I thought everyone backstage was madly changing. How's Carolus doing?"

"As well as can be expected in the circumstances, I suppose," Dittany answered vaguely. "The last I knew, he was having trouble with one of his boots."

"One of his boots? How ridiculous!"

"Well, that's showbiz. Excuse me, I have to speak to your father on a general question of theatrical expertise."

"Such as how to get a boot off?"

Wilhedra's smile was painful to see. Dittany only smiled back and kept moving. Fortunately for her, Jenson was with Osbert at the moment. Archie was there, too, looking about the way Osbert's father had looked at the wedding reception before Bert got him out back at the picnic table and began telling him eyewear salesman stories. Dittany slipped her arm through Osbert's and gave him a squeeze out of sheer necessity. He squeezed back, perhaps for the same reason.

"Howdy, pardner. How's it going back there?"

"Wilhedra was just asking me pretty much the same thing, funnily enough. Jenson, we need you backstage on a question of theatrical expertise." Dittany couldn't suppress a yawn as she spoke, and Osbert squeezed her arm again.

"Going to sleep without rocking tonight, eh, kid? Come on, what's happening?"

"Roger's coping as you told him to, Andy's better nature has prevailed again, and Sergeant MacVicar wants to ask Jenson something, so would you please go backstage right now, Jenson?"

"Why, certainly, if I'm needed. It's not going to take long, is it?"

"I fervently hope not," Dittany answered. "We're all about ready to drop. Archie, Andy McNaster's changing now. He'll drive you and Daniel back to the inn and we'll see you for breakfast about half past nine. Will that suit you?''

Archie shook his head. ''I'm afraid that's not going to work, Dittany. The only plane we could get seats on leaves at half past ten. That means we ought to be on the road by eight or a little after, wouldn't you say?''

''I would, unfortunately. Then breakfast will have to be at seven, unless you'd rather we just came a little before eight and picked you up. I could drive while you and Osbert talk. What a pity you have to leave so soon.''

''Isn't it,'' Archie replied politely. ''However, we've done what we came for. I have to tell you Daniel's quite excited about the play, though it's never safe to count chickens that haven't hatched yet. Why don't we leave it that I'll give you a ring first thing in the morning when I find out what Daniel wants to do? Would half past six be too early?''

''Not if you expect Osbert and me to be ready on time. Ethel usually wants her breakfast about then anyway.''

Ethel had been able to sleep through the entire second act. Dittany had seen her a minute ago, fresh and rested, taking an intelligent interest in the work of the scene shifters. She'd spend another five or six hours in restful slumber tonight, God willing, get Dittany up two minutes before dawn cracked to serve her breakfast, take her morning stroll up Cat Alley, check out a few fence posts, and exchange compliments with any neighbor who happened along. Then she'd come home and flake out beside the stove for a few hours while her alleged master and mistress dragged themselves off to deliver Archie and Daniel to the airport assuming Sergeant MacVicar would let them leave town. A dog's life, forsooth! Dittany leaned on Osbert's arm and let him steer her backstage to see how Jenson Thorbisher-Freep was making out.

Jenson was a most unhappy man, that much was clear at a glance. He was standing listening to Sergeant MacVicar, running his hands through his frosty mane but forgetting to look leonine. As the sergeant finished explaining what had happened, Jenson simply stood there staring at him. Then he shook himself together, much as Andy McNaster had done.

"What a dreadfully shocking thing to happen! Where is the dear fellow now? My daughter will want to go to him at once. Dittany, have you broken the news to Wilhedra?"

Of course she hadn't, why on earth should she? "I didn't think it was my place to," Dittany answered rather curtly.

"No, of course it wasn't." Jenson clutched another fistful of hair. "What am I thinking of? But you say Carolus is in no great danger, Sergeant?"

"I can say naething on that count, sir, until I receive an official report from the hospital."

"He cussed a lot while they were getting him out the back door on the stretcher," Dittany volunteered to make amends for her brusqueness. "That's always a healthy sign, don't you think?"

Sergeant MacVicar gazed down on her corkscrew curls with an indulgent eye. "Nae doot, lassie."

He was lapsing into his old habit of regarding her as a wee, fatherless bairn. She really ought to go and get out of this pinafore, but she couldn't bear not to hear what Jenson might have to say about the cartridge.

Sergeant MacVicar must be anxious, too. He lost no time getting to the point. "Noo, Mr. Thorbisher-Freep, I understand the gun McNaster fired belongs to you."

"You're quite right, Sergeant. It's an old Smith & Wesson that came from my collection of theatrical memorabilia. As it happened, I'd carried the gun myself when I played Jack Rance in *The Girl of the Golden West*. The four blank cartridges I brought along with it were left over from that production. Is that what you wanted to ask me? I'd like to get back to my daughter."

"In guid time, Mr. Thorbisher-Freep. How long had yon cartridges been in your possession?"

"Far longer than I like to think. Twenty years at least, perhaps nearer thirty. But they worked perfectly all right at rehearsals, Sergeant."

"They made lovely bangs," Dittany confirmed.

"Aye," said Sergeant MacVicar. "I misdoubt they banged louder than new ones. The powder would hae dried out and gained rather than losing strength. Am I no' correct, Mr. Thorbisher-Freep?''

"I should not presume to judge, Sergeant. My stage manager at the time got hold of the cartridges somewhere and showed me how to load the gun, which I'd bought originally not to use but simply as a collector's item. I was told it had been carried on Buffalo Bill's Wild West Show's first European tour in 1887. This may have been Bill's own gun. The initials W.F.C. are engraved on the butt, as you see, though I realize they're no positive guarantee of authenticity. However, I'm sure you're not interested in historical footnotes just now. My point is simply that my knowledge of firearms has never progressed beyond that one small experience.''

"You've ne'er used the gun for target practice?''

"One doesn't need target practice to shoot off a blank, Sergeant. I do know that much. And I know the difference between a blank cartridge and a live bullet.'' Heat was creeping into Jenson's pear-shaped tones. "I can assure you the four blanks I turned over to the Traveling Thespians' property man were in fact blanks. Don't ask me how Andrew McNaster got hold of that bullet he shot my good friend Carolus Bledsoe with. I can only tell you he didn't get it from me.''

Sergeant MacVicar favored the wealthy collector with an Augustan nod. "Weel spoken, Mr. Thorbisher-Freep. Tell me noo, did you yoursel' handle yon four cartridges before you gave them to Roger Munson?''

"Handle them? What an odd question. But yes, as a matter of fact, I did. The blanks were in the gun, you see, and I didn't much like the idea of leaving them there while I was carrying it around. I know so little of firearms, I thought perhaps they might all explode at once if I hit a big pothole or something. The roads are in wretched condition this time of year, as I'm sure I don't have to tell you. Anyway, however unnecessary it might have been, I unloaded the gun and put the cartridges in a box with cotton around them. That's what I normally do with any small item from my collection if I take it anywhere.''

"And when you took them out, did you happen to

notice that one of the cartridges was heavier than the others?''

"No, I can't say that I did. Why should it be? On account of the powder's shrinking, as you mentioned earlier?''

"That would make no detectable difference in the weight, Mr. Thorbisher-Freep. Has it ne'er entered your ken that there exists sic a thing as a wad-cutting bullet?''

"A wad-cutting bullet? No, that's a new one on me. What do they look like?''

"They look like blank cartridges. The cardboard wad on top is not the same color, but that can easily be got around. The one feature impossible to conceal is that the wad-cutter weighs more than a blank because it has a bullet concealed inside the cartridge casing.''

"Then I'd have noticed," said Jenson. "I have a highly developed sense of touch. Collectors do, they say. Maybe that's why we collect, so we can have lots of pleasant things to fondle. And I handled the cartridges quite a lot, actually. First I took them out of the cylinder one by one, you know, and laid them in the box, as I said. Then I took them out again one at a time, to load the gun. Finally, having been assured it would be safe to do so, I loaded the one remaining blank into the Smith & Wesson before I brought it over here this afternoon. By that time, you see, I'd had plenty of chances to get used to the heft of them. It's absolutely impossible I wouldn't have felt the difference if that last cartridge weighed more than the others had.''

Sergeant MacVicar nodded. "I incline to the same opinion, Mr. Thorbisher-Freep.''

"Then how could Carolus have been shot? Unless somebody took out the blank I put in and substituted one of those wad-cutting bullets you speak of. By mistake, I'm sure. Some youngster playing in the gym could have fired off the gun, then realized he might get in trouble for wasting the blank. So he ran home and got one of his father's bullets, not being able to tell the difference. You all have guns over here, I expect.''

That just showed how much Jenson Thorbisher-Freep knew about Lobelia Falls. Dittany expected Sergeant

MacVicar to set the man straight, but all he said was, "Nae doot Roger Munson will be able to cast light on the matter when he gets back from the hospital. Noo, Mr. Thorbisher-Freep, could you tell me just for the record what you did after you dropped off yon gun and left here?"

"Yes, of course. Dear me, this reminds me of the time I played Sherlock Holmes in *The Hound of the Baskervilles*. Let's see, I came over this morning to break the sad news about the opera house. I'm sure you know all about our olfactory disaster, so I shan't go into that. Once I saw how ably the Traveling Thespians were coping with the emergency, I took Miss Monk out to lunch. That was at Dittany's suggestion, actually, but of course the pleasure was mine. Where is our lovely heroine, by the way?"

"In the girls' locker room unhooking her Merry Widow, I expect," Dittany told him. "She had to be grilled, so she's late getting changed."

Jenson winced. "How painful you make it sound. I hope Arethusa's not unduly upset by what happened to Carolus?"

"That depends on how you define unduly. We're none of us any too happy about it."

Except maybe Roger Munson because he liked nothing better than a situation he could rise to, but Dittany thought she wouldn't say so in front of Jenson Thorbisher-Freep. Why didn't the old gasbag quit nattering about Arethusa and finish what he had to say? She really was ready to drop, and poor Osbert must be asleep on his feet. She hadn't heard a yip out of him since they came backstage. Now he was leaning against her as if she were a gatepost, not that she minded.

"So then you brought Arethusa back to the gym," she prompted to get Jenson back on the track. "That was just after half past one, as I recall. You stood talking to Carolus for a while, then you left."

"Thank you for refreshing my memory." Jenson was looking pretty shopworn, too. "I'm flattered that my movements made so deep an impression on you in the midst of so much turmoil. As you say, Dittany, I left. My object in talking with Carolus had been to find out whether he'd be able to attend a little tea my daughter was planning in order to celebrate his debut as a leading man. However, it was obvious by then that he couldn't get away, so I went home to tell Wilhedra she'd better postpone her tea party.''

"Miss Thorbisher-Freep and Mr. Bledsoe are good friends, then?'' Sergeant MacVicar asked almost as innocently as if he didn't know.

Jenson Thorbisher-Freep smiled. "I think you might say so, Sergeant. Strictly between us, they're only waiting for this regrettable lawsuit over his divorce settlement to be done with before they announce their engagement. Carolus's former wife is a woman of volatile temperament, as you may have heard, and they don't want to provoke any public scenes from her like the one we were treated to at the dress rehearsal. By the way, I must compliment the Lobelia Falls police force on the superb job your man Burlson did in averting a possible repeat of last night's episode.''

Sergeant MacVicar made a noise like the final wheeze of a distant bagpipe. He wasn't used to hearing much but complaints about Ormerod, except from owners of stray livestock. Ormerod did have an affinity with the larger quadrupeds.

"Rm'ph. Did you leave yon revolver with the Traveling Thespians before or after you took Miss Monk to eat, Mr. Thorbisher-Freep?''

"Oh, before. I'd brought it with me from home not knowing whether or where it might be needed later and not wishing to face a possible extra trip back and forth from Scottsbeck. Once I learned the performance would be held in Lobelia Falls, I was glad to turn the revolver over to Roger Munson. I'd have felt ridiculous toting the thing into a restaurant with me like one of our friend Osbert's gunslingers, and I'd never have dared leave it in the car.''

"A commendable caution, Mr. Thorbisher-Freep. And what happened after you dropped Miss Monk off?''

"I didn't drop her off, exactly. I came back here with her just to see how matters were progressing. I stayed for—what, Dittany? Not more than fifteen minutes at the most, wouldn't you say?''

"About that,'' Dittany conceded.

"By then my conscience was giving me twinges about the tea party, so I went straight home and explained the situation to my daughter. Cad that I am, I left Wilhedra to handle the cancellations, and went upstairs to take a nap. And there I stayed, reading and dozing, until our upstairs maid called me to dinner. My daughter and I dined together with the maid in attendance as usual, then Wilhedra drove me here, since she knows I dislike driving after dark. Now she's waiting to drive me back and it really is getting awfully late, Sergeant, so if you—"

"Indeed I'll no' keep the leddy waiting any longer," Sergeant MacVicar replied gallantly. "I'll just write you a wee receipt for yon firearm, thank you for your patience, and wish you a very guid e'en, Mr. Thorbisher-Freep."

Chapter 11

"I know what you're thinking," said Dittany.

"Oh aye?" Sergeant MacVicar gave her the kind of look an elderly Scot would naturally give a wee bairn who was being a pain in the neck. "Then ye ken mair than I do, lass. That a distinguished citizen like yon Thorbisher-Freep would plot a bloody vengeance against his daughter's fiancé just because Bledsoe's attentions hae been temporarily diverted to another and I must say far handsomer wumman is mair than I'm prepared to swallow."

"That's not what I thought you were thinking. What you darn well ought to be thinking, eh, is about letting Mrs. MacVicar know what's keeping you. Unless of course you're prepared to sit down to breakfast in the morning and find out she's sprinkled sugar on your porridge."

"She wouldna! Mrs. MacVicar is a God-fearing wumman. She kens weel that sugar on parritch is against nature and releegion." The sergeant paused to reflect. "Howsomever, lass, as a matter o' common courtesy, it wouldna hurt for you to step out there and kindly explain that I might be held up here yet for some wee while."

"Doing what?" Osbert asked, somewhat to Dittany's surprise for she'd thought him still asleep. "Everybody's gone home, pretty much."

"Aye," said the sergeant, "an' that presents a problem. Did it no' occur to you, Deputy Monk, that they should all be held for interrogation?"

"Sure it did, but how could I? They all had families in

the audience waiting to drive them home. It was either let
them go or start a stampede. Anyway, you'll have a
chance to grill them all in the morning. I've invited the
whole cast and backstage crew to breakfast at our house.''

"Osbert," cried Dittany, "you might have told me!"

"Oh, didn't I? I'm sorry, dear, it slipped my mind. I
think I said half past nine. Or maybe half past ten. Half
past something, I'm fairly sure."

They'd find out fast enough come morning. What the
flaming heck was she going to serve all those people?
Dittany went off on her peacekeeping mission feeling pretty
warlike herself. She found Mrs. MacVicar sitting alone in
the gymnasium, somewhat pinched around the lips.

"Your husband sent me out with an olive branch in my
beak," she explained. "He's awfully sorry to keep you
waiting, but he may be tied up here for another wee while.
Would you like to come backstage?"

"Candidly, I should like to go home to bed," Mrs.
MacVicar replied. However, she got up and followed Dittany through the green curtains. "Whatever is keeping
him?"

There was no point in not telling her now, so Dittany
did. "Somebody switched the blank cartridge in Andy
McNaster's six-shooter for a real bullet, and he shot Carolus Bledsoe in the foot."

"Indeed?" said Mrs. MacVicar. "That seems a remark-
ably ill-natured prank for someone to have played. But I
suppose we shouldn't pass judgment before we've discovered the facts. I expect Donald is hoping something like
that about myself just now. Have you ever wondered why
you got married, Dittany?"

"I'm wondering right now, if you want to know. Osbert
just this minute informed me that he's invited the whole
cast to Sunday breakfast and I doubt whether we've got
three eggs in the house. I'd intended to grocery shop this
morning. Or is it yesterday morning by now? Anyway, I
never got the chance and now I'm stuck."

"Fortunately I'm in a position to unstick you," Mrs.
MacVicar consoled her. "I don't know whether you've
ever met my daughter-in-law Nancy? She's one of those
incredibly talented people who can't seem to help making

a roaring success of anything they put their hands to. Last year she adopted a couple of chickens that some neighbors had ill-advisedly given their youngsters for Easter. Now she's got a flock of thirty hens and they're laying so fast she can't keep up with the surplus. I've got four dozen of Nancy's eggs in my fridge right now and I'm afraid she's going to give me some more tomorrow. You'll do me a big favor by taking the overflow off my hands. And people will bring things, too, you know. I can't imagine Hazel Munson doesn't already have a coffee cake wrapped up and ready to go."

Dittany managed a small chuckle. "I've got one of Hazel's coffee cakes in the freezer myself, come to think of it. And I can make a big batch of—oh gosh, I can't. I've promised Osbert's agent we'll take him and the man he brought with him to the airport first thing in the morning. They have to catch a plane at half past ten."

"Well, dinna fash yoursel', as Donald would say. Things always work out one way or another. Oh dear, he's going to ruin that good suit, and I just paid to have it pressed."

The sergeant was down on his hands and knees, crawling around the by now empty stage in what would have been an undignified manner if anybody else had been doing it. Mrs. MacVicar watched quietly for a moment, then walked over and spoke to him across the space where the footlights had been.

"Donald, if it's that unfired blank cartridge you're looking for, you'll find it caught in the crack where the left-hand steps don't quite butt up against the stage. I'm surprised nobody has noticed it before."

"Say," said Pierre Boulanger, who was just getting ready to leave, "I'll bet that's what I kicked. I remember my foot touching something and hearing it rattle across the floor while we were taking down the last flat. I looked down but didn't see anything, so I figured it must have been a nail out of the scenery or something and thought no more about it."

"Where were you when you kicked it, Pierre?" asked Osbert. He must have been awake all the time, after all.

"Seems to me I was standing right about where we'd set

that little table Andy'd been playing cards on. Is that the blank, Sergeant?''

Sergeant MacVicar had by now budged the dull brass cylinder out of the crack, using a couple of scenery nails as pincers. "So it would seem. Here we hae a .38 cartridge with its wad intact. The brass is tarnished and the wad discolored as if with age.''

Using the nails, he slid the cartridge on to a sheet of paper from his notebook, folded the paper into a little cradle, and lifted it.

"Frae the light weight, I judge this to be indeed a blank. Pending an affirmatory statement frae Mr. Thorbisher-Freep, we may tentatively assume this to be the fourth of his old blank cartridges, ta'en frae his gun and replaced by a deadlier missile. Nae doot we'll discover the spent bullet imbedded in the timbers beneath this stage, and much good will it do us.''

Sergeant MacVicar straightened up and dusted off his trousers as a small commotion heralded the return of Roger Munson. "Guid man, Roger. What's the vairdict?''

"Carolus lost the first joint of his left middle toe,'' Roger reported. "He's darn lucky it wasn't worse, but it turns out Carolus has unusually long middle toes so he has to buy his shoes half a size too large. What Andy shot away was mostly empty boot, he'll be relieved to know.''

"Aye, and what of yon Bledsoe? Did they keep him at the hospital?''

"Yes, but they said he could leave tomorrow morning if no symptoms develop.''

"What kind of symptoms?'' Dittany wanted to know.

"They didn't say. Lockjaw, blood poisoning, heart failure, whatever. I'm supposed to call in the morning and see if Carolus needs a lift.''

"Why you? Can't his own people collect him?''

"He seems to be quite alone in the world, now that he's divorced. When they asked for his next of kin, he just shook his head. It was rather pathetic,'' Roger added. He wasn't given to sentiment as a rule but no doubt succoring a man with half his middle toe shot off established some sort of bond.

Dittany shook her own head. "Carolus is practically

engaged to Wilhedra Thorbisher-Freep, Roger. Her father told us just a little while ago.''

"Is he, i' faith?" remarked Arethusa, who'd finally emerged from the girls' locker room with her Merry Widow over her arm. "Osbert, I want to go home. Now.''

"Then why the heck don't you?" her nephew replied politely.

"Churl! I require transportation.''

"Moulting mavericks, that's right! You're fresh out of boyfriends aren't you? How is it back there? All cleaned out?''

"Nobody's left, it's neat as a pin, and there's nothing to eat.'' Arethusa whirled on Sergeant MacVicar, her huge, dark eyes flashing sparks. "Stap me, sirrah, do you mean to keep us here all night?''

"That's a very good question, Arethusa,'' said Mrs. MacVicar.

Even the sergeant himself had to concur. "Aye, leddies, it is, and my answer is no. Your nephew and his wee wifie hae invited us all to breakfast, Arethusa. We can most advantageously resume our endeavors to get at the heart of this matter then. Nine o'clock was the hour you set, gin memory serves me, Deputy Monk.''

Osbert looked mildly surprised but didn't contradict him. The wee wifie gave her husband a less than adoring glance, but didn't say anything, either. If Sergeant MacVicar remembered the time as nine o'clock, then nine o'clock it would be, and that was that. Not half past anything. They'd just have to wheedle one of the Munson boys into driving Archie and Daniel to the airport.

"Nine o'clock will give the cast members time enough to eat their breakfasts, give their testimony, and meet their respective spouses at church in time for services,'' Mrs. MacVicar pointed out.

Sergeant MacVicar raised his eyebrows. Dittany understood.

"Mrs. MacVicar's coming, too, you know. She has to. She's bringing the eggs.''

"Then all is settled and I'll say nae mair. Noo, Margaret, let's gang awa' hame.''

Of course none of them left immediately. Any group of

people who've been doing anything complicated together always have to do a little extra puttering around before they call it quits. At last, however, the last piece of scenery was stowed in the basement, the last prop carried out to somebody's car, the last discarded program picked up and stuffed into a wastebasket, and the somewhat complex system of shutting off all the lights figured out. Roger Munson made sure everybody was out, then locked the gym door. The premiere performance of *Dangerous Dan McGrew* was now another item in the Thorbisher-Freep collection of theatrical memorabilia.

But the melodrama was still going on. Dittany rolled out of bed about half past seven the next morning, aghast that she'd slept so late even though she'd have preferred to sleep a few hours longer. She leaped in and out of the shower, dragged on a pair of black wool pants chosen to blend with Ethel's shed fur, and added her most colorful top to lift her spirits, should that be feasible. She let Ethel out and was thinking she absolutely must wake Osbert and phone the Munsons, even though she hated the thought of getting them up, when the phone rang. It was, as she'd expected, Archie.

Now came the moment of truth and she didn't have the faintest idea what to tell him. That didn't much matter, though. She got no farther than "Oh Archie" before he interrupted.

"Look, Dittany, I can't tell you how sorry I am to have got you up so early for nothing. I know you must be worn out from last night and itching to get us off your backs so you can relax. But the thing of it is, Daniel doesn't want to leave."

This time she only managed an "Oh."

"Daniel's absolutely riveted by Lobelia Falls," Archie babbled on. "He says he's already seen better melodrama here than they've had on the theater circuit in ages, and he's not budging till the final curtain. Can you possibly bear us awhile longer, Dittany?"

"I can bear having you stay a darn sight easier than I could have coped with getting you to the airport," she told him frankly. "Osbert and I got our wires crossed and he's invited the whole cast here for breakfast so Sergeant

MacVicar can conduct a mass grilling. You and Daniel might as well buzz along and join the party. I'll have somebody pick you up about a quarter to nine.''

"Oh, that's marvelous. Daniel will be tickled silly. You're quite sure we shan't be putting you out?''

"Believe me, you won't even be noticed in the general confusion. Just don't expect anything fancy.''

Such as a place to sit down or the exclusive use of a butter knife. Most of the other guests would be familiar with the traditional freewheeling Henbit-Monk style of entertaining, she needn't worry about them. Andy McNaster and the Thorbisher-Freeps wouldn't be, but they probably weren't even intending to come and who cared about them, anyway? Just the relief of not having to find a way out of that airport dilemma made the prospect of a getting breakfast for somewhere between twenty and thirty people with no advance preparation seem like a relative bagatelle.

Dittany filled Ethel's food bowl, got out the big mixing bowl, her three remaining eggs, and a few other odds and ends, and began slapping together a triple batch of muffins. With Mrs. MacVicar's four dozen eggs and the canned ham they always kept in the fridge for emergencies, they'd manage well even if nobody else brought anything at all.

But people did bring things, of course; everything from jars of cream to flowers for the table. There were pitchers of juice, bowls of fruit, plain doughnuts, cinnamon doughnuts, jelly doughnuts, biscuits, rolls, sticky buns, white bread, brown bread, cheese bread, pumpkin bread, banana bread, date bread, cranberry-nut-raisin bread, and something Zilla Trott made that none of the rest could identify and nobody liked to ask.

"If this is your idea of nothing fancy," Archie asked in understandable bemusement a couple of hours later, "what happens when you put on a real bash?"

"We use matching napkins," Dittany replied with her mouth full. For quite a while, she'd been too busy scrambling eggs and frying ham for the crew to feed herself. By now, though, supply had caught up with demand and she was free to do a little browsing among the fleshpots.

The Thorbisher-Freeps hadn't shown up, which didn't hurt her feelings any. Andy McNaster had, and was sitting knee-to-knee with Arethusa, watching her eat a sticky bun. Daniel was near them, watching Andy. Their faces made an interesting study. Andy's wore the goofy expression of a man besotted with adoration. Daniel looked more like Minerva Oakes's old cat Emmeline doing sentry duty at a mousehole. Emmeline was a truly dedicated mouser. Daniel appeared to be dedicated, too, but to what?

Dittany had no time to go and find out. Sergeant MacVicar was standing up at the head of the dining room table laying down his napkin as if it were the Magna Carta. Hazel Munson, who'd been going around with the teapot because Hazel couldn't bear not to make herself useful for long at a stretch, caught the last drop from the spout and tiptoed over to set the pot down on the buffet as if she'd been caught doing something mildly improper. Others paused with last bites of doughnut of muffin halfway to their mouths. This was a moment fraught with portent, and fraughtly did they view it.

The sergeant wasted no time on preliminaries. "I needna tell you, ladies and gentlemen, that a situation of deepest gravity has arisen. It appears that yon Andrew McNaster has been made the unwitting tool of a pairfidious plot to assassinate your fellow performer, Carolus Bledsoe. I willna waste your time wi' idle conjectures as to why this outrage may hae been plotted. What we must try to do here and noo is detairmine who could hae switched a live bullet for the last of the blank cartridges supplied, I am told, by Mr. Jenson Thorbisher-Freep. It appears the switch could hae been made either before or after the gun was loaded by Carolus Bledsoe himsel' and laid on the table that held various properties required in the play. Roger Munson was in charge of these, so I shall ask him to recapitulate for us."

Everybody knew in advance what Roger was going to say, but they all listened attentively nonetheless. Even though they'd been talking about little else ever since they got into the house and probably before, Roger's crisp summation of the events leading up to the shooting left them with a satisfactory feeling that now they were really getting somewhere. There was a tentative movement to give him a round of applause, but it was checked as being not quite the thing under the circumstances. Sergeant MacVicar's Augustan nod of approval was enough.

"And noo," the sergeant went on, "who has further information to contribute?"

"I have," said Osbert, who'd been acting as waiter and busboy. "I think you ought to know there were some pretty harsh words passed about Carolus late yesterday in the dining room at the inn. Aunt Arethusa, do you want to tell it?"

Arethusa was engaged with the last of the sticky buns and indicated by sign language that she didn't.

"How about you, Andy?"

"I am but an unlettered building contractor-cum-innkeeper and have no gift of narrative," Andy replied modestly. "You tell 'em, Osbert."

So Osbert told them, and he told them well. Skilled storyteller that he was, he saved the best line for the last. "So when I saw Leander Hellespont backstage at the gym before the performance, I couldn't help wondering."

"Um ah," said Sergeant MacVicar, which was quite a commitment, from him. "And precisely what was Leander Hellespont doing backstage, Deputy Monk?"

"Looking for the men's room, I guess. At least that's where he went. I watched him to make sure."

"And did you wait to see him come out again?"

"No, I didn't have time. Somebody wanted me onstage to check the set. Anyway, I didn't think too much of Hellespont's showing up for the performance. I knew he was a spy from the Scottsbeck Players, and I had other things on my mind just then."

"Aye, nae doot," Sergeant MacVicar conceded. "And what aboot the rest of you? Did anyone else see a tall, thin man, dressed up like Dracula frae the sound of him, wandering backstage?"

If they had seen Hellespont, they hadn't paid much attention to him. There'd been a number of unauthorized persons milling around before the performance. The Thespians had tried as best they could to ignore these interlopers. The cast had all been in the locker rooms nursing their stage fright and putting on each other's makeup. The stagehands had been running back and forth doing this and that, seeing extraneous persons only as obstacles to be got around or shooed away.

Roger Munson had kept an eye on the properties table as best he could, but Roger had been doing more running than anybody else, checking to make sure there was enough cold tea in the whiskey bottles and performing other vital missions. He hadn't noticed any strangers backstage but he wouldn't have been apt to. As a disciple of the higher efficiency, he'd trained himself to focus his whole attention on the task at hand.

"So naebody has any idea how long yon Hellespont stayed backstage?" Sergeant MacVicar asked at last in a somewhat disheartened tone.

Dittary looked at young Sammy, who in the interests of higher efficiency had seated himself beside the jelly dough-nuts. Sammy looked at Dittany, caught her signal to speak up and did.

"I can't say how long Mr. Hellespont was backstage because I didn't see him there, but I do know he wasn't in the audience until about three minutes before curtain time. He took the outside aisle seat, fourth row, next to the fire exit."

"That's right," Dittany confirmed. "Sammy and I both saw him come in because we'd meant for Ormerod Burlson to take that seat. Carolus Bledsoe's ex-wife was sitting directly in front of it. Ormerod was supposed to have picked her up at the door and ridden herd on her all evening in case she'd brought along some more tomatoes, but he evidently got sidetracked at the lemonade stand. Anyway, Ormerod still wasn't with her then, and he certainly wasn't anywhere near her when she came backstage."

Chapter 12

"You saw Mrs. Bledsoe backstage?"

The cry came from several sets of lips, albeit not those of Arethusa who was still having difficulty with the sticky bun. Dittany raised her eyebrows.

"How could I have missed seeing her? Doesn't anybody remember that woman in the burgundy storm coat and dark glasses who poked her head into the girls' locker room claiming she was looking for the Ladies'?"

"You mean she was the same one who threw the tomato?" shrieked Hazel.

"None other than. Didn't you recognize her?"

"How could I? She startled me, popping in all bundled up like that, and I stuck the darn mascara brush in my eye. I couldn't see a thing but midnight sable for about five minutes. Anyway, how would I have known? She was in and out so fast at the rehearsal—"

"Actually she wasn't," Dittany corrected. "She'd been there all the time. Mrs. Bledsoe was that blond woman in mink sitting behind the Thorbisher-Freeps."

"I thought the mink one was Wilhedra."

"There were two minks."

"Well, I only remember one," Hazel insisted rather huffily.

Hardly anybody else appeared to have noticed a second fur-bearing biped at the opera house Friday night. They'd all been too preoccupied trying to remember what they were supposed to do, as was right and proper.

"Then I guess I must have been the only one," Dittany had to concede. "I had a perfect lookout post, you know, back there on the piano bench with not much to do when I wasn't playing. I'd had my eye on the woman off and on all evening, wondering who she was and what she'd come for. I saw her stand up but of course I had no idea she was going to throw the tomato till it was too late to stop her. I recognized her right away when she came into the locker room."

"Then why didn't you say something?" Desdemona Portley demanded.

"How could I? You were all so dithery by then, you'd have gone up like a bunch of skyrockets. Carolus had already told me he'd hired an off-duty policeman to ride herd on her in case she had any bright ideas about getting into the act tonight, so I just snuck out front and enlisted Sammy here to make Ormerod do his job. But if Mrs. Bledsoe had already got hold of the .38 and changed the bullet—oh, why didn't I speak up before it was too late?"

"Darling, you mustn't blame yourself," Osbert protested. "Chucking a tomato is a far cry from putting a live bullet into a gun that you know is going to be fired point-blank at somebody's chest. Why didn't I jump on Leander Hellespont when I found him backstage? He's a darn sight likelier prospect than Mrs. Bledsoe."

"But she bopped Carolus with a ham and macaroni casserole."

"Hellespont uttered threats in public. You heard him yourself."

"So did I," said Andrew McNaster. "And I should of decked him then and there, eh, but I stayed my hand on the paltry grounds that it wouldn't be good for business. Mea is the culpa."

"Hold, sirrah," cried Arethusa. "Tua is not the culpa, forsooth. If your nobler nature hadn't prevailed, Carolus Bledsoe would by now be a well-ventilated corpse. The culpa is mea for having accepted his invitation to dinner when he was already engaged to Wilhedra Thorbisher-Freep."

"But how were you supposed to know he was when he never said?" Dittany reminded her. "Anyway, he wasn't. Jenson told us they're waiting till after the lawsuit gets settled. Isn't that right, Jenson? Oh gosh, I wonder if we have any eggs left.''

It had occurred to her that she was talking to a man who hadn't been present a moment ago and still wasn't fed. ''Is your daughter with you or over at the hospital soothing Carolus's fevered instep?''

''Neither,'' Jenson replied sadly. ''Poor Wilhedra's at home soothing her own fevered instep. She took a tumble on the stairs this morning, which is why I wasn't able to get here sooner. The doctor assured us that it's only a nasty sprain, but he insists she's to stay off the foot for at least a week and maybe longer. He's given her something for the pain and I've left her in the maid's care just long enough to come here and let you know that the Traveling Thespians have been unanimously though still unofficially declared the winners of the Thorbisher-Freep collection of theatrical memorabilia.''

''Oh, that's marvelous!'' Everybody put on a dutiful show of being tremendously excited by the news, though in fact nobody was. Winning the contest seemed terribly unimportant compared to seeing a fellow player barely miss being shot to death in their midst. Perhaps Therese Boulanger summed up their feelings best when she said, ''But you'll eat something now you're here?''

Jenson seemed surprised that she could end the rejoicing so readily, but he agreed. ''Perhaps a cup of black coffee if you have any left. It's been an extremely trying time all around.''

As Therese fetched the coffee, Hazel asked Jenson sympathetically if he wouldn't like a doughnut to go with it. Roger, though, was more solicitous for his ex-patient.

''Then what about Carolus? Hasn't anybody been over to see how he's making out?''

Jenson shook his silver mane. ''Not to the best of my knowledge. My daughter and I intended to go, of course, and I suppose I could swing by the hospital for a few minutes on my way home. But I do want to get back to Wilhedra. We'd already promised the maid she could have the day off to attend her great-nephew's christening and I can't very well insist she change her plans. You know what the servant problem is these days.''

In Lobelia Falls there was no servant problem because nobody had any servants. People hired help when they needed it and the neighbors were always glad to pop over and lend a hand in a pinch. Things must be different in Scottsbeck. Anyway the Thorbisher-Freep mansion was not the sort of place a person would pop to. Murmurs of condolence arose but it was clear that not even Hazel Munson was planning to drop in on Wilhedra with a few cheery words and a bowl of fruit Jello-O.

"So what happens to Carolus?" Roger was insisting.

"I suppose one might telephone the hospital and ask for a report," Jenson replied.

He'd refused the doughnut on the grounds of extreme perturbation but accepted one of Dittany's excellent muffins at Zilla Trott's insistence that he had to keep up his strength. Perhaps the muffin had helped him to collect his wits and offer so cogent a suggestion. Roger went at once to make the call, the telephone being in the kitchen next to the pantry door where Gram Henbit had ordered it installed back when telephones were wooden boxes that had to be cranked before you could get Central to say, "Number, please?"

While they were waiting for Roger to report back, Sergeant MacVicar asked Jenson to take a look at the blank cartridge that had been picked up after the performance. "Does it look at a' familiar, sir?"

"Oh yes, no question," the older man agreed readily. "I couldn't swear to it, of course; but as far as I can tell, this one's identical to the other three that had been in my old Smith & Wesson ever since I played Jack Rance. I noticed how dingy and tarnished they looked, and how the color of the wads had been dulled by time. Frankly, I was a little ashamed to bring them along but I told myself it didn't matter because the audience wouldn't get to see them. It's as well I overcame my scruples. The discoloration serves as an identification of sorts, wouldn't you say? Ah, Roger. What news of Carolus?"

"The doctor's been in and says he can go home but he'll have to go straight to bed and stay there."

"Dear, dear. Now what are we going to do? It's absolutely out of the question for him to go back to his flat.

Carolus was forced to move out of his house, you know, because of that ridiculous litigation with his ex-wife. Pending the settlement, he's been living in bachelor quarters. The flat's a third-floor walkup and he has no help except a professional cleaning service once a week. Wilhedra and I had planned to put him up for the duration, but now she's immobilized herself and I can't possibly ask the maid to wait on two invalids at the same time. She'd quit in a wink, then where should we be?''

"But hasn't Carolus any other friends in Scottsbeck?" asked Samantha Burberry.

Jenson shrugged. "Professional friends, hardly the sort who'd care to fetch his breakfast and change his bed. I'm afraid the ex-wife has pretty well succeeded in alienating their former social acquaintances. No, it looks like a nursing home for Carolus, assuming we can find one willing to take him in on such short notice. Rather a dismal outlook for the poor chap, but what else can we do?''

Minerva Oakes started to say something but Zilla Trott hissed at her so savagely that she kept quiet. Minerva had already had some spectacularly bad luck with temporary occupants of her spare room. It wouldn't behoove her to add a shooting victim with a rampageous ex-wife to her list of calamities. Besides, Zilla had what she evidently thought was a better idea.

"Arethusa, you've got plenty of room and Carolus is more your friend than any of ours. Why don't you take him in?''

Only Zilla could have made such a suggestion in all innocence. Andrew McNaster actually bared his teeth. Arethusa very nearly bared hers.

"Zounds, woman, what kind of friends do you think we are? Methinks 'twould be the height of unseemliness. Me also thinks Wilhedra Thorbisher-Freep would hit the roof.''

Jenson gave her a wry smile. "I'm afraid you're right about that, dear lady. Furthermore, the distraction of nursing an invalid might keep you from being able to concentrate on your writing, and we can't have that. Think of your vast reading public! No, I'm afraid our dear friend Carolus must e'en dree his ain weird, as the gracious Sergeant MacVicar would doubtless express it. Unless we might find some hospitable and as yet childless couple with a house as big as their hearts,'' he added with a wistful sigh.

Roger Munson cleared his throat. "Actually, Osbert, if you hadn't written that shooting scene into the play—"

All of a sudden the air was full of ifs: If the boys didn't take up so much space at the Munson house, if Samantha Burberry didn't have the Development Commission's annual report to write, if the Boulangers' daughter Felice hadn't just got engaged and wanted a hurry-up wedding because her bridegroom was being transferred to Oslo, and a good many other variations on the same basic theme. What it all boiled down to was what Dittany had known in her heart of hearts it was going to boil down to, because everything in Lobelia Falls always did.

Despite a last-ditch "What about Osbert's vast reading public?" she found herself laying out the fancy towels and a fresh cake of soap in the upstairs bathroom. At least she wasn't having to clean up the kitchen. A squad of her clubmates had volunteered to do the dishes, thus assuring that she wouldn't be able to find any of her favorite cooking utensils for the next month or so.

Osbert didn't appear to share Dittany's qualms about the prospect of having a casualty of the Malamute saloon shoot-out lying around. He went off quite happily, driving the ranch wagon with Roger Munson beside him and Ethel in the back, a small flask of brandy tied to her collar in case Carolus took a fainting fit on the way back from the hospital.

Desdemona Portley had given Archie and Daniel a warm invitation to drop over and examine her scrapbook of earlier Traveling Thespians productions. Andrew McNaster had countered with a suggestion that he and Arethusa take the two visitors on a sightseeing tour of Lobelia Falls and environs. They'd asked for a raincheck on the scrapbook and accepted the ride. Desdemona wasn't the least bit offended. She said in that case she'd just go home and put her feet up while her husband read the Sunday comics to her, as was his pleasant habit.

By now, from around the corner and up the street, the sounds of church bells could be heard. Mrs. MacVicar was putting on her coat and giving her husband a look. A sudden dreadful recollection struck Dittany and she gave him a look, too. Her look must have expressed all the awfulness she was feeling, for the sergeant immediately came over to her.

"What's the matter, lass?"

"I've got to talk to you. Can you stay a minute after the rest?"

"It willna take lang?"

"You know I wouldn't make you miss the collection."

Muttering something to the effect that Dittany was getting more like her mother every day of her life, Sergeant MacVicar went off to have a word with his wife. Mrs. MacVicar drew on her gloves much more briskly than he wished she would and said she'd walk on ahead with Minerva and Zilla.

By now everybody else had gone, too, except for the cleanup squad, and they were all busy running back and forth between the dining room and the kitchen. Dittany drew the sergeant out into the front hall where they wouldn't be overheard, and spoke her piece.

"I didn't want to say this in front of the rest, but you have to know. Carolus Bledsoe is Charlie."

"Oh aye?" The sergeant seemed less thunderstruck by her revelation than she'd anticipated. It occurred to her that he probably hadn't the ghost of an idea what she was talking about.

"Don't you remember that time when we were trying to save the Enchanted Mountain from being developed and I eavesdropped on that meeting where Andy McNaster was trying to get his lawyer to pull a dirty deal for him? The lawyer said he'd done plenty of dirty deals for Andy but he wouldn't do this one, though he knew somebody who would. Andy called the lawyer Charlie, and Charles is the same name as Carolus. And that's who he is."

"Dittany, why did you no' tell me this before?"

"Because I didn't realize it myself till day before yesterday. By then it was too late to get somebody else to play the feedbag man and I couldn't bear to ruin Osbert's play. I'd never seen Charlie, you know, I'd only heard his voice. I did get a sort of familiar feeling when Arethusa introduced us at the airport that day, but I couldn't place

him. I'd thought about it off and on ever since. Then all of
a sudden while I was in the midst of making cookies, it
hit me like a ton of bricks. You know how those things
do.''

Sergeant MacVicar scratched his chin.

"Oh, stop scratching your chin at me! Why should I
have told, with Andy being reformed all over the place and
the pair of them working off their aggressions by insulting
each other onstage? I didn't even tell Osbert because he
was so wound up about the play, what with Archie bringing Daniel and us trying to win the competition and everybody rushing in and out of here pestering him about one
thing and another.''

"Aye?"

"Aye, darn it. And yesterday there wasn't even time to
breathe, and to top it all off, Osbert went ahead and
invited the whole crowd here for breakfast without even
bothering to ask me whether we had anything in the house
to feed them. Those four dozen eggs of your daughter-in-
law's saved my bacon and I hope you'll be kind enough to
tell her how grateful I am when you see her. The fact that
you had four dozen eggs to give might also suggest to her
the possibility that she ought to find somebody else to wish
off her surplus eggs on.''

Dittany paused to reflect. "On the other hand, maybe
you'd better not say anything. I'll probably have to be
making a lot of eggnogs for Roger to feed Carolus. I don't
know why the heck I always have to be the one left
standing on the burning deck.''

She got no sympathy from Sergeant MacVicar. "Did it
ne'er occur to you that considering their earlier pairfidious
association and wi' the two of them presently at logger-
heads over Arethusa, that the ill-feeling between McNaster
and Bledsoe might develop into a serious confrontation?''

"Of course it occurred to me. It also occurred to me that
they only had the dress rehearsal and the actual performance left to play, and that neither one of them was loopy
enough to start mixing it up in front of an audience,
specially since Arethusa was their co-star and would have
stapped their garters good and proper if they loused up her
act. Sergeant, you don't honestly believe Andy McNaster

deliberately went out and bought himself a real .38 caliber bullet so he could shoot off Carolus Bledsoe's left middle toe and keep him from chasing after Arethusa?''

''I can believe there may be other reasons why Andrew McNaster might commit an assault upon the former partner of his skulduggerous machinations.''

''So can I,'' Dittany had to admit. ''But whatever else Andy McNaster may have been in the past and may still be for all we know, I've never heard anybody call him stupid. Besides, it's not as if he were the only one clamoring for Carolus Bledsoe's guts in a bucket. What about Leander Hellespont? What about Carolus's ex-wife? What about Wilhedra Thorbisher-Freep, for that matter? Though I'll grant you it seems a bit premature for Wilhedra to try to kill Carolus when they're not even married yet.''

''The point is well taken,'' Sergeant MacVicar conceded with a nervous glance at his watch.

''And what about some stranger we don't yet know anything about?'' Dittany went on. ''Carolus in his Charlie persona could still be pulling dirty tricks for other skulduggerers, couldn't he? In fact I should think he'd pretty much have to if he expects to keep eating now that he's lost Andy's business.''

''All avenues shall be explored,'' said the sergeant with his hand on the doorknob. ''I'll be back to interrogate yon Bledsoe once he's recovered frae the trauma of being brought from the hospital and I hae succeeded in placating my leddy wife. In the meantime, lass, keep mum an' gae canny.''

Chapter 13

Keep mum and go bonkers would be closer to the mark, Dittany thought as she watched Osbert help Roger Munson and his sons Ed and Dave juggle Carolus Bledsoe up her front stairs lashed to a stretcher. Everybody but Carolus appeared to be having a good time. He, on the other hand, was looking pretty much the way he'd looked last night when he'd caught sight of the hole in his boot.

"His bed's all turned down," she told the rescue squad. "Is he going to need pajamas and things?"

"No," said Roger. "We stopped at his apartment and packed a bag. It's all organized."

Naturally it would be. "Then we girls will leave you to get him tucked in. Come on, Ethel, let's put the kettle on. I expect everybody would like a cup of tea."

"I'd like a stiff drink," said Carolus through clenched teeth.

"Sorry," Roger told him. "Not while you're still on antibiotics."

Dittany didn't wait for the discussion, if there was going to be one. She went back to the kitchen, filled the kettle, let Ethel out for a run, and started wondering where the dishwashers had hidden the cream jug. In a couple of minutes, Osbert came down and kissed her on the back of the neck.

"That the best you can do?" she grumbled. "What's happening upstairs?"

"Roger's getting Carolus organized. Where's Sergeant MacVicar?"

"Gone to church. He's coming back to grill Carolus later on, assuming there's anything left of the man by the time Roger gets through playing doctor. Osbert, there's something I have to tell you."

He seized her in fervent embrace. "Darling, you don't mean—"

"Of course I don't mean. Quit looking so happy. It's Carolus. He's Charlie."

"What's so awful about being Charlie? I'd be Charlie too if I were Carolus. That's the trouble with Osbert, I'm darned if I'll be Ozzie and we've already got a Bert. What I'd really like to be is a Luke. I wish I'd picked Luke Laramie instead of Lex for my writing name. Luke means bringer of light."

"But Osbert means divinely brilliant, which suits you much better. Besides, Luke makes me think of lukewarm, and you're certainly not that."

"I am sometimes," Osbert insisted. "I'm sort of luke-warm about having Carolus here now that the initial euphoria has died, if you really want to know. I wish we hadn't said we'd take him."

"Not to be contentious," Dittany replied, "but I don't recall that we did, if by we you mean to include me."

"Of course I do, dear. There's only one we for me, you know that. I always think of us as two hearts that beat as one. Which ventricle would you rather be, right or left?"

"I honestly haven't given it much thought. Listen, Osbert—"

"How's the tea coming?" That was Roger, bustling into the kitchen, fairly radiating efficiency. "Carolus needs a stimulant."

"Who doesn't? Fix the tray since you burn to be help-ful." Dittany slapped loose tea into a small pot and peeked to see if the kettle was boiling yet. "What happened to the boys?"

"They've gone along home. They thought they might get in a few shots before Hazel calls us to dinner." The Munson boys would soon be eligible for promotion from the Junior to the Senior Male Archers' Target and Game

Shooting Association and were naturally eager to hone their skills. "Where's the little cloth that goes on the tray?"

"What little cloth that goes on the tray, for Pete's sake?" Dittany exploded. "Roger, this is not the Royal Hotel and I don't give two hoots in heck whether Carolus Bledsoe likes the way I set a tray or not. Just take this tea up to him and tell him for me he's darned lucky to get it."

"Well, I just wondered. Hazel always puts on a little embroidered cloth."

"Dittany never does," said Osbert. "She maintains tray cloths are inefficient."

"Bless my soul," cried Roger. "So they are. And to think I never realized that myself! I must tell Hazel."

"I hope she beans you with a tray if you do," Dittany snarled. "Scat, Roger."

Roger picked up the clothless tray and scatted. Osbert turned to his somewhat distraught wife.

"Darling, why don't you sit down in the rocking chair and let me bring you a cup of tea? Better still, why don't we both curl up on the couch and have a nice little snuggle while you tell me all about Carolus being Charlie?"

"There, see? I said you were divinely brilliant," Dittany replied. "The only flaw I can see in your highly attractive scenario is that in about thirty seconds Roger's going to come cavorting back to say Carolus wants a ham sandwich."

"Why should Carolus want a ham sandwich?"

"As a hypothesis, because he's hungry. Maybe it won't be a ham sandwich, but it'll be something. Want to bet?"

Actually it was almost a minute. They'd had the chance to get their own tea poured and were even set to drink it when Roger did indeed return. What he wanted was a little handbell that Carolus could ring whenever he needed attention.

"Carolus just had attention," Osbert protested. "Is he asking for more already?"

"Well, he did say something about a ham sandwich," Roger answered. "Apparently the hospital breakfast was not to his liking."

"There, see," said Dittany, "what did I tell you?"

She checked the fridge and managed after considerable pawing around to locate all that was left of the ham. There was just about enough for one respectable sandwich. She might have sent Roger back up to find out which kind of bread Carolus preferred, but she felt just mean enough not to. He'd take white because that was the kind she and Osbert were least fond of, and if he didn't like it he could darn well lump it.

Dittany did add lettuce and mustard pickle because after all one had one's standards even if one didn't go in for embroidered tray cloths. She also fixed Carolus a sauce dish full of leftover fruit compote that somebody had contributed to the breakfast. It had to be eaten up anyway because it wouldn't keep, and the extra vitamins might help to speed the healing process.

Roger nodded approval. "That's fine. Now the bell."

Dittany shook her head. "No bell."

"You don't have one? That's all right, I can bring—"

"Don't you dare, Roger Munson! Carolus Bledsoe is not getting a bell. Men are the world's worst invalids. They get bored lying in bed and start pestering for attention. I'm not going to stand for being dingalinged at every two minutes by somebody I don't even particularly care for, if you want the honest truth. Osbert or I will go up and check on Carolus at reasonable intervals, and we'll decide for ourselves what's reasonable so don't bother to tell us. We'll provide him with books, jigsaw puzzles, a radio, crayons and a coloring book, or whatever else will keep him amused. We'll keep him warm and fed and—oh gosh, we won't have to do baths and bedpans?"

"No," Roger assured her. "He's allowed to get up long enough to attend to his personal needs. He'll need crutches or a cane and perhaps some assistance getting in and out of bed. A bell would—"

"No it wouldn't. We have a pair of crutches Carolus can use. Mum bought them for Dad the time he broke his leg trying to learn the samba. If he needs help getting up he can holler down the stairs. Why don't you scoot along home to your dinner and let us take it from here? Since you have everything so well organized," Dittany added, for she did like Roger Munson despite his perfectionistic tendencies.

"Yes, I'd better get cracking," he agreed. "I mustn't upset Hazel's schedule. I'll drop over again later on and bring that portable television set Dave won last year in the hockey club raffle. Nobody at our house ever watches it anyway."

That stood to reason. Few Lobelia Falls residents ever did have much time to spend with the tube, not that they cared. Everyday life there was far too crammed with action and drama for the prepackaged variety to hold much attraction. Being from Scottsbeck, however, Carolus Bledsoe would no doubt welcome the diversion.

Roger didn't really have to bring his set over as the Monks had a perfectly good one of their own that they didn't watch often, either, but they said it was very nice of him and handed him the tray to take up. He came back downstairs a few minutes later with a list of commissions from the invalid, explained at some length what he was going to do about them, and finally, to the Monks' ineffable relief, went home.

"Okay, pardner, now what about Charlie?" Osbert asked when he'd got Dittany arranged to their mutual satisfaction.

Dittany repeated what she'd told Sergeant MacVicar. Osbert understood perfectly.

"That was positively noble of you, darling. And how could you possibly have anticipated what happened? After all, whoever had it in for Carolus could just as easily have got at him before the performance. Easier, I should think, and nothing happened then. As it is, we'll be able to keep him under guard until his toe heals and by then we ought to have found out who switched those cartridges. I just wish Sergeant MacVicar would get back here. He didn't say when he was coming?"

"No, but three o'clock probably wouldn't be far off the mark, unless Nancy comes with some more eggs."

Sunday dinnertime for Lobelia Falls was from half past one to half past two, allowing half an hour's leeway in either direction for getting the kids' hands washed, making the gravy, organizing the dishwashing, and taking post-prandial snoozes. This was not a municipal ordinance, merely a way of causing the smallest number of persons the least amount of inconvenience in scheduling archery meets, rehearsals of the madrigal society, family visits, and the myriad other activities in which all the townsfolk got involved to a greater or lesser degree. Dittany supposed she ought to be thinking about their own dinner, although she and Osbert were the neighborhood iconoclasts when it came to keeping on schedule.

She'd as soon not bother, herself, but what about Archie and Daniel? Was Andy planning to bring them back here in time for the meal he might assume she was cooking when in fact she wasn't, or would he keep up his angel of mercy act long enough to feed them someplace else? She asked Osbert, but he didn't know.

"Couldn't we just make some ham sandwiches?" was his suggestion.

"No we couldn't," Dittany said. "Carolus got the last bit of ham."

"Then an omelet?"

"The eggs are all gone. We're still pretty well fixed for doughnuts, jelly, and dog food."

"Well then, not to worry. Ethel won't mind sharing in a pinch. Will you, faithful friend?"

It need hardly be said that Ethel had joined them on the couch. Rather, roughly half of her had joined them. The half there wasn't room for remained sprawled on the floor or suspended in between. She seemed comfortable enough. The interlude was a pleasant one and they'd all three have been happier if the doorbell hadn't put an end to it.

"Oh gosh," Dittany groaned, "don't tell me they're back already. What the heck did they go to the front door for? Arethusa knows we're always in the kitchen."

"That's not Aunt Arethusa," said Osbert. "She'd be thumping and hollering by now. I'll go, dear. You stay here and rest yourself."

"Hah! As if anybody in this dad-dratted town was going to let me." She wiggled off the couch and straightened her blouse. "No, let us both be up and doing with a heart for any fate. You can be the right ventricle this time. Come on, Ethel, why should we break up the party?"

Their expedition proved to be not only over-manned but

also over-womanned and over-dogged. Nobody was at the door. However, a long white box from the Scottsbeck florist lay on the doormat.

"Oh how lovely," Dittany cried. "Mum and Bert must have ordered flowers by phone."

"Nope," said Osbert, who had eyes like an eagle's but more amiable. "The card says they're for Carolus. Here, let me—Ethel, get out of the way."

The dog had leaped in front of him and straddled the box, baring her teeth. As Osbert tried to get it out from under her, she actually growled at him.

"Ethel, what's got into you?" Dittany scolded. "You know better than that. Osbert, stop her!"

But there was no stopping Ethel. She caught up the box by its cord, leaped over the veranda railing, and raced off to Cat Alley with Carolus's present clutched in her jaws like a giant bone.

"She's gone plumb loco," yelled Osbert. He was over the railing, too, racing after her. "Ethel, you mutt, come back here."

"She'll ruin those flowers."

Dittany ran down the steps and joined in the race, though she wasn't much of a runner herself. Osbert was fast, but Ethel easily outdistanced him. Before he could get anywhere near her, she braked and started ripping at the box like a hunger-maddened malamute. Growling, snapping, pawing, she had it apart in no time. But no broken blossoms appeared. Instead, something long, thin, and brown slithered out of the wreckage, reared about a third of its length upright, spread an ugly hood of skin over its head, and hissed.

"Galloping longhorns, it's a cobra!" yelled Osbert. "Dittany, stay back! Ethel! Ethel, come here. Come on, old girl! Come on!"

No longer a raging, snarling demon-dog, Ethel bounded back to them, ears flapping, tail churning, delighted with herself as well she had reason to be.

"She saved his life," Dittany marveled. "Ethel risked her own life to save Carolus Bledsoe's."

"I doubt if Ethel read the card, dear." Osbert had one arm around Dittany and the other around their faithful friend. "Ethel, old pard, I don't know how to—Dittany darling, have we a really big steak in the house?"

"No, but we'll get you one, Ethel." Dittany was sniffling into the thick black fur. "We'll get you anything you want, forever and ever. Oh Ethel, what if the cobra had bitten you? Osbert, what are we going to do about that thing? We can't leave it crawling around loose."

"I don't think any snake's going to crawl far in this weather, dearest," he reassured her. "Look, it's already got its hood down, it'll be torpid in a minute. So will we if we stay out here any longer without our coats. Come on back in the house before you catch pneumonia."

"Ethel wouldn't let a germ get near us," Dittany laughed, rubbing away her tears on Osbert's sleeve. "Would you, old buddy? Are you quite sure that cobra's not about to start chasing us, Osbert?"

"What it's about to do is freeze to death if it doesn't find a place to get warm pretty soon. I see a bunch of tissue paper in what's left of that box, which would have given it some insulation against the cold. Probably not quite enough, though, which was a lucky break for us. If it were warm it would have reacted a darn sight faster."

The cobra would have warmed up fast enough once it got inside the house. Dittany realized she was shivering. "Darling, don't you find this totally unbelievable?"

"Oh, I don't know, dear. I shouldn't say a cobra was any more unbelievable than the tarantula that showed up on Carolus's coat at the airport."

"But that came out of Arethusa's corsage. Didn't it?"

"Darling, Aunt Arethusa must have been toting that mess of shrubbery around for hours before we met her. Even she'd have had a hard time not to notice a spider the size of a kitten somewhere along the way."

"Then it must have been in the bouquet Andy McNaster—darling, Andy wouldn't have done a thing like that. Would he?"

"Your guess is as good as mine, darling. People were coming and going all the time, you know. We weren't paying any attention to them because we were talking among ourselves. It could have been anybody. Come on, it's wiggling. Let's get away from here."

Safe inside the door, Osbert turned around for a last look at the deadly reptile. It was flat on the snow now, trying to crawl away but getting no traction on the cold, slippery surface. Loathesome as the snake was, he felt a twinge of pity.

"What a rotten thing to do. Darling, I think I'll put on my high boots and heavy gloves and see if I can rig a snare at the end of my fishing pole. We can't just let it die out there."

"It would have let Ethel die," said Dittany soberly. "But after all, it's only a snake. I don't suppose it understands how we feel about her. I'll go find one of those heavy cardboard boxes Mum bought the time she was going to get organized. Then I'll put on my own boots and come with you."

"No, darling, I'm afraid it would be too traumatic for Ethel if we both went. You'd better stay here and be ready to administer first aid if she swoons."

Ethel's was, after all, the greater need. "All right, darling," Dittany conceded, "but I move we give the cobra a few minutes' more refrigerating time before you go back out there."

Chapter 14

As things turned out, capturing the cobra was no great feat. By the time Osbert had rigged a wire noose on the end of his fly rod and Dittany had got him togged out in a manner that suggested the White Knight's safeguards against the bites of sharks, the cobra was so thoroughly refrigerated that Osbert could simply have picked it up by the tail and tossed it into the box. However, he carried out the operation by the book, then set the box down cellar next to the furnace with a cord around the middle and a brick on top in case the cobra should revive feeling frisky.

"Maybe we should have set a saucer of milk inside," Dittany fretted. "The poor thing will be hungry when it thaws out."

"Are you quite sure cobras drink milk, dear?" Osbert was having a tough time getting out of his protective gear, and spoke in short grunts.

"That's what the villain fed the snake in *The Speckled Band*."

"Possibly his was a milk snake. Would you mind helping me off with these boots? They're so full of socks I can't budge them."

"Not at all, dear," Dittany replied, suiting the action to the word. "That third pair was probably redundant, but I wasn't about to take any chances of his biting you in the calf. Or her, as the case may be. Darling, has it occurred to you that Roger Munson's going to be awfully miffed because we didn't let him tell us how to catch the cobra?"

"Actually, it hadn't. What does occur to me is that we've got to find out pronto who left that box. Would you mind calling the Binkles and asking them if they saw a messenger stop here?"

"I'll call but they won't be home. They both sing in the choir at St. Agapantha's."

"One of them could have come down with laryngitis," Osbert pointed out.

Evidently neither of them had; Dittany got no answer. That was bad. At this end of Applewood Avenue, there were only themselves and the Binkles. The road, which was no avenue at all, petered out into a cul-de-sac connecting only with Cat Alley, the lane that rambled across to the Enchanted Mountain and trickled up and over into the country road on the opposite side of what was really no mountain, either, but only a fair-sized hill.

Cat Alley hadn't been plowed all winter but the young bloods of Lobelia Falls had done plenty of skiing, sliding, and snowmobiling on it. By now the snow was packed down so hard that a four-wheel-drive vehicle could probably get through from the other end without much trouble. As could a skier or a snowmobiler, of course. The hitch there was that the Monks' kitchen windows gave them clear views of the lane and the mountain, and Osbert and Dittany had been in the kitchen some little while when the doorbell rang. Granted, they hadn't been concentrating on the scenery but they could hardly have missed anybody approaching the house.

"I can't believe that messenger came the back way," said Osbert. "We'd surely have seen him. Or her."

"But we didn't hear a car in the road," Dittany argued.

"The messenger could have parked at the corner and walked in. Or ridden a bike. Or a horse with muffled feet. Hooves, I mean," Osbert amended, as he was a stickler for technical equine accuracy. "Darling, why don't you phone around to a few of the neighbors and see whether anybody saw anything? I'd better check on Carolus."

"You're not intending to question him?"

"Oh no, that would hardly be according to protocol. We have to wait for the sheriff."

"What sheriff?"

Osbert blushed a little. "I mean Sergeant MacVicar. I like to think of him as the sheriff. You understand, don't you, dear?"

"Of course, dearest. You're not going to get to brooding on distant mesas up there and forget to bring down the tray, are you?"

"Nary a brood, pardner. I wonder whether Carolus would like some of my Max Brands to read."

"Why don't you give him that new book of Arethusa's instead?" Dittany suggested. *"Perfidy in a Peruke* ought to send him galloping back to Wilhedra's waiting arms, though what she wants of him is beyond me."

She gave Osbert a bon voyage kiss to help him upstairs and went to the telephone. Three numbers later, she was still dialing in vain. Everybody and his grandfather must have gone to church. Was this a sudden mass craving for divine guidance, she wondered cynically, or an urge to buttonhole fellow congregants after the services and exchange views on the play, the Architrave's acquisition of the Thorbisher-Freep collection, and Carolus Bledsoe's middle toe? Why the heck couldn't a few of them have stayed home and peeked through the front room curtains? Dittany gave up after the sixth try and went to see what she could scrape together for dinner assuming she got stuck with having to cook one.

She didn't. Arethusa and her entourage rolled in about half past two burbling about the marvelous pizza they'd stopped for at a place Andy knew and insisting they couldn't possibly eat another bite. Unless Dittany had been planning to offer them tea and some of that leftover coffee cake, Arethusa added thoughtfully. Dittany replied with relief that she had in fact been about to do just that, and sat them down around the kitchen table because she was darned if she'd mess up the dining room twice in one day.

It didn't take long to discover that Arethusa had another fish in her net. Archie was keeping his eyes fixed on her as if he were Coventry Patmore gestating some sentimental line like, "Ah, would I were that blob of raspberry jelly upon thin alabaster cheek."

Andy was looking similarly moonstruck, though that was nothing to write home about, and Carolus Bledsoe was no doubt wondering why Arethusa wasn't up there cheering his bed of pain instead of down here gobbling up everything edible. Only Daniel seemed immune to her allure. His full attention was still fixed upon Andrew McNaster.

Dittany, having refilled the teapot and got its cosy tugged firmly down over its fat brown sides, fixed her own attention on Daniel. She knew, of course, about the boy bees and the girl bees. She accepted the fact that boy bees sometimes preferred boy bees to girl bees, whereas girl bees might choose to buzz along with other girl bees to the total exclusion of boy bees. It was not her place to pass judgment on their proclivities even though she herself was firmly aligned with the boy bee-girl bee faction. But Daniel's interest in Andy didn't strike her as that of a boy bee getting up his nerve to invite another boy bee to join him at the next buttercup for a sip of nectar and maybe a little roll in the pollen. What the heck was Daniel up to?

Daniel was up to eating another slice of coffee cake, at any rate. Dittany cut it for him and went on making tea-table conversation even as she pondered his odd behavior. She wasn't able to get in much pondering time, however, as Sergeant MacVicar showed up on the dot of three in strict accordance with local protocol.

He'd changed into his customary uniform, which didn't make him any less awe-inspiring a figure. He refused tea, to Dittany's relief since Arethusa had by now pretty much cleared the table, and got straight to business.

"Deputy Monk, hae there been any new developments?"

Osbert swallowed the last of his own cake and made his brief report. "We've acquired a cobra."

Whatever Sergeant MacVicar might have been expecting, it clearly was not a cobra. He actually went so far as to raise his eyebrows.

"Oh aye?"

"The box was addressed to Carolus Bledsoe," Osbert amplified, "but Ethel wouldn't let him have it."

"Zounds," cried Arethusa. "That dog takes entirely too much upon herself, in my considered opinion. Why should Carolus be deprived the solace of herpetological companionship at the whim of an ill-bred and quite possibly bogus canine?''

Dittany flew to her faithful friend's defense. ''Ethel was afraid the cobra would bite somebody, for Pete's sake.''

''Mere pusillanimous conjecture. It's probably quite an amiable cobra. Carolus could have whiled away his convalescence playing the flute for its enjoyment. Cobras are notable music lovers.''

''Cobras are deaf as fence posts,'' Osbert contradicted. ''They don't hear those flutes the snake charmers tweetle at them. They weave back and forth pretending to dance, but what they're really doing is trying to make up their minds where to bite the guy for waking them.''

''I' faith? If the creatures are that fuzzy-minded, I can't see where they offer any serious threat,'' Arethusa retorted, licking jam off her fingers. ''As far as I'm concerned, your cobra's a mere tempest in a teapot.

''If I might be permitted to get a worrd in edgewise,'' Sergeant MacVicar remarked ith ponderous dignity, ''I'm still waiting for Deputy Monk to finish his reporrt.''

''Oh, all right, if you're goi to start gargling r's at me.''

Arethusa lapsed into sullen silence, leaving Osbert the floor. His account of the cobra's arrival was crispiy delivered and variously received.

''Diabolical,'' breathed Daniel, his sharp little dark eyes glistening.

''Trite and cliché,'' sneered Archie.

The agent was all set to harangue the gathering on how many third, fourth, and fifth-rate novels he'd got stuck with reading in which venomous reptiles had been sent to unwitting victims, but Andy McNaster cut him off.

''What have you done with her?''

''Her who?'' asked Osbert, startled by the intensity of Andy's demand.

''Her. The cobra. Where is she?''

Osbert regarded his frantic interrogator narrowly. ''How do you know it's a she?''

Andy licked his lips. ''I always think of a cobra as a she. I thought everybody did. They have that feminine grace about them, and they wear hoods. Fascinators, my grandma used to call them. Like I said, what have you done with her?''

''She's down cellar in a box.'' Osbert sounded somewhat bewildered, as well he might. ''We put her next to the furnace to thaw out.''

''I must go to her.''

Andy leaped from his chair, raced into the pantry, raced out again, found the door that really did lead to the cellar, and galloped down the stairs. Osbert, Sergeant MacVicar, Daniel, and Archie galloped after him. Dittany was all set to gallop, too, but Arethusa snatched her back.

''Hold, wench. Who's going to cook supper if that thing fangs you?''

''Unhand me, Arethusa.'' Dittany wrenched free and stuck her head down the cellarway. ''Osbert, you come straight back upstairs and get your extra socks on.''

''Don't worry, dear,'' Osbert called back. ''We're just going to lift the lid a tiny crack and peek in to see how she's doing. Oh gosh, she doesn't look—''

He probably finished what he'd intended to say, but the words were drowned out by McNaster's anguished howl.

''Arethusa!''

''What is it, Andrew?'' Arethusa Monk also had her head in the stairwell by now, but Andrew McNaster was not addressing her. The lid was in his hand and his grief-contorted face was bent toward the brownish streak that lay pitifully sprawled at the bottom of the former Mrs. Henbit's organizing box.

''She's gone,'' he choked.

Osbert tried to console him. ''Maybe she's only resting.''

''No.'' Andy's broad shoulders were heaving with ill-suppressed grief. ''I know my snake. She's shuffled off her mortal coil. But why, gosh darn it? Answer me, why?''

''I'm afraid it's because she'd got too chilled before we could catch her and bring her inside,'' Osbert told him. ''She was slithering around on the snow after the box got broken open.''

Andy sniffed and nodded. ''Cobras can't handle the cold. I always kept her nice and warm. She had a glass aquarium only I guess you'd call it a terrarium on a stand next to the radiator, with moss and plants in it and a little miniature model of the Taj Mahal to make her feel at home. She had the best of everything. I brought her meatballs and spaghetti, whatever she wanted to eat. And to think she had to end like this? Oh, Arethusa!''

"How come you named her Arethusa?" Daniel wanted to know.

"Foolish sentimentality, I suppose."

"Andrew," Arethusa Monk was at the mourner's side, her great, lustrous dark orbs abrim with unshed tears. "Did you really name your cobra after me?"

"She was all I had that I could call my own," McNaster replied simply.

The scene was a touching one, but Sergeant MacVicar was not one to let sentiment interfere with duty. "Mr. McNaster, how did yon venomous reptile come to be in your possession?"

"She was sent to me."

"By whom?"

"An anonymous donor."

"Tumultuous tumbleweeds," shouted Osbert, "do you mean to tell us you got her in the mail?"

"Yup. I just opened the box and there she was. At first I was kind of peeved, I have to admit. I'd of turned right around and mailed her back, eh, only there was no return address on the label. So I stuck her in this old aquarium I'd had kicking around empty since my goldfish died, and then I—well, I kind of got attached to her."

"But you never found out who sent her?" Osbert pressed. "Couldn't you even guess?"

"Well, yeah, I had a couple of ideas but nothing I could pin on anybody."

"Was Carolus Bledsoe one of your ideas?"

Andy became suddenly very still.

Sergeant MacVicar stepped to the fore. "We ken fine about you an' your former sidekick, Mr. McNaster. Yon Bledsoe, whom you called Charlie, was your lawyer, and had been for some time before you and he had a difference of opinion over your attempt to obtain municipal lands for private purposes. How long after that did he continue to work for you?"

Andy's face turned from ruddy to pale then back to red, but no word did he utter.

"You are in a ticklish position, Mr. McNaster. I advise you to answer."

"With all respect, Sergeant, I think my lawyer, whether it was Charlie Bledsoe or anybody else, would advise me to keep my big mouth shut. Look, I know you folks over here in Lobelia Falls don't like me—"

"Oh, but we do."

Strangely, it was not Arethusa but Dittany who protested. "We like you quite a lot, Andy, now that we're used to you. Since you haven't been reformed all that long, though, you probably don't realize how unaccustomed we here in Lobelia Falls are to having real bullets switched for blank cartridges and finding live cobras on our doorsteps. Things you people in Scottsbeck appear to take in stride tend to make us want to get hold of whoever's doing them and make them stop. Or her, if you were planning to get sniffy over the masculine pronoun."

"I don't get sniffy over masculine pronouns. I get sniffy about my cobra being made the sacrificial goat for some lousy bugger's foul perfidy."

"Then you ought to be as anxious as the rest of us to catch the snakenapper, so why can't you answer Sergeant MacVicar's question?"

"Why can't he answer mine?" Andy bawled back. "How come my cobra got killed?"

"I told you she didn't get killed," Osbert insisted. "She died of exposure."

"Want to bet?" said Dittany, who'd been keeping an anxious eye on the open box. "Look at her now, she's trying to coil. I move we put the cover back on, pronto."

"Hey!" Ignoring her warning and heedless of what the dusty cellar floor might do to his natty pinstriped trousers, Andy dropped to his knees. "Come on, Thusie girl, hiss for Papa."

Chapter 15

Arethusa Monk, though not unmoved by the tableau before her, did a rapid about-face. "*Allons, mes enfants*, let us hie ourselves hence. Methinks we should leave them alone together."

"What a splendid idea," cried Archie. "Allow me to offer you my arm, Miss Monk."

Osbert approached Dittany with equal gallantry. "Want a piggyback up the stairs, pardner?"

Daniel showed himself quite ready to abandon his absorbed scrutiny of Andrew McNaster for the nonce, and even Sergeant MacVicar beat a hasty though not undignified retreat. Andy was not long in coming after them.

"She's going to be okay," he told the group now reassembled in the kitchen. "I guess I made kind of a jackass of myself down there, eh."

"*Au contraire*," Arethusa told him kindly. "You but revealed a facet of your inwardly sensitive and compassionate character which you'd hitherto kept veiled against the prying scorn of unfeeling eyes behind a mask of ruthless inscrutability."

Normally Osbert would have had something grammatical to say about the prying scorn of unfeeling eyes. Today he only nodded. "Every one of us would have felt the same, Andy, if Arethusa had been our cobra. Wouldn't we, everybody?"

Dittany, Archie, and especially Daniel assured Andy that they would. Sergeant MacVicar made a Caledonian noise that might not go quite so far as to signify assent but did at least evince a degree of sympathetic understanding.

"And noo, Mr. McNaster, pairhaps we might address the conundrum of how yon cobra got from your house to the Monks'. Hae you any thoughts on the matter?"

"Well, what it looks like to me is, somebody must of broke into my place and took her."

"Aye? Who might that have been?"

"Somebody who needed a cobra in a hurry and knew I had one?"

"That would seem a reasonable surmise," Sergeant MacVicar conceded. "Who knew you possessed sic a creature? Do you hae frequent visitors to your house?"

"No, I never have anybody. See, it's not much of a place, just a little what you'd call an efficiency flat in an apartment house I own over in Scottsbeck. If I'm seeing anybody on business, we meet in my office over at the construction company. If it's social, which it mostly isn't, I take 'em to the inn. At the flat there's just me and Thusie."

Andy sighed. "I suppose it's not much of a life for a cobra now that I come to think of it, me being away so much and all. I ought to get her out more, let her meet other snakes, catch a few bugs, live a little. That's the heck of being a lonesome bachelor, you never know how to handle relationships."

"Being a bachelor has naething to do wi' it," said Sergeant MacVicar with some feeling. "How long has yon cobra been in your possession?"

"Since just before Christmas. She came gift-wrapped with a big red bow on the box."

"You were alone when you opened yon box?"

"Yes, it was delivered to the apartment. I was surprised because I hardly ever get mail there."

"Ah, and naebody save yoursel' has access to your rooms?"

"Well, Fitzy does. He takes care of the building, see, and comes in to clean for me once a week or so. And Ceddie Fawcett was in last week to fix a busted pipe. Ceddie's one of the Fawcett brothers who run a plumbing business over in Scottsbeck," Andy explained to Daniel, who was hanging on his every word. "They do all the plumbing work for McNaster Construction."

When there was work to be done, Dittany amended silently. Jim Streph had told Roger Munson that things were pretty quiet around McNaster Construction now that Andy had stopped making crooked deals. Hazel had passed on the news in strictest confidence, so of course Dittany kept quiet about that. She did, however, observe "No doubt Fitzy and Ceddie have spread the word about your pet cobra to all their friends and relatives."

"I suppose," Andy agreed wearily. "I'm sure Ceddie told the bartender at the inn because lately all the waitresses and busboys and everybody have been snickering behind my back about me getting a cobra for Christmas which I guess they figure it couldn't have happened to a nicer guy. I know what goes on around that place and they needn't think I don't. Not that I care," he added with a bravado which fooled nobody now that the veil of ruthless inscrutability had been dropped.

"Aye, news does get aboot," said Sergeant MacVicar. "Would your flat be hard to break into, Mr. McNaster?"

Andy shrugged. "Not particularly. It's on the ground floor and I haven't bothered with fancy locks or burglar alarms. There's nothing in the place worth stealing, just my clothes and a few sticks of furniture and a portable TV. I keep all my papers and stuff in the safe at the office. Anyway, after I got Thusie, I figured she'd scare away any robber who happened along. So what happens? They bust in and steal my snake. There's irony for you."

"Irony indeed, Mr. McNaster. Was the cobra in her usual place when you left your flat this morning?"

"I didn't leave the flat this morning, I slept at the inn. I do that sometimes when we're not booked up. Last night was kind of exhausting between the play and what happened in the last act, so when I took Archie and Dan here back to the inn I figured what the heck, I might as well stay there myself."

"You didna gae back this morn for a change of clothing?"

"I didn't have to. I keep clean shirts and stuff there."

"You werena worried about yon cobra?"

"Oh no. Snakes aren't like a dog you have to feed two

or three times a day and take out for a walk, you know. They only eat about once a week and I'd fed Thusie yesterday morning. She had water in her little dish that's supposed to look like a pond and she'd have been plenty warm enough there by the radiator. Even if the heat went off, which it shouldn't have, Fitzy being on the job like I said, the terrarium would have stayed warm enough. With the lid on it's like a greenhouse.''

"As a matter of curiosity, Mr. McNaster, how do you manage to keep frae being bitten when you take care of Arethusa?''

"Easy enough. I wear heavy gloves with big gauntlets halfway up my arms and I've got a stick with a noose on the end of it that I get around her neck. I use that to lift her out and put her in a special cage with a sliding door to it while I'm getting the terrarium fixed up. When I'm through, I just slide open the door of the cage, shake her out into the terrarium, and slap the lid on it fast.''

"And what do you do wi' yon gauntlets and stick after you've finished using them?''

Andy grinned sheepishly. "More often than not I just leave 'em wherever they happen to fall. I'm not exactly the neatest guy in the world.''

"Then the snake thief would hae found them ready to hand, and thus would hae been able to extract your cobra frae the terrarium without difficulty?''

"Sure, provided he had a steady hand and iron nerve and was plenty quick on the draw with that noose.''

"We may assume that such was the case, sin' the cobra was then placed in the florist's box and transported to this house. Would the florist's box in which your cobra was concealed also hae come frae your flat, by the bye?''

"Heck, no. Nobody ever sends me flowers. Not that a few people I know wouldn't like to,'' Andy added lugubriously, "provided I wasn't alive to smell 'em.''

"Fie, Andrew,'' cried Arethusa. "Dispel such dire and darksome deemings.''

"Aye,'' said Sergeant MacVicar. "Let us stick wi' the facts. What is germane is that twice in less than twenty-four hours Mr. Bledsoe has had narrow escapes from being assassinated. In both cases, you, Mr. McNaster, hae been made in some sense the instrument of his intended murder. It seems therefore not ootside the bounds of logical conjecture that the perpetrator of these ootrages may be known to both you and Mr. Bledsoe. Do you not agree that is possible, Mr. McNaster?''

"Aye. I mean yeah. Sure. You bet."

"Than can you think of any person who might be guilty of these dreadfu' crimes?"

"Well, not to be ungallant toward the fair sex, but there's that loony ex-wife of Charlie's."

"The temperamental Mrs. Bledsoe. Has your acquaintance with her continued sin' the divorce?"

"Look here, Sergeant, if you're hinting there was ever anything between Ermeline and me, you're out to lunch. In the first place, do you think I'm dumb enough to go horsing around with a lawyer's wife? Or anybody else's wife," Andy added with a nervous glance at Arethusa Monk.

"In the second place, I don't call myself a coward exactly but I'm sure not reckless enough to grab a tigress by the tail which I didn't mean in the rude and lascivious manner it might of sounded like and no offense to the ladies present."

"None taken," Dittany assured him. "Did you dump Charlie, or did Charlie dump you?"

"Ar-h'm," said Sergeant MacVicar. "Perhaps Mr. McNaster is impatient to return yon cobra to her wee glass hoose, gin he deems her weel enow to undertake the journey. And perhaps, Arethusa, you'd care to assist in meenistering to your namesake."

"And perhaps you'd like us to go with them," Archie and Daniel volunteered in chorus, both obviously delighted at the prospect for whatever their respective reasons might be.

"An excellent suggestion," Sergeant MacVicar replied blandly. "Mr. McNaster, it's understood that you will hold yoursel' in readiness for further interrogation."

"Sure, Sergeant, any time you say. I'm a darn sight more anxious than you are to get this mess cleared up."

"As weel you might be, Mr. McNaster. Noo, Deputy

Monk, would you kindly step up to yon guest room and ascertain whether Mr. Bledsoe feels up to an official visit?''

"Yes, Chief. Archie, give us a ring when you've got the cobra delivered and let us know what you and Daniel would like to do later on. Dittany and I will be right here. Barring further unexpected developments," Osbert added prudently, things being as they'd been ever since he'd sat down to write *Dangerous Dan*.

Her husband's effort to be a good host in the face of all obstacles reminded Dittany that she had her own responsibilities as a hostess. "Perhaps Thusie would like a drink of milk for the road," she suggested as Andy carried the box up from the cellar.

"Thanks," he replied, "but she'd better wait till she gets home. I don't want her getting carsick on top of everything else. Maybe you could lend me an old blanket or something to wrap around the box just so she won't get chilled again."

"Of course." Dittany fetched an afghan her mother had crocheted in stripes of orange, vermilion, scarlet, and deep crimson. "This ought to keep her warm. Here, let me help you wrap."

They'd got Thusie nicely tucked up and Andy was on his way out the door when the telephone rang. It was Wilhedra Thorbisher-Freep, wanting to talk with Carolus.

"I'm sorry," Dittany told her, "but that won't be possible."

Wilhedra's "Oh?" was reminiscent of a January night in Aklavik. "May I ask why not?"

"Because the phone's downstairs and he's up."

"Don't you have an extension?"

"Nope. My grandmother considered them an effete and decadent notion leading to hardening of the arteries for lack of exercise, so we've refrained from having one installed out of filial piety."

"How quaint. But then how can I get in touch with Carolus?"

"We might bring Roger Munson and his sons back here with the stretcher to carry him down, but I hate to ask because they had such an awful time getting him up. I'm not sure Carolus would go for the idea, anyway. He did some pretty fancy cussing en route the first time," Dittany explained. "Couldn't you just write a note?"

"And ask your Aunt Arethusa to deliver it, perhaps? I suppose she's up there with him, playing Florence Nightingale to the hilt."

"Nope. She's gone off with Andy, Archie, and Daniel."

Wilhedra digested that information in silence for a moment, then she inquired in a less hostile tone, "How is Carolus bearing up?"

"As well as can be expected. He ate a hearty lunch a while ago. Osbert's checking on him now. I can yell up the stairs and see whether he has any message, if you like."

"No, don't bother. I'll write the note. By the way," Wilhedra added in an offhand manner that didn't fool Dittany a bit, "who are Archie and Daniel?"

"Didn't you meet them last night at the play? Archie is Osbert's agent and Daniel's a producer who's going to buy *Dangerous Dan*, we hope."

"Oh yes, I remember now. One tall and thin, one short and stout. Dot and dash, Father called them. And where does Andy McNaster come in?"

"He's putting them up at the inn and helping Arethusa show them around because Osbert and I are stuck here with Carolus. Thanks to your father," Dittany couldn't help adding in view of that crack about dot and dash.

"My father? What did he have to do with it?"

"Everything. He dropped by during breakfast to explain why he wasn't able to come, and made a lovely speech about how Carolus couldn't go to your house when he left the hospital because you'd sprained your ankle and the maid would leave if he asked her to take care of you both. Your father claimed the only alternatives were for Carolus to pine alone and desolate in a nursing home or else be offered a haven by kind and compassionate friends, namely us."

"Why you in particular?"

"Your father can answer that better than I. Anyway, the upshot was that Roger Munson went to the hospital and got Carolus and brought him here; and here Carolus has to stay until the doctor says he's fit to leave. Wilhedra, I'm sorry about your ankle. I'm sorry about Carolus's toe. But right now I'm sorriest for Osbert and myself. So why don't I just go tell Carolus you were asking for him and if you have any further objections to the way his convalescence is being handled, I suggest you share them with your father."

"Yes, Dittany, of course. I simply didn't understand the situation. And it's so frustrating being laid up like this when I desperately want to be making myself useful to Carolus. I must say it does seem—Arethusa might have managed to squeeze out a few minutes' time for him after he practically had to carry her on his back all through the play."

"I'll tell her you said so. Good-bye, Wilhedra."

By this time, Osbert was back downstairs. "He's all curried and watered and feeling his oats, Sergeant. Do you want to go up now?"

"Aye, let's get on wi' it."

"I'll go too," Dittany said, "and give him Wilhedra's message."

What with one thing and another, this was the first she'd seen of their less than welcome guest since Roger and his boys had lugged him up the stairs. She found Carolus, almost unrecognizable in apricot silk pajamas, propped up against Gram Henbit's best pillowcases. Trust Roger Munson to pick out the ones with the crocheted edges she'd been saving for when Osbert's mother came to visit.

"Wilhedra just called," she told him after the ritual inquiries as to his current state of being had been adequately dealt with. "She's laid up with a sprained ankle. Did anybody tell you?"

"Yes, Roger mentioned it on the way from the hospital. How did she do that?"

"Slipped on the stairs, her father said. She wants you to know how sorry she is that she can't take care of you."

"Nice of her." Carolus didn't sound much interested. "What's on your mind, Sergeant MacVicar?"

"A vast deal, Mr. Bledsoe, and none of it pleasant. Are you aware that two different attempts on your life appear to hae been made sin' last you supped?"

"Two different attempts? Whatever do you mean?"

"Firstly, as you know, you narrowly escaped a mortal

wound frae a live bullet exchanged for the blank cartridge Andrew McNaster was supposed to fire at your chest. Secondly, you were apparently intended to sustain a fatal bite frae a cobra delivered to this house late the day's morn in a florist's box addressed to you."

"What?" Hurling bedclothes left and right, Carolus struggled to get up. "I hate snakes! Get me out of here."

Osbert pushed him back. "Whoa there, Carolus. Hold your horses. Ethel saved you from the cobra and Andy McNaster took it home."

"Andy McNaster? And you simply let him?"

"Why not?" said Dittany. "It was his cobra. Her name's Arethusa and she lives in a glass box next to his radiator."

"I'm sure she does, when she's not off helping Andy run his business."

"That is a verra strong statement, Mr. Bledsoe," said Sergeant MacVicar. "I assume you, being a lawyer, hae firm grounds for making it."

"I believe I'd have little difficulty supporting my observation if I had to," Carolus replied coolly, "though I'd been under the impression that as the aggrieved party in this case, I had the right to express myself without being jumped on."

"Nae censure was implied, Mr. Bledsoe, nor will any be given unless it's deserved. Then you hae reason to believe Mr. McNaster constitutes a threat to your well-being, notwithstanding his refusal to shoot e'en a supposed blank cartridge at you yestreen?"

"Mr. McNaster showed no such reluctance at the dress rehearsal, Sergeant. I might also remind you that he did in fact succeed in maiming me for life. Whether this was done in total innocence as he alleges or as the result of his losing his nerve about committing a cold-blooded murder in front of several hundred witnesses, I leave you to discover. As for this morning's incident, I can only repeat what Dittany just told me. It was McNaster's cobra."

Chapter 16

"Could you perchance gie us a hint as to whyfor yon McNaster might take a notion to murder you, Mr. Bledsoe?" Sergeant MacVicar asked politely.

"There's nothing I'd rather do, Sergeant. What it boils down to is that I've had certain professional dealings with Mr. McNaster in which serious questions of illegal procedures were involved. I'm afraid I can't go into specific details without committing a breach of client confidentiality. However, I can assure you that McNaster has sound reason to fear that his so-called reformation is going to rest on extremely shaky ground for as long as I'm allowed to remain alive."

"Yoursel' having been always on the side of law an' order, nae doot?"

"Always," Carolus replied sweetly.

Dittany started to say "I object" but snapped her mouth shut before the words could escape. Since she and Osbert appeared to be stuck with taking care of the lawyer for at least the next few days, it would be easier on all three of them if Charlie didn't know his cover had been blown. Carolus had noticed her lips begin to move, though. Fortunately he guessed wrong about what she'd been about to say.

"Perhaps, Dittany, you were wondering whether it would be tactless to mention my, shall we say, increasingly close friendship with Osbert's aunt, and the all-too-obvious effect it appears to be having on Mr. McNaster. Ridiculous, I know."

"Yes, isn't it," Dittany agreed. "Andy knows as well
as the rest of us that you've already plighted your troth to
Wilhedra Thorbisher-Freep."

That was not the reply Carolus Bledsoe had expected,
and it certainly wasn't the one he'd wanted. "Does he,
indeed? Then Andy must know a good deal more about my
personal business than I do."

"Stuff it, Carolus," said Osbert. "You needn't try to
play cozy with us. Jenson spilled the beans about your
secret engagement to the whole cast and crew at breakfast
here this morning."

"Ah yes, Jenson." Carolus looked much like a man
who'd just bitten into a juicy red apple and discovered half
a worm. "He does have a flair for the dramatic gesture,
doesn't he? I expect Jenson's decided I'm eligible for his
theatrical collection now that I've been shot onstage during
a performance."

"Then if Wilhedra calls again, do you want us to tell
her the engagement's off?" Dittany asked him.

"I'd far rather you didn't tell her anything at all. Whatever you said could only lead to hurt feelings and the
Thorbisher-Freeps are old friends whom I don't want to
offend. I'll have a little chat with Wilhedra as soon as I'm
back on my feet. She and I understand each other very
well, I'm thankful to say."

"I should think you might be, eh," said Dittany. "It
would be awful to get slapped with a breach of promise
suit while your ex-wife's still trying to have you bagged
for fraud."

Carolus tried hard to portray mild amusement. "You do
have a charming way of bringing comfort to the afflicted,
my dear. Let me assure you, Jenson Thorbisher-Freep
would never set himself or his daughter up to play a
courtroom scene unless he could officiate as judge, and
even he might have a hard time convincing himself that
was possible. Anyway, Wilhedra has another admirer, as
you must have gathered from that absurd scene in the
restaurant last night. During which threats against my
person were uttered, Sergeant MacVicar, in case you hadn't
heard."

"I hae heard, Mr. Bledsoe. Leander Hellespont made

another appearance backstage in the gymnasium whilst you an' the rest of the cast were getting ready for the performance.''

"I didn't know that! How did you find out?"

"It's my business to find out, Mr. Bledsoe. Yon Hellespont is already being investigated by the Scottsbeck police, as is your ex-wife who was also seen backstage.''

"What about that chap who was supposed to be tailing her? I gave him strict orders to keep her out of trouble.''

"You didn't give him orders to keep her out of the women's rest room, did you?'' asked Dittany.

Carolus grunted. "How could I? Anyway, I can't believe it's Ermeline who's trying to kill me. She'd rather keep me alive so she can watch me squirm. But I'm relieved to know some action's being taken. Let's hope somebody comes up with results before my would-be murderer gets lucky. Can't you put a guard on this house?''

"You've been guarded e'er since you arrived, Mr. Bledsoe,'' Sergeant MacVicar informed him sternly.

"Then how did that cobra get here?''

"Yon cobra did not get to you, Mr. Bledsoe. You were in nae mair danger whilst it was on these premises than you are noo that it's been taken away. Gin you deem yoursel' unsafe here, however, I can arrange for your transferral to a place of maximum security.''

"Where, for instance? The Scottsbeck jail?''

"Aye, or the county mental hospital. Tak' your pick.''

"Thanks for nothing, I'll chance it here. Osbert, have you any whiskey in the house?''

"Yep.'' Osbert had settled himself beside Dittany in the window seat. He continued to sit.

"Then would you mind getting me some?'' Carolus asked him in no gracious tone.

"Sorry. Roger said not while you're on antibiotics.''

Carolus said something luridly uncomplimentary about Roger Munson. Osbert heard him unmoved.

"No more Mr. Nice Guy, eh? You might as well get this straight, Carolus; you're here because the Thorbisher-Freeps couldn't have you and a nursing home wouldn't take you. My wife and I will do our best to make you comfortable, but that isn't going to include anything that might interfere with your speediest possible recovery. You're welcome to a cup of tea if you want it.''

"Don't bother,'' Carolus replied sulkily. "Since I'm only here on sufferance, I mustn't put you to any extra trouble.''

"Why not?'' said Dittany. "Everybody else does. I'll put the kettle on. Don't anybody say anything interesting while I'm gone.''

Sergeant MacVicar stood up. "I believe everything has been said that needed to be said at this stage of the investigation. Mr. Bledsoe, gin you happen to think of any further information that might be of use, it will be in your best interest to pass it along to Deputy Monk or mysel' with all dispatch. In the meantime, you can best serve yoursel' and us by keeping calm and following your doctor's orders. I see Roger Munson getting out of his car wi' a television set in his arms, so I'll leave you the noo to suffer his attentions in whatever manner you see fit.''

Dittany went downstairs to let the sergeant out and Roger in. Then she put on the kettle, sat down in the kitchen rocker to wait for it to boil, and fell asleep. She woke with the kettle ready to dance off the stove and Osbert bending over her, smoothing back her light brown hair.

"Are you all right, darling?''

"I guess so.'' She yawned and did a little experimental stretching. "I don't know what got into me, I never sleep in the daytime. Do something about that kettle, will you, darling? Carolus must be yammering for his tea. Do you think we made a mistake telling him about the cobra?''

"He had to know, dear.'' Osbert filled the teapot and started fixing a tray. "Shall I give him some of this stuff Zilla brought?''

"No, don't, for heaven's sake. He's had enough shocks to his system already. Give him that last bit of coffee cake and a few of Therese's cookies. Those ought to hold him till suppertime, whenever that may be. Is Roger still here?''

"No, he went straight home as soon as he'd got the television set working. Hazel's brother Euonymus and his wife are visiting and they were in the midst of a Chinese checkers tournament. What are we having for supper, by the way?''

"Could you eat beans on toast?"

"Us old cowhands can always eat beans on toast, pardner. I wonder what Archie and Daniel are doing."

"As a guess, ogling," Dittany answered. "I hope Arethusa offers them supper at her house for a change. It's going to be slim pickings around here if we have to stretch one can of beans among six or seven of us. Unless you want to take them out to eat and I'll stay here with Carolus?"

"Not on your life, sweetheart. Ethel and I will ride herd on Carolus and you can go with the boys. Let them treat you on Archie's expense account. He's had it pretty easy so far."

"How could I sit eating filet mignon knowing you were back here with a can of beans and a crabby invalid?" Dittany protested. "We'll manage one way or another, we always do. Do you think we ought to make a conciliatory gesture and have our tea upstairs with Carolus?"

Osbert shrugged. "As long as we're stuck with him, we might as well make a decent pretense of enjoying his company. Here, you take the cookies and I'll carry the tray."

They found Carolus flipping the remote control switch from station to station and not finding anything he liked. "Ah, my bodyguard has arrived," he remarked sarcastically. "Why three cups? Is the dog coming, too?"

"Two cups for us and one for you," said Dittany, refusing to be annoyed. "Ethel's up on the Enchanted Mountain trying to find something to bark at. Do you want to pour or shall I?"

"You, by all means."

They took their cups and cookies and sat for a while watching a program from British Columbia about how to carve a totem pole. Gradually they drifted into conversation, trying to stay away from controversial subjects. That meant mostly talking about the play, which led inevitably to talking about the lady who'd been temporarily known as Lou.

"I'd rather hoped Arethusa might drop by and say hello," Carolus remarked with a sigh of self-pity.

"I'm sure she will as soon as she has a chance," was Dittany's consolation. "The thing of it is, we'd expected Osbert's agent and his friend the producer to leave early this morning, but they've decided to stay over. That means somebody has to entertain them and Arethusa's been the only one free to cope. She did mention something about coming back here at suppertime."

Carolus brightened up. "Then I ought to start trying to make myself presentable. I didn't get much of a shave this morning at the hospital. The nurse gave me a stupid little disposable plastic razor which was about as useful as nothing at all. There's a good one in my shaving kit. It's in that suitcase Roger picked up at my apartment this morning. I always leave a bag packed because I never know when I'm going to be called out of town in a hurry."

He probably meant whether he'd have to take it on the lam, Dittany thought, but she didn't say so since this was meant to be a peacekeeping operation. Osbert went over and started to open the brown pigskin suitcase that was sitting on the floor beside the dresser. Then he hesitated.

"Wait a minute, Carolus. You said your kit was already packed. Did Roger open it?"

"He opened the suitcase to get my robe and pajamas out, but I don't believe he opened the shaving kit. Why should he?"

"I don't know." Osbert lifted the lid of the suitcase, fished around under a clean shirt, and pulled out a small zippered case that matched the bag. "Is this what you want?"

"Yes. If you'll be kind enough to help me to the bathroom—"

Osbert hesitated. "This is going to sound pretty silly, Carolus, but I think it mightn't be a bad idea for me to take this kit outdoors and open it there. Using those lazy tongs Dittany's grandfather had for when his lumbago was acting up. Do you remember where we keep them, darling?"

"Hanging in the cellarway next to the wire carpet beater,"

Dittany told him. "Darling, that case isn't hissing, by any chance?"

Osbert held the kit to his ear. "No, it doesn't seem to be doing anything. I'm probably being foolish."

"Better you a fool than I a corpse," Carolus replied grimly. "Go ahead, Osbert. Open the damned thing anywhere you want except here. God, I feel like a trapped rat."

"I'll get the tongs," Dittany said. "Osbert, why don't you throw the kit out the window? If there's a bomb inside, it will go off when it hits and you won't be running the risk."

"Sound thinking, dear. Is there anything breakable inside, Carolus?"

"Just some after-shave lotion. I don't care, go ahead and chuck it."

"I'll aim for a snowbank." Osbert opened the window, leaned out, and lobbed the kit neatly into a high drift out by the road.

"No bang," said Dittany. "That's a hopeful sign, but you'd better put on those extra socks anyway."

She got him bundled up against almost any contingency except total immersion, which wasn't likely to happen anyway, and watched in apprehension from the top of the front steps.

Osbert approached the shaving kit much as he had the cobra. It took some fiddling to get the case wedged firmly enough into a cleft branch of the lilac bush so that he could get a grip with the tongs on the zipper tab, but Deputy Monk was not one to back away from difficulty. Satisfied, he backed off, extended the lazy tongs to their full length, grappled with the zipper, and tugged.

Crack! He leaped back as Dittany yelped, then retracted the tongs and stared in semi-disbelief at the object that had attached itself to the bottom gripper.

"Roistering rattlesnakes, it's a rat trap! And the spring bar that's supposed to snap down over the rat's head has been filed to a sharp edge and smeared with something or other."

"Cobra venom, I'll bet." Heedless of the cold and her

thin shoes, Dittany was out on the path now, craning her neck for a better look.

"Or else plain old-fashioned rat poison mixed with molasses to make it stick," Osbert suggested. "I expect the idea was for the sharpened wire to slam down and cut Carolus's fingers open when he reached into the kit, so that the poison would enter the bloodstream. If it is poison, of course. It might just be something nasty like lye or itching powder. Come on, darling, let's get back inside before you catch pneumonia."

"Don't forget the shaving kit. Carolus will want his razor."

"He'd better use mine till we find out what that stuff on the wire is. Some of it might have dropped off." But Osbert retrieved the kit from the lilac bush anyway. "We'll keep this for evidence. Gosh, I don't much look forward to telling Carolus what we found."

"He ought to be darned glad you found it instead of him," said Dittany. "I'm betting Sergeant MacVicar isn't going to relish what his wife will say when we call him away from his tea. But we should, don't you think?"

"Oh, no question. He'll want Carolus's permission for a thorough search of his flat. Some ornery coyote is anxious to see Carolus Bledsoe dead, pardner."

"This coyote's more than ornery. Crazy as a coot, if you ask me. Tarantulas and bullets and cobras and rat traps right and left! It must be that goofy ex-wife, wouldn't you think?"

"Carolus says not."

"So what? Men never know anything about women. Except you, dear." Dittany kissed Osbert's cowlick as it emerged from his parka. "Go ahead, call the sergeant. I'm going to take a prowl through the freezer and see if I can't find something for supper besides baked beans."

Both missions were crowned with success. By the time Dittany emerged from the cellar with a package of frozen leftover turkey, a plastic container of giblet gravy, a bag of broccoli, and some passion fruit ice cream she'd bought in a spirit of scientific research and hadn't yet found occasion to try, Osbert had Sergeant MacVicar with him in the kitchen, holding Gramp Henbit's lazy tongs and shaking his head over the rat trap.

"A vicious machination, indeed. Carolus Bledsoe would hae lost a finger or two, belike. An' perchance his life, gin yon sticky substance smeared on the wire is what you conjecture it to be. Aye, Deputy Monk, a diabolical mind is at work here."

He fished his eyeglasses out of his breast pocket, perched them halfway down the majestic sweep of his nose, and scrutinized the rat trap more closely. "Supersnapper, eh. Not a brand wi' which I am familiar. The trusty auld Ratsbane has aye been the favorite around these parts."

"Then if we can find a shop that sells Supersnappers instead of Ratsbanes, we may be able to trace the person who bought the trap," said Dittany.

"It's a possibility, but a weary and belike fruitless task it may prove to be."

Sergeant MacVicar returned his spectacles to his pocket and picked up the plastic bag in which Osbert had stowed the shaving kit. "We may be able to get some fingerprints off this wee poke. Dittany lass, you did me a guid turn when you showed the perspicacity to marry this bright lad."

"I did myself an even better turn."

Osbert grinned and blushed and gave his wife, though not the sergeant, an affectionate squeeze. "And here I'd been thinking I was the lucky one. We'll get married again tomorrow, Chief, if you think it'll help the case along. Is there any chance of getting that wire analyzed today?"

"We can try. My daughter-in-law will nae doot be willing to drop off the trap at the chemistry teacher's hoose on her way home frae bringing the eggs. Hae you a stamp pad in the house?"

"Two of them," Dittany told him. "One green for getting out the Grub-and-Stakers' newsletter, one black on general principles. What do you want stamped? Oh, I know. Carolus Bledsoe's fingerprints."

"Aye, lass, they'll be on the kit along wi' Deputy Monk's."

"Would ordinary typewriter paper do to take the fingerprints on, Chief?'' Osbert said. ''That's what we have mostly.''

''I dinna see why not.''

They experimented on Osbert and found typewriter paper worked just fine. Then they had to take the pad and paper upstairs, explain to Carolus about the rat trap in the shaving kit, and get his fingerprints, also. Finally they had to fetch him a tot of brandy, antibiotics or no antibiotics. Even a lawyer could take only just so much in the way of being assassinated without beginning to fray around the edges.

Chapter 17

Osbert had made a thorough search of Carolus's luggage to make sure there were no more booby traps and was playing cribbage with the patient to settle him down. Dittany was in the kitchen, wondering whether she ought to defrost that whole big lump of turkey or just hack off enough for the three of them and put the rest back in the freezer, when Arethusa blew in with Archie in tow.

"What happened to Daniel?" Dittany asked her.

"He's gone where the woodbine twineth."

"Could you be more specific? There's a fair amount of woodbine around, you know."

Since Arethusa appeared to be more interested in the turkey, Archie took over the explanation. "We stopped at the inn for a drink with Andy, and found out two of the kitchen helpers had got into a fight. They'd been throwing crockery and knives and both of them were rather impressively cut up. So Andy had to drive them over to the hospital to get stitched together, then go back to stir the soup and make the salads, the cook being by now short-handed and the usual biggish Sunday night supper crowd expected. Daniel stayed on to help Andy. He had to do a fair amount of KP in the army, he says, so he's handy in a big kitchen. Arethusa and I decided to leave them to it and walk over here. It's a lovely evening for a stroll."

The day had been bleak and raw at its best. As the light failed, the temperature had dropped and the wind picked up. Archie must have a fairly serious case.

"I'm glad you came," Dittany replied as a thoughtful hostess must. "I was wondering whether to plan on you for supper."

"Also for drinks and hors-d'oeuvre," Arethusa assured her. "Where's that useless nephew of mine, forsooth?"

"Upstairs entertaining our invalid. Carolus has been asking for you, by the way. He got shaved on purpose when we said we more or less expected you here, so you'd better go up."

"For how long, prithee?"

"That's between you and your conscience."

"Stomach," Arethusa corrected. "What time are you planning to serve?"

"Anon."

"And as to the drinks?"

"Help yourself. You know where we keep the liquor. Archie, what would you like?"

"Let me fix them."

Archie bounded out of the chair he'd barely got settled in and followed Arethusa into the pantry. That was where Osbert had proposed to Dittany on the strength of a four-day acquaintance. She watched with interest to see whether Archie was going to beat Osbert's time, but evidently he wasn't quite that beglamored yet. He came out after only a minute or so, carrying a whiskey and two sherries. Arethusa followed with a plate of crackers. Both acted content enough, but neither showed that stunned and starry expression which betokens a rapid-fire betrothal.

"Archie's going to stay here and keep you company," said Arethusa, taking the two sherries from him and handing one to Dittany. "I'll send Osbert down to set the table. You did say the turkey would be ready in half an hour or so?"

"Actually I didn't, but it probably will be. Ask Carolus what he wants to drink that isn't alcoholic."

"Silly wench. If it isn't alcoholic, Carolus won't want it."

Arethusa took a sip of her own sherry and went upstairs, carrying a separate plate of crackers and a hefty wedge of cheddar to tide her over. Archie gazed after her like a lovelorn whippet.

"You know, it seems totally incredible that a woman like her could be Osbert's aunt."

"Osbert often finds it so," Dittany agreed. "You don't mind if we eat supper here in the kitchen? We always do, when it's just family."

"Not at all." Archie proved his point by sitting down again. "Agents count as family, pretty much. This Bledsoe fellow, has Arethusa known him long?"

"Only since she was crowned reigning queen of the roguish regency romance. They happened to sit together on the plane coming back and he gave her his smoked peanuts. But it wasn't the start of something beautiful, if that's what you're wondering. Don't you remember Jenson Thorbisher-Freep mentioning this morning that Carolus is going to marry his daughter?"

"Did he really? I must have been thinking of something else at the time. So the fact that Bledsoe happened to be playing Arethusa's husband in *Dangerous Dan* has no bearing whatsoever on their real-life relationship."

Archie, who'd shown no appetite hitherto for the cheese and crackers, now helped himself to a lavish handful. "Merely the easy camaraderie of the stage," he amplified, spraying a few crumbs in his eagerness to get his point across. "Just a couple of ships passing in the night."

"That seems to be the drift," Dittany agreed. With a what-the-heck gesture, she dumped the rest of the turkey into the pan. "Has Daniel said anything yet about the play?"

"Not the kind of anything you mean. He's talked a great deal about acting techniques and so forth, mostly with Andy. Arethusa rather seems to prefer to talk with me."

The poor, deluded fish, Dittany thought sympathetically. The only person Arethusa genuinely enjoyed talking to was herself. What she'd probably been doing all day was lolling around with a queenly smile playing about her ruby lips, letting Archie natter on as he pleased while she spun herself yet another sugary fantasia about her dauntless though often boring hero, Sir Percy, and his pea-brained light of love, Lady Ermintrude; which she'd subsequently write down and expect Dittany to type for her. Archie burbled on about Arethusa's astonishing depth of understanding while Dittany allowed a queenly smile to play about her lips and wondered whether to serve noodles, rice, or potatoes with the turkey.

Noodles, she decided, those were quickest. She was in the pantry trying to discover whether in fact she had any on hand when Archie interrupted himself to remark, "Somebody's at the door, Dittany."

Roger Munson with the Chinese checkers board? No, Roger knew better than to come calling just at suppertime. Dittany started to wipe her hands on her apron, realized she wasn't wearing one, took a quick swipe with a paper towel instead, and went to find out who it was. She found herself staring at a solid mass of black wool broadcloth.

"Jenson!" she exclaimed. "Why aren't you home with Wilhedra?"

"Well may you ask."

The sepulchral voice was not Jenson Thorbisher-Freep's. Nor, for that matter, was the cloak. The inopportune visitor was unequivocally Leander Hellespont.

"For goodness' sake," was her reaction. "You're the last person I expected to see. What can I do for you, Mr. Hellespont?"

"You can lead me to Cleopatra."

He stalked into the kitchen like the statue of the Commendatore coming to dine with Don Juan. When he was directly under the light, he flung back his head, contorted his gaunt visage into an expression that might be intended to depict the extremity of emotional suffering or a bad case of gastritis, and clenched his two fists against those upper breadths of his cloak under which his breast was presumably located.

"I am dying, Egypt, dying; only I here importune death awhile, until of many thousand kisses the poor last I lay upon thy lips."

"Are you sure you've got the right house, Mr. Hellespont?" said Dittany. "Cleopatra isn't here."

"The devil damn thee black, thou cream-faced loon! Where got'st thou that goose look?"

Archie leaped up from his chair to Dittany's side without appearing to touch the linoleum in between. "Now look here, you—"

"No more o' that, my lord, no more o' that! You mar all wi' this starting."

"I'll mar you with some finishing if you don't quit insulting my client's wife. What do you think you're raving about?"

"Some say he's mad; others that lesser hate him do call it valiant fury; but for certain he cannot buckle his distemper'd cause within the belt of rule. What I am talking about, sirrah, is that I crave utterance with my Lady Macbeth, my Desdemona, my Gertrude, nay, e'en perchance my Iphigenia!"

"You said you were looking for Cleopatra."

"O ye that have ears and hear not! I seek her in histrionic association with whom my loftiest aspirations as a thespian may yet be fulfilled. 'Twas but yestreen I did observe her strutting and fretting a wasted hour upon the stage in a paltry melodrama penned, I was told, by one who styles himself her nephew, resident of this dwelling."

Light began at last to glimmer. "Would you by any chance be looking for my husband's Aunt Arethusa?" Dittany asked him.

"Yes! Yes, i' sooth, 'tis she!" Hellespont flung himself to his knees, letting his cape swirl artistically about him regardless of the fact that the linoleum was by now somewhat badly tracked up, and lifted clasped hands in the classic gesture of supplication. "Oh, lead me, lead me to her!"

Dittany shook her head. "Sorry, she's busy just now. Mr. Hellespont, I don't like to seem inhospitable but you've called at an awfully inconvenient time. I was starting to get supper on the table and I'm afraid I can't ask you to join us, eh, because there's just about enough to go around as it is."

"Food!" He dismissed the entire subject of gastronomy with a disdainful wave of his hand. "I offer food for the spirit, food for the intellect, and five percent of the gate."

"Ten," Archie replied automatically as a conscientious agent naturally would. "Mr. Hellespont, are you trying to tell us you want Miss Arethusa Monk to join you in some theatrical enterprise?"

"I will elevate her to the heights!"

"She's already elevated," said Dittany.

The actor did a commendable job of registering amused disbelief, considering that his Irvingesque features were not well adapted to levity. "Not as Arethusa Monk, surely. I've never come upon that name in *Variety.*"

"Try the *Hearts and Flowers Gazette.* She's the reigning queen of regency romance, didn't you know that?"

"Pah! Who does regency drama these days?"

"Who's talking about drama? Arethusa's an author."

"A what?"

"She writes books."

"Books!" He dismissed the entire subject of bibliography, too. "I will make her rich beyond the dreams of avarice."

"She's already richer than she needs to be and she doesn't dream of avarice. She dreams of being abducted by a member of the Hellfire Club."

"I'll abduct her!"

"You'll be sorry if you do. She'll eat you out of house and home."

"I will bring the world to her feet," the would-be Pygmalion insisted, though Dittany detected just a hint of lessening fervor.

"It's already there," she assured him. "Some of it anyway. Mr. Hellespont, you don't seem to understand. Arethusa Monk has achieved a position of preeminence in her chosen sector of the literary field."

"Writing sentimental drivel."

Then he did understand. However, Dittany was not about to give ground. "If you want to talk business with my husband's aunt, why don't you telephone her some day this week at her own house and ask her for an appointment?"

"Appointment? Faugh! I come as a harbinger of immortality and you try to fob me off with an appointment."

Hellespont turned away from her in haughty disdain, whipping his cloak in so wide a circle that it almost knocked the pans off the stove. He'd had dress weights sewn into the hem, the old popinjay, was Dittany's surmise. But where was this other whirl coming from? All of a sudden, the kitchen had become a veritable maelstrom of flapping black broadcloth.

"Ungh!"

"Urff!"

"Confound—"

"You!"

Jenson Thorbisher-Freep was first to recover his aplomb. "Sorry, Dittany, I should have knocked before I barged in. Leander, I never expected to find you here."

"He was looking for Cleopatra," Dittany took it upon herself to explain, as Hellespont seemed completely preoccupied with getting his cloak untangled from the towel rack.

The thespian furled the last breath of his cloak and gave her a cold look. "I was looking for a leading lady," he amended. "Surely, Jenson, you must agree that the superb actress who chooses for some reason I cannot fathom to let herself be known as Arethusa Monk was grievously miscast in that trumpery bit of fustian we were constrained to sit through last night. And yet there were moments of transcendence. That ineffable gesture, for instance, when she clasped the dying feedbag man to her bosom! Tender, protective, ferociously possessive! The eternal mother! The anguished spouse! *Vénus toute entière à sa proie attaché.*"

"Actually, Carolus was squirming around and Arethusa was trying to make him lie still," said Dittany.

"Ah yes, Carolus." Jenson became all solicitude. "How is the dear fellow?"

"Bearing up, more or less. He's playing cribbage with Osbert. And Archie is helping me get supper." She hoped Jenson would take the hint and leave, preferably accompanied by Hellespont. She could do without what would no doubt ensue should the two discover that Arethusa was actually in the house.

Jenson did get her message, though he got it wrong. "No, no, my dear, I can't stay. I wouldn't dream of imposing on your hospitality twice in one day. I came out to get Wilhedra's prescription filled and though I might as well pop over for a moment to see how our other patient is doing. You're quite sure Carolus is resting comfortably?"

"I'm sure he'd let us know if he weren't," Dittany assured the putative father-in-law. "Carolus isn't the bashful type, we've discovered. Wilhedra's doing all right, I hope? I spoke with her on the phone a while back."

"You are the soul of kindness, dear lady. I'm sure your call was a great comfort to her. But I mustn't keep you from your cooking. I'll come again at a more convenient time. Leander, can I offer you a ride back to Scottsbeck?"

"Thank you, Jenson. My own conveyance awaits. Yet I shall not return to my ancestral soil until I have achieved my sworn purpose."

"You mean persuading Arethusa Monk to join the Scottsbeck Players?"

"Nay, more! Far more! I will mold her, I will shape her. I will—"

"You will do no such thing!" Jenson thundered. "Arethusa Monk will have nothing to do with you or your claptrap crew of bumbling amateurs. If you try to badger her, Leander, you'll answer to me!"

Hellespont bristled, but it was Archie who yelled. "How dare you take it upon yourself to speak for Miss Monk? She's not your client. You don't own her!"

Jenson Thorbisher-Freep drew his black cloak about him, threw back his hoary head, and gave Archie the kind of smile Sir John A. MacDonald might have given Louis Riel if they'd happened to meet in the kitchen of a very tired young housewife who was trying to warm up a panful of leftover turkey in giblet gravy. "That, my good man, is what you think. *A bientôt,* Dittany."

Chapter 18

Dittany picked up the glass of sherry she hadn't yet got to taste, and took a calming sip. It failed to calm.

Archie shook his head and drained the last of his whiskey. That didn't seem to be doing much good, either. "It can't be true! Can it?"

"That would depend on what you mean by it," Dittany replied cautiously.

"You know perfectly well what I mean. That Arethusa could have—that she and that fatuous lump of affectations—"

"Which fatuous lump of affectations? Want me to pour you another drink?"

"I'll get it, thanks."

Archie retired to the pantry. Perhaps he needed to be alone with his thoughts. Dittany checked the noodle water, discovered it was boiling, and put in the noodles. It was a good thing she'd decided on noodles; by now the half hour Arethusa had stipulated with such misguided optimism was well past.

Dittany herself was feeling the need of a good, hot, sit-down supper in contrast to the snacks she'd been subsisting on all day. She started to suggest that Archie hurry along the preparations by bringing some plates out with him, then decided she hadn't better. She was fond of the ancestral ironstone and he was pretty shaky at the moment.

So was she, now that she had a moment's peace to take stock of her condition. The possibility of Arethusa's becoming stepmother to Wilhedra was not one Dittany cared to contemplate with any degree of seriousness. Even Andy McNaster's cobra would, as far as she was concerned, be a more acceptable addition to their family circle.

Taking things all around, she was sick and tired of the Thorbisher-Freeps. She was sick of having backwater thespians barge in and emote all over her kitchen while she was trying to get a meal on the table. She was sickest of being niece-in-law to the reigning queen of regency romance.

Why couldn't life be the way it used to be back in those halcyon days before Jenson Thorbisher-Freep decided to get rid of his collection? Even now, she and Osbert could be sitting side by side at their respective typewriters, he chasing a gang of rustlers down some sun-baked arroyo, she answering his fan mail. She adored writing long, chatty letters back to those kind readers who'd taken the time to pour out their admiration for Lex Laramie's books and their own secret yearnings to be literary cowboys, too. Osbert adored having her write them because he himself always got bashful and couldn't think of anything to say.

Ethel could be sprawled out here by the kitchen stove where she'd always loved to lie before traffic got so thick as to make the floor unsafe for tail and paws. Arethusa could wander in unescorted with no thought in her head beyond snaffling the little pearl onions out of the mustard pickle dish before Osbert beat her to them. All these lovesick swains cluttering up the place were a plain bloody nuisance. Dittany went and got the plates herself. Archie wandered over to the rocking chair and sat there brooding. She let him sit.

As she was putting the plates around, Osbert and Arethusa came down from the sickroom together. Their respective utterances were, "Hope we didn't keep you, darling," and "Gadzooks, not ready yet?"

"Another few minutes," she replied curtly. "I was interrupted. Namely and to wit by Leander Hellespont, who wants to mold Arethusa, and by Jenson Thorbisher-Freep, who says he can't."

"Does he, i' faith?" Arethusa replied absently, her fathomless gaze on the table. "Were you planning to set out some of that plum jam Therese brought? And perchance bread and butter and a few rolls and biscuits? And pickles and preserves and a simple appetizer like *paté en croute* or *oeufs en gelée?*''

"We're having warmed-up *dindon au sauce d'abatis* and passion fruit ice cream in honor of your recent coronation. If that doesn't appeal to you, there's always the pizza parlor."

"Don't be absurd." Arethusa fished in the pot with the stirring spoon, managed to trap a slithery noodle, blew on it, and bit. "Not quite done. Whatever possessed you to invite Leander Hellespont here, ecod?"

"I didn't invite him. He came. As did Jenson, ostensibly to inquire after Carolus, which he could perfectly well have done by telephone. Arethusa, you haven't really gone and got yourself engaged to that man?"

"What man?" Arethusa spoke abstractedly, being engrossed with trying to snare another noodle.

"Will you get your head out of that pot and answer Dittany's question?" snapped Osbert. "Are you or are you not engaged to Jenson Thorbisher-Freep?"

"I thought she said Leander Hellespont."

"Either or both. Or anybody else," Osbert added in the hope of getting to the crux without further preamble.

Arethusa secured her noodle, nibbled at it, and pondered. At last, with Archie watching in an agony of suspense, she shook the purple turban she'd taken to wearing draped tiara-wise atop her raven tresses. "To the best of my recollection, no."

"Then why was Freep talking as if he had an option on you?" Archie cried hotly.

"Perchance because he likes to hear himself talk? You can drain the noodles now, Dittany."

"Thanks for letting me know. Fix Carolus a tray, why don't you? There's a jug of white wine in the fridge if anybody wants some."

They all decided they did, so the euphoric Archie poured while Dittany dished up and Osbert made a fast trip upstairs with the invalid's tray. The food was good, the wine agreeable. The fire crackled in the old wood stove. Ethel returned from her wanderings, had a companionable bowl of dog food laced with the leftover giblet gravy, and stretched out in her favorite spot. Now and then she emitted a contented whoofle or thumped her tail to let the others know she was with them in spirit. She would have been content to lie there all evening long, thinking doggish thoughts, but Osbert decided she'd better go up and guard Carolus, so she went.

This was the first peaceful time the Monks' house had known in weeks. The diners chatted in soft, slow voices. Osbert talked of archery and last roundups, Dittany of archery and the Grub-and-Stakers' plans for expanding the beds of plantain-leaved pussytoes on the Enchanted Mountain if spring ever came. Arethusa talked of archery and the Moonlight and Roses coronation. Archie talked lovingly of royalties. They were all in a state of utter content when the knock came at the door. Osbert got up reluctantly.

"I'll go."

"Maybe it's Roger Munson coming to tuck Carolus in for the night," said Dittany, though she really couldn't believe they were going to get off that easily. They weren't.

"Good evening," a high-pitched, somewhat nasal voice shrilled from the doorstep. "This is the Monk residence, isn't it?"

"Yes, that's right."

Osbert found himself confronted by a great deal of mink. He stepped back instinctively, and the mink stepped in.

"Carolus Bledsoe is staying here, I'm told," said its occupant.

Osbert agreed cautiously that such was indeed the case.

"Then could I just run up and say hello to him? I'm his former wife, Ermeline Bledsoe. I've brought him some fruit."

"I'm sorry," said Osbert. "Carolus isn't allowed visitors. Or fruit. Doctor's orders."

A burst of incredulous laughter greeted his words. "No fruit? That's crazy. All invalids are allowed fruit. It's the rule in every hospital. For the vitamins, you know."

"Vitamins disagree with Carolus," Osbert insisted doggedly.

"They do, eh? Then how do they strike you?"

Again Dittany watched the mink-clad arm fly up, again she saw an object hurtle through the air. Osbert ducked

aside. The object flew across the kitchen to impale itself
on the damper handle in the stovepipe. Another followed,
and another and another, in rapid-fire succession.

By now, Osbert had stationed himself at shortstop and
was catching them on the fly. Archie, playing the outfield,
intercepted the few Osbert missed. Dittany, with great
presence of mind, fetched out the dishpan so they could
dump their catches and leave their hands free for the next.
By the time Mrs. Bledsoe quit pitching, the pan was full of
fruit. All lemons.

"Feel better now that you've let off steam, Mrs.
Bledsoe?" said Osbert not unkindly. "You're under arrest, of course."

"Arrest? Who do you think you are, Renfrew of the
Mounted?"

"Nope. Just Deputy Monk of the Lobelia Falls police
force. The charge is assaulting an auxiliary officer of the
law and making a mess of my wife's kitchen. Of course if
we should happen to find any bombs or anything of that
sort inside these lemons, we'd have to book you on a more
serious charge. Dittany, darling, why don't you give Sergeant MacVicar another buzz?"

"Wait a minute," shrieked Mrs. Bledsoe. "Can't you
take a joke? I was just having a bit of good, clean fun. It
always amuses Carolus when I throw things at him."

"It doesn't amuse me a bit," Osbert said obdurately.
"Furthermore, I don't remember Carolus being particularly overcome with glee when you bopped him with that
tomato at the dress rehearsal."

"And what about that ham and macaroni casserole you
forgot to take out of the dish, forsooth, before you chucked
it?" Arethusa put in. "Carolus will carry the scar to his
grave."

Mrs. Bledsoe favored her with a haughty sneer. "I suppose he showed you his scar?"

"Did he? I don't recall." Arethusa had located a cookie
which had hitherto escaped her all-devouring gaze, and
was giving it most of her attention. "Was yours a good
casserole?"

"It was a superb casserole! And he had the nerve to say
it tasted like wallpaper paste."

"I' fegs? What did you put into it?"

"Oh, ham and macaroni and a bit of this and that. You know how it is with casseroles."

"I always add a few dashes of Worcestershire sauce, myself," said Arethusa. "And a good pinch of dried basil if it's anything fishy or chickeny."

"A dollop of mustard in the cream sauce works wonders with ham and macaroni," Mrs. Bledsoe responded. "I also put in about a tablespoonful of marmalade more or less, depending."

"Marmalade? Stap my garters, what an excellent idea. Was there marmalade in the casserole you slugged Carolus with?"

"No. The brute had pigged it all up at breakfast. So it was his own fault, really. Carolus never understood me. I'll bet he doesn't understand you, either, for all his big talk. I suppose he goes on and on."

"Perchance he does," Arethusa conceded willingly.

That wasn't enough for Mrs. Bledsoe. "What do you mean, perchance? Don't you listen?"

This, like the marmalade, was clearly a new concept to Arethusa. "Oh, is one supposed to listen? I've been thinking of his voice more in the context of background music. Be fair, Mrs. Bledsoe. The worm may have entered the bud and the bloom be off the rose, but surely even you have to admit that Carolus's timbre is more agreeable than the banal bleats and squawks one hears over the telephone when one's waiting for an airline reservation."

The former Mrs. Bledsoe paused to reflect. "I must confess I'd never thought of Carolus as Muzak. Perhaps if I had, things might have been different between us."

"Even now it may not be too late," Arethusa urged.

"Stuff it, Arethusa," said Dittany. "Not to dash any hopes of a reconciliation, but isn't Mrs. Bledsoe aware that Carolus is about to become engaged to somebody else?"

Mrs. Bledsoe emitted a short, bitter laugh. "Oh, that silly business with Wilhedra Thorbisher-Freep? Forget it, that's just another of her father's bright ideas. Jenson's been encouraging Carolus to think he's going to get his grabby mitts into the Thorbisher-Freep family money the way he did into mine, but what those two don't know is that Wilhedra's already secretly engaged to Leander Hellespont.''

''You're kidding!''

''Ask the girls at the bridge club. Wilhedra's had the hots for Leander ever since she saw him in his kilt as Macbeth. You wouldn't believe it, but that wilted string bean has the sexiest knees a woman ever dreamed of.''

''Do women actually dream about men's knees?'' Archie was obviously making a mental note to send back to Toronto for his own kilt at the earliest possible moment should Arethusa reply in the affirmative.

However, Arethusa voiced no opinion on the matter. Dittany, on whom the modest amount of wine she'd drunk was having an unusually mellowing effect because by now she was so desperately in need of mellowing, did.

''I never dream about knees. I dream about that adorable cowlick behind Osbert's left ear.''

''Shucks, ma'am, you didn't ought to say things like that in front of mixed company.'' Blushing so furiously he forgot he was Deputy Monk, Osbert allowed his arms to encircle Dittany's torso.

What might then have transpired became moot as Sergeant MacVicar came along and Osbert had to switch back to being Deputy Monk. The sergeant was carrying a green plastic bowl full of lovely brown eggs.

''Margaret sends these in case I wind up staying for breakfast.''

Dittany took the bowl. ''Thanks, but do I detect a note of acrimony?''

''Aye, lass, you do. I hae a wee suspicion that my guid wife is nane too pleased wi' the events of this weekend. Nor am I, gin you want the truth. Is this our latest miscreant? Mrs. Bledsoe, I believe?''

''She was chucking lemons,'' Osbert explained.

''Only in a spirit of japery,'' Arethusa intervened. ''In my opinion, she's more to be pitied than censured. She says Carolus told her the ham and macaroni casserole she threw at him tasted like wallpaper paste but it was his own fault because he'd eaten all the marmalade.''

''An' how does she explain yon lemons?''

"She meant them for Carolus. To cheer him up. Can't you see her as a woman grievously wronged?"

"I can see her as a woman wi' a most peculiar sense of humor," Sergeant MacVicar replied severely. "Mrs. Bledsoe, gin sae you still style yoursel', you are known to hae committed an assault upon your former husband in the Scottsbeck opera house on Friday e'en."

"I beaned him with a tomato, if that's what you call an assault. Any ex-wife in my position would have done the same."

"Other ex-wives would hae conducted themsel' wi' dignity an' propriety, Mrs. Bledsoe. What were you doing backstage at the gymnasium last night?"

"Who says I was there?"

"I do, for one," Dittany told her. "You poked your head into the girls' locker room while we were dressing. I recognized you from the opera house. I was the piano player, you know, and I'd been watching you all evening."

"So what if you were? How was I supposed to know it was the girls' locker room? I was looking for the loo. The fact that I happened to have a package of itching powder in my hand at the time was merely an amusing coincidence."

"Amusing to whom, for instance?" asked Osbert.

"Your question is irrelevant and immaterial," Mrs. Bledsoe retorted, "since I never got to use the itching powder."

"Was that because you happened to catch sight of Jenson Thorbisher-Freep's old six-shooter lying on the props table? Recognizing it as the one he'd carried when he played Jack Rance, because it's unthinkable Jenson wouldn't have told you if he ever got the chance, and deducing that it carried a blank cartridge Andy McNaster was going to shoot at your ex-husband, did you or did you not decide to play an even merrier prank and substitute a live bullet for the blank?"

"I don't carry live six-shooter bullets around with me! Even if I did, how was I to know Andy was going to fire the gun at Carolus? I left the dress rehearsal before the shooting began, as Little Mary Sunshine here should be able to tell you since she's so darned observant."

"You could have lurked in the vestibule," Osbert insisted.

Mrs. Bledsoe sneered. "Planting stink bombs, maybe? I suppose you'll try to hang that on me, too."

Chapter 19

"Er-hm." Sergeant MacVicar wasn't about to let the situation get out of hand. "Mrs. Bledsoe, what is your relationship wi' Andrew McNaster?"

"That chiseling two-timer? Whatever he says about me, it's a lie!"

"Then it's no' true that yours has been a mere acquaintance based solely on Mr. McNaster's business connection with your former husband?"

The ex-Mrs. Bledsoe goggled. "Is that what Andy says?"

"I'm spiering the questions, Mrs. Bledsoe."

"Oh. Well, sure, that's true. Certainly it's true. Why shouldn't it be true?"

Mrs. Bledsoe fumbled in her handbag. The others watched her nervously, but all she brought out was a lipstick with a little mirror attached to it, which she proceeded to use in the customary manner.

"I've barely laid eyes on Andy since Carolus and I split up," she told them, speaking through clenched teeth and holding her lips stiff so she wouldn't smear her paint job. "I went away to nurse my broken heart. But then Carolus started trying to get funny about Auntie's property, so I came home to Scottsbeck."

She slammed the lipstick back in its case and hurled it into her handbag. "I've seen Andy once in the shopping mall to say hello to and that's all. We were right outside the Cozy Corner Tea Shop and he never so much as offered to

165

buy me a sandwich,'' she added so pettishly that it would have been almost impossible to doubt her word.

Nevertheless, Sergeant MacVicar shook his head. ''You saw Mr. McNaster both Friday and Saturday nights of this past week, Mrs. Bledsoe.''

''Only in the play,'' she protested. ''That doesn't count.''

''You didna happen to meet him backstage yestreen before the performance, near the props table?''

''I was never near the props table! That's entrapment, buster, and you needn't try to pull it on me because I know my rights, eh. I went in through the wrong door, is how I happened to be backstage. So I went back out the same way, walked around to the front entrance, and bought a ticket in the lobby. I realized I'd made a mistake from not knowing the building, you see, and didn't want to be accused of gatecrashing. A lady such as I would find it extremely painful to be the focus of an embarrassing public scene, as even a clod like you must realize.''

Mrs. Bledsoe drew her minks about her and gave the sergeant a particularly haughty stare. He responded with a kindly nod.

''Oh aye, I ken fine how embarrassed you'd be. So you hae nothing to tell us about Andrew McNaster save that he's a two-timing chiseler.''

''I was only repeating what my ex-husband told me when he found out Andy was turning over a new leaf. That's hearsay evidence and not allowable in court, in case you didn't know.''

Sergeant MacVicar nodded again. ''I thank you for the free legal advice, Mrs. Bledsoe. Would there be any information concerning Mr. McNaster that you could give us of your own pairsonal knowledge?''

''There would not and I wouldn't anyway because I don't like your face.''

Mrs. Bledsoe looked around, presumably for something to throw, but Osbert and Archie closed in on her and she went back to being haughty. ''I shall now wish you a very good evening and take myself off.''

''One moment, Mrs. Bledsoe,'' the sergeant reminded her. ''There's still a wee matter of a disorderly conduct charge to be dealt with.''

"Oh, pooh to disorderly conduct. That was just a bit of good, clean fun. Deputy Monk isn't going to press charges now that he understands my tragic situation."

"Like heck I'm not," Osbert insisted. "I don't understand the situation at all. You came waltzing in here uninvited and started chucking lemons around like confetti at a wedding, just because I wouldn't let you go upstairs and commit bodily assault on your ex-husband, who's in a pretty fragile nervous condition already."

Mrs. Bledsoe sneered. "From what, pray tell? There's never been anything fragile about Carolus's nerves from my personal observation. And believe me, I've had plenty of opportunities to observe."

"Have you ever observed Carolus after he's been the victim of three and possibly four separate murder attempts within a span of less than twenty-four hours?"

"Four murder attempts? What are you talking about? Is this some kind of joke?"

"Carolus isn't finding it particularly funny, Mrs. Bledsoe, and neither are we. Would you mind telling us what you've been doing all day?"

"I rose early for morning prayers and breakfast with my cousin the Reverend Leviticus McLazarus, at whose house I'm temporarily residing. Also present were his wife Zilphah, their sons Amos and Nahum, their daughter Keren-Happuch, and their exchange student M'Bwongo M'Bwungi. After breakfast, we all went to church together and stayed through the coffee hour, after which we returned to the parsonage for a light collation. We sang a few hymns around the melodeon, then went back to the church to attend a concert presented by the Young People's Group, assisted by members of the Sunshine Choir. We again returned to the parsonage, where I helped my cousin's wife prepare Sunday high tea, of which we partook *en famille,* and I'm due at evening service in half an hour so you'll really have to excuse me. Cousin Leviticus will be dreadfully upset if I fail to show up because I'm in jail for disturbing the Sabbath peace. Cousin Leviticus is very big on the Sabbath."

"How did you ever escape to come here?" Dittany asked, as well she might.

"I'm comforting the afflicted and doing good to him

who despitefully used me," Mrs. Bledsoe explained. "This was Cousin Leviticus's idea, not mine."

"Do tell. Which of you thought of the lemons?"

Mrs. Bledsoe simpered. "Those were an inspiration of the moment. I happened to pass a convenience market that was still open, and it came to me in a flash."

"Clever you. But how did you know Carolus needed comforting? Was it on the morning news broadcast about his toe getting shot off?"

"I wouldn't know about the news, but it's certainly being broadcast. I heard about Carolus right after service, from one of my cousin's parishioners who happens to be an emergency room nurse at the Scottsbeck Hospital. It was an agonizing moment for me, I can tell you. Cousin Zilphah was right beside me shaking hands, and I almost fractured my upper lip trying not to smile. Who's murdering him?"

"We were hoping you might be able to enlighten us on that point," said Dittany.

"You mean you were hoping I'd break down and confess. I wish I knew myself, I might be able to drop the person a few helpful hints. But if anything occurs to me, I'll let you know right away. May I go now, Sergeant? I'll come over first thing tomorrow if you want, and polish Mrs. Monk's stovepipe as an act of humility."

"Aye, go." Sergeant MacVicar sounded awfully tired. "Just don't get any more inspirations, Mrs. Bledsoe, such as leaving town without due notice."

"I'll hae a sharp word wi' yon Scottsbeck police chief," he added after Mrs. Bledsoe had taken her leave. "She was supposed to have been kept under observation."

"But surely she can't have been setting booby traps and abducting cobras if she spent the day getting washed in the blood of the lamb," Arethusa protested. "And she forgot her lemons. Shouldn't somebody run after her?"

"We're impounding the lemons as evidence," Osbert told his aunt firmly.

"Including that one stuck on the damper handle, forsooth? You've got fried pips all over the stove."

"It wouldn't occur to you to wipe them up?"

"And disturb the evidence?" Arethusa flung her purple

cape about her. "Well, now that the show appears to be over, methinks I'll betake myself houseward."

Archie leaped to her side. "I'll walk you home!"

"You'd better put your coat on first," Dittany reminded him. "It's pretty nippy out there by now."

"And aren't you going to slip upstairs and smooth Carolus's pillow for him before you go, Auntie dear?" Osbert suggested with what he meant for a sly leer, but Osbert was no earthly good at leering and it came off as an amiable grin. Arethusa didn't notice anyway because she was already out the door.

"Actually, we had better check on Carolus," said Dittany. "I suppose he ought to know his ex-wife called to express her sympathy, or whatever. And Ethel's about due for a shrubbery break."

"Ethel is in attendance on the invalid?" Sergeant MacVicar asked.

"Well, we didn't dare leave him alone after the awful things that have been happening, and she was the one who sniffed out the cobra. I only wish we could teach her to lug trays."

"Oh aye? I thought Roger Munson was helping."

"Roger's already done more than his share. I expect Hazel and some of the others will be over tomorrow, after they've had a chance to rest up. Everybody's been dead on their feet today, myself included."

"Why don't you slide on up to bed, dear?" said Osbert. "I'll see to Carolus."

"I might as well look in on him since I'm going up anyway. I'll send Ethel down and you can let her out."

"And I shall drop a wee flea in the ear of the Scottsbeck police, then get back to the station," said Sergeant MacVicar. "May I use your telephone on official business, Deputy Monk?"

"Sure thing, Chief. Want me to dial the number for you?"

Dittany left them to it and went ahead upstairs. She found Carolus and Ethel watching some dreary nonsense on the Munson boys' television. Several cars were chasing each other through a complicated maze of alleys and highways in a reckless and inconsiderate manner. Carolus appeared to be well enough entertained, but Ethel looked bored.

Dittany released the dog from duty, changed the water in the invalid's carafe in case anybody'd happened to catch the pair of them napping and sneaked in a pinch of strychnine or a few typhoid germs, and went to put on her nightgown. She was propped up on two pillows reading an old Angela Thirkell to quiet her mind and dispose her to slumber when Osbert came into their bedroom, obviously perturbed.

She closed her book. "What's up, Deputy Monk?"

"Sergeant MacVicar called the Scottsbeck police."

"And so?"

"So they've been talking to some woman who lives in Andy's apartment building. She claims she watched Andy leave the place about two o'clock this morning with a florist's box under his arm. Sergeant MacVicar's mad as a wet hen."

"Is he going to arrest Andy?"

"I don't know, dear. He was sounding awfully Scotch when he left for the inn."

"But Andy told us he spent last night there. He can get the night clerk to testify he didn't go out, can't he?"

"The clerk would know whether he went past the front desk, I suppose, but there's more than one door to the place."

"And Andy must have his own set of keys." Dittany sighed. "The woman could have dreamed it, couldn't she?"

"She said she'd got up to make cocoa because she couldn't sleep, and heard the outside door shut so she went to see who could be going out so late. She recognized Andy because he's so big and burly and always walks as if he were getting ready to toss the caber. She didn't get a good look at his face, but she said she could see his black hair and the curly ends of his mustache sticking out. It sounds awfully circumstantial, darling."

"Too darn circumstantial, if you ask me. She's probably mad at him for raising her rent or something, and is trying to get him in trouble."

"But how would she have known to mention the florist's box? She said that was what really struck her as peculiar. It wasn't so much Andy's going out late. She's used to his coming and going at odd hours because the construction business gets him out early and the inn keeps him up late. Besides, he's a bachelor and she knows what that means."

Dittany sniffed. "It probably doesn't mean what she thinks it does, unless he's been two-timing Arethusa. She's just trying to blacken his name."

"I don't think so, dear," Osbert demurred. "She did say Andy used to be a rotten landlord, but the past year or so he's been a saint. He even painted her kitchen and didn't slap a penny extra on the rent."

"She could still be sore from all the times he didn't paint the kitchen," Dittany insisted.

"Darling, I understand how you feel, but consider the facts. Andy did fire the gun, and he did have it in his possession during the entire second act. He could easily have switched the cartridges during the dance hall scene, when he was back there by himself playing solitaire and nobody was paying attention to him."

"But he wouldn't have risked Thusie's life keeping her out in the cold ever since two o'clock!"

Osbert shook his head. "I'm not so sure, dear. That scene he put on was pretty touching, but Andy's a first-rate actor. And the mind does tend to boggle at a grown man's getting sentimentally attached to a cobra."

Dittany struggled to produce a smile. "You know what Arethusa would say to that. 'Nonsense, it happens all the time.' Darling, do you suppose Daniel sees through Andy's facade of injured innocence and that's why he keeps sticking to him like a fly to molasses?"

"I don't know, pardner. I did drop a word to Archie and he doesn't know, either. He says Daniel usually prefers the companionship of tall, gorgeous, redheaded actresses who read a lot of Aristotle and Plato."

"That may explain why Daniel's immune to Arethusa, but it still doesn't tell us what he sees in Andy. Unless Andy once wronged his dear old gray-haired father in a shady business deal and Daniel's come to seek a dire and secret vengeance."

Osbert wasn't ready to buy a dark and secret vengeance. "Why should he keep trying to murder Carolus just to get Andy in trouble?"

"Because Carolus was Andy's accomplice back then, of course. Daniel's out to get them both. Only how could he have switched the cartridges? There's no way he could have gone backstage before the show. He and Archie didn't get to the gym until about a minute and a half before curtain time. Lemuel from the inn drove them over and brought them right inside the gym door. I watched him turn them over to one of the ushers. I was playing the overture then, you know, and I could see out through a crack in the curtains. I'd been wondering where the heck they were because those two front seats you saved for them were right in front of me, still empty. And Archie stuck to Daniel like glue all through the show to make sure he didn't fall asleep from all those brandies and miss any of the lines. He's bound and determined to get us that contract. You know Archie."

Osbert said yes he knew Archie but he didn't know how Daniel could have managed to set that rat trap in Carolus's shaving kit or stolen a cobra from Andy's flat. "Unless he brought along a trusted confederate we still don't know about," he added generously.

"A trusted confederate would stick out like a sore thumb in Lobelia Falls," Dittany had to admit. "All right, we may as well wash out Daniel's dire vengeance. It has to be somebody local, which brings us straight back to Andy. Dad-blang it, why couldn't he have kept on being his old rotten self? Then at least we wouldn't feel bad about suspecting him."

Chapter 20

Wilhedra Thorbisher-Freep's eyes were sunk into her head like two burnt holes in a blanket. Her face was a ghostly pale gray, the skin hanging from the bones in serried ranks of wrinkles. She looked, in short, awful. Dittany hoped to heck Arethusa wouldn't take a notion to tell her so.

The best that might be said of her was that she blended into her surroundings. The armchair she sat in was slipcovered in a once flowered chintz now faded to about the same color as her face. The bathrobe she had on might originally have been blue but wasn't much of anything at this stage in its deterioration. The bedroom wallpaper had presumably started out light green with a Japanesey pattern of white bamboo; now the green was the color of bile and the bamboo a dirty yellow. Blotches of stain from a leaky roof failed to add much in the way of design interest. The ceiling was peeling in scabrous flakes and the carpet on the floor was no great shakes, either.

Wilhedra had a crutch leaning against the arm of her chair and her bad ankle propped up on a hassock. When she saw her visitors, she tried hard to smile and reached for her crutch. They were urging her not to get up when her father bustled into the room.

"Ladies, I do most humbly beg your pardon. For some unfathomable reason, Norah failed to tell me you were here."

"I expect that's because we asked for Wilhedra, not you," Dittany told him flat out.

Wilhedra wasn't her favorite person, but she was beginning to wonder what sort of life this rich man's daughter must have been leading all these years, and whether she'd been giving any serious thought to the advisability of landing her dear old penny-pinching, spotlight-hugging daddy a poke in the ego with that handy crutch. Arethusa must be wondering too; she made rather a protracted business of giving Wilhedra a peck on the cheek and bestowing the flowers and cookies they'd brought her.

Jenson chose not to be deceived by any charitable ruse. "Oh, come now, my dears. Kind of you to show an interest in Wilhedra, of course, but I know what you're actually here for is to enjoy a good, long gloat over the treasures you've won for the Architrave. I'm quite at your disposal. As for Wilhedra, the only cheering up she needs is good news of her beloved Carolus. How is the dear lad this morning?"

"Well, I can tell you there's nothing much wrong with his appetite," said Dittany. "He polished off three fried eggs and a stack of toast for breakfast and complained because we were out of ham. That's why we came over to Scottsbeck so early, as a matter of fact, instead of waiting to make a more seemly afternoon call. We have to go shopping at the supermarket because he's eaten us right down to the nubbins."

"Ah, yes. I can see my daughter will have her hands full cooking for her bridegroom. Now come along, come along. I know you're absolutely thirsting to examine the whole collection piece by piece."

"Dittany can thirst," said Arethusa. "I'd fainer stay and talk to Wilhedra."

"Not on your life," Dittany retorted. "I baked the cookies so I get to stay with Wilhedra. You're chairman of the board of trustees; you can darn well do the thirsting yourself."

Arethusa emitted a regal snort but consented to being led from the sickroom. Jenson would no doubt rather be alone with Arethusa, but couldn't help himself from snapping, "Then join us in the exhibition parlor as soon as you feel you've done your duty. Wilhedra, don't keep Dittany too long."

He took Arethusa's arm and hustled her from the depressing room. Dittany raised her eyebrows.

"What happens if I don't go?" she asked with her usual tact and finesse. "Will he take away your teddy bear?"

She was sorry she'd said it. A dark flush rippled up and down Wilhedra's wrinkles.

"You have to understand, Dittany, that Father's a bit upset with me just now. My being laid up through my own clumsiness makes a lot of extra work and he's not used to coping. Besides, I'm afraid he's none too happy about being forced to part with his collection."

"But who's forcing him? He didn't have to run the contest, did he? Wasn't it all his own idea in the first place?"

"Oh yes, you may rest assured of that," Wilhedra answered in a tone dry enough to sour milk. "It's been a long, long time since anybody tried to persuade Father into anything he didn't choose to do."

She fiddled with the fringe of a somewhat motheaten tartan rug that was spread over her lap and legs, the room being none too warm. Dittany could feel a dank chill even through her boots and the coat she hadn't been invited to take off.

"Father's always been something of an autocrat," Wilhedra went on rather shyly, as if she wasn't used to sharing confidences. "The—imperiousness, I suppose you might call it—seems to be growing on him as he gets older. Sometimes I wonder if he's altogether—" She fell silent and went on picking at the fringe. Dittany thought maybe it mightn't be an unkind idea to change the subject.

"How did you sprain your ankle? Did you fall on the ice? We noticed your front walk hadn't been shoveled lately."

"I know, isn't it awful? The neighborhood kids ask so much more for shoveling nowadays than they used to that Father gets angry with them and won't have it done. He still thinks fifty cents is enough to pay."

Wilhedra essayed a merry laugh, but she certainly hadn't inherited her father's histrionic talent. "Actually what I did was trip yesterday morning going downstairs to breakfast. Don't ask me how I managed to do such a stupid thing.''

"You weren't wearing a long bathrobe, by any chance?''

"To sit at the table with Father? Perish the thought! No, I had on my usual daytime clothes and sensible low-heeled shoes. Those back stairs are rather poky, I will admit, and I did have my hands full. Father likes his cup of tea first thing in the morning, so Norah brings it up as soon as she gets the kettle boiled. When I go down, I take the tray with me to save her the steps.''

She shook her head. "I've done that every morning for more years than I care to count and never so much as rattled the cup on the saucer, but yesterday I don't know what happened. It felt as if something had caught at my ankle and tripped me, but Father said that was nonsense. He even went to the bother of checking the stairs and said there was nothing I could possibly have tripped over. He was quite put out that any daughter of his didn't know how to get down a staircase without falling over her own feet. The tray went flying, of course, and one of his good Crown Derby cups had its handle knocked off.''

"Can't you glue it back on?''

"I suppose so, but what's the use? Father hates mended china.''

How did he feel about mended daughters? Dittany managed to refrain from asking and confined herself to sympathetic murmurs. Wilhedra asked about Carolus again as if she hadn't heard the first time, and Dittany assured her he was getting along as well as could be expected, all things considered. She didn't say what things. Wilhedra probably was in no mood to hear about cobras, and Dittany couldn't remember which lethal poison it was that the sharpened wire of the rat trap had turned out to be smeared with.

She did mention the ex-Mrs. Bledsoe and the basket of lemons because it made a pretty funny story. She kept quiet about Leander Hellespont's visit. That had been even funnier, but she had a strong feeling Wilhedra wouldn't see the humor. Conversation languished. Wilhedra was patently uneasy about keeping Dittany away from the exhibition parlor. Her fringe-plucking took on a more accelerated tempo. Dittany caught the hint.

"Well, I expect I'd better go play chaperone. You don't really want Arethusa for a stepmother, do you?"

"God, no!" Wilhedra blurted. Then she flushed again. "But of course that's up to Father."

"I should say it was equally up to Arethusa," Dittany retorted.

"That's because you don't know my beloved parent the way I do." Wilhedra was too far gone to hide her bitterness. "Thank you for coming. In case you don't remember, you go down the front stairs and turn right."

But Dittany chose to go down the back stairs, the ones on which Wilhedra had taken her toss. They were indeed poky, she noticed, and neither well lit nor well maintained. Probably Jenson never used them. Luckily the former Mrs. Henbit, gadget-minded as ever, had stuffed a little flashlight on a key chain into her daughter's Christmas stocking. Dittany used it now to scrutinize the woodwork as she picked her way down.

Three steps from the bottom she found what she'd been looking for. The tack driven into the wall on the left-hand side must have been pulled out when Wilhedra tripped; all Dittany could find was the tiny hole. The right-hand tack, with a wisp of transparent fishline still clinging to it, was hard to spot against the varnished woodwork, but it was definitely there.

So the Thorbisher-Freep mansion was under attack, too. Was Carolus's would-be assassin trying to get at him through his intended second wife, or had Wilhedra been tripped on her own account?

Jenson couldn't have bothered to look all that hard for the cause of his daughter's so-called accident, but then he didn't seem to be much concerned about Wilhedra in general, except as the prospective wife of a divorced man with a shady background and a lawsuit hanging over his head. Why was a pompous old coot like him so heck-bent on marrying her off to Carolus Bledsoe when neither of them seemed to be all that keen on the match?

From the front of the house, Dittany could hear Jenson declaiming about Minnie Maddern Fiske and Arethusa interjecting an occasional zounds or forsooth. She must be bored stiff. Well, that was what she got for being a femme fatale. Dittany had no intention of being likewise bored. She had different fish to fry.

During their earlier visit to the mansion, Jenson had given them a quick peek into what he'd called his library. This was, she recalled, a relatively unpretentious room at the back of the house that contained a good many books, a carved walnut desk with a big swivel chair behind it, and not much else. Dittany crept along the hallway, sticking to the somewhat threadbare runner so her boots wouldn't clunk, let herself into the library, and shut the door behind her.

Jenson was not a tidy man or, it would appear, a diligent one. His desk was awash in unanswered correspondence. Dittany knew it was ill-bred to read other people's mail, but this was no time for scruples. Anyway, she could hardly avoid seeing all those big red PLEASE REMIT stickers on the unpaid bills, of which there were more than anything else. The only letters she could find were duns. A particularly sniffy one from the Scottsbeck Bank reminded Mr. Thorbisher-Freep that his checking account was grievously overdrawn, his savings account was down to nil, and unless he deposited sufficient funds forthwith to cover all those rubber cheques he'd been writing, steps would have to be taken.

What could this mean? Was Jenson turning into a pathological miser? Was that why he wouldn't pay to have the front walk shoveled or buy his daughter a new bathrobe? But he'd been treating Arethusa to all those lunches and dinners, and the reigning queen of regency romance was no cheap date when it came to food.

Rummaging further, Dittany came upon a letter from the same stockbroking firm Osbert's father used. In answer to Mr. Thorbisher-Freep's complaint about their failure to follow through on his orders, Mr. Thorbisher-Freep was reminded that over the past several years he'd been steadily creaming off the choicer stocks in his portfolio. The ones he was unsuccessfully trying to peddle now were, not to put too fine a point on it, junk. Mr. Thorbisher-Freep might be further reminded that the said stocks had been purchased over the stockbroker's strenuous protest. The letter didn't come straight out and call Mr. Thorbisher-Freep a pigheaded old fool who had nobody to blame but himself, but the intimation was definitely there.

So Jenson wasn't a miser, he was broke. That was why he'd been trailing Arethusa like a big-game poacher after an elephant. He wanted her tusks!

More specifically, he wanted her money, her jewels, her glass-topped dining room table with the gilded crocodiles holding it up. He wanted that imaginary crystal and gold fishbowl Dittany had improvised at their first meeting, when she'd got so annoyed at being upstaged by poor old Wilhedra in that elderly and balding mink, as she now knew it to be. It must have been the fishbowl that set him to stalking Arethusa. This was all Dittany's own fault.

No it wasn't, how could it be? Arethusa was quite capable of attracting men on her own hook, as witness the fact that she'd also collected Andy, Carolus, and Archie without even trying. But maybe Carolus was after her money, too, and maybe Archie was hoping to annex her as a client. Was it only Andy McNaster who loved her for herself alone? Or was Andy, too, working some dark and devious scheme with Arethusa as his cat's-paw or gull?

Dittany experienced an increasing sense of alarm. She'd better get into that exhibition room fast, before Jenson decided to abduct Arethusa to the attic and exercise his evil wiles on her. And also before Jenson came looking to see why Dittany hadn't appeared as bidden in the exhibition room. She inched the library door open, made sure the coast was clear, and scuttled down the hall.

She was in the nick of time. Jenson had Arethusa backed up against one of those glass display cases Mr. Glunck so coveted, and was pouring out his soul.

"Surely, dearest lady, you cannot but be aware of the deep regard in which I hold you. Ah, could I but find words to express the fervor which enkindles this throbbing heart when I gaze into those limpid pools of mystery and feel my being thrill with a rapturous tremor of—dare I say passion?"

Arethusa blinked. "Sorry, I was thinking about Minnie Maddern Fiske. Would you mind repeating the question?"

"He was wondering if he dared say passion," Dittany took it upon herself to explain.

Arethusa considered the matter, then frowned slightly. "I find passion a sadly overworked word. He might consider vehemence, infatuation, or fervor."

"He's already used fervor."

"In what context?"

"In the context of its enkindling his throbbing heart when he gazes into your limpid pools of mystery."

"Limpid pools of mystery isn't so bad, though I'd be inclined to substitute fathomless orbs of inscrutability, myself. Did Wilhedra enjoy the cookies? Speaking of which, hadn't we better be going? We don't want to miss lunch, you know."

"It's only eleven o'clock," Dittany protested. "I'll tell you what, why don't I run on ahead and buy the groceries while you and Jenson get on with your interesting exercise in vocabulary-building? Oh, and I'd better stop at the bank while I'm out. I have all those cheques of yours to deposit."

"What cheques, prithee?"

"Those royalty cheques I found scattered all over your office while we were looking for that emerald-studded silver paper knife you mislaid."

Dittany turned to Jenson with an amused little chuckle. "That's so like Arethusa, she never remembers to cash half her royalty cheques. They come in so fast that she can't keep track of them. She just uses them for bookmarks or grocery lists or stuffs them away and forgets where she put them."

"Ah, you famous writers." Jenson edged even closer and boldly seized one of Arethusa's hands in both of his own. It was, Dittany noticed, the hand on which Arethusa wore that nice diamond ring she'd inherited from her Aunt Melissa who married the railroad baron. "It's plain to see you need somebody to handle those dull, mundane business details so you can devote yourself more fully to your muse."

Arethusa turned her fathomless orbs of inscrutability first on Jenson, then on Dittany. Although one could never be sure what might be going on in that strangely convoluted brain of hers, Dittany thought it quite possible Arethusa was reflecting that (a) she didn't own an emerald-studded silver paper knife and wouldn't mislay it if she did, because Arethusa was surprisingly chary of her personal possessions, and (b) she would be most unlikely to use a royalty cheque for a bookmark or a grocery list because she was even charier about her financial returns, as her beleaguered agent could testify. Therefore (c) Dittany must be telling these egregious lies for some useful purpose and it behooved Arethusa to play along with them or risk having to cook her own meals for a week or two. Arethusa Monk knew which side of the toast her beans were on. She nodded.

"Jenson, I'm afraid you'll have to excuse us for a moment. I gather I'm constrained to endorse some cheques. One does endorse them, doesn't one? I seem to recall having done something of the sort at various times in the past."

Jenson assured her that endorsement of cheques was in fact standard procedure and that he'd be delighted to excuse her. "Certainly, my dear. Why don't I leave you two to yourselves while I nip down to the kitchen and tell Norah to fetch us a cup of tea? We'll have our elevenses while Dittany does her errands. You'd like that, wouldn't you?"

"Lovely. With perchance a morsel of toast or a bun? Or two?"

Arethusa was fishing in her handsome leather purse for her gold pen, dredging up a tortoiseshell and gold comb case and a compact paved in brilliants as she fished. They were only rhinestones, but Jenson didn't know that. Positively licking his chops at this casual display of wealth, he left the exhibition parlor, shutting the door behind him lest his prey escape.

"Now what's all this balderdash about royalty cheques, ecod?" Arethusa hissed.

"It's a delaying tactic," Dittany hissed back. "Arethusa, you've got to stall him along. Employ your feminine wiles."

"What wiles?"

"Any wiles that will keep him here in this room till I

get back. Let him draw you out about how much money you have stashed away.''

''What business is that of his?''

''He plans to make it his business. Lead him on. You needn't tell him anything. Just hint vaguely of accounts in banks from here to Halifax and thousand-dollar bills tucked under the dining room carpet. But for Pete's sake don't commit yourself to anything. Ask yourself what Minnie Maddern Fiske would do in a case like this and act accordingly.''

''For how long, egad? Where are you going?''

''Not far. I'll be back before lunch, never fear. Here he comes, start batting your eyelashes.''

Jenson breezed into the room, all smiles. Dittany made a feint of stuffing a handful of cheques into her pocketbook.

''All finished with your tiresome little bit of business, ladies? Norah has the kettle on, Arethusa my dear.''

''I'm all set.'' Dittany patted her handbag and buttoned her coat. ''I'll pop up and see whether Wilhedra needs anything from the drugstore while I'm out, then I'll be on my way rejoicing. Do try to remember what you did with that lot of bond coupons, Arethusa. Bye for now. Have fun.''

Chapter 21

Dittany ran heavily up the front stairs, then lightly down the back. In accordance with the popularly-held belief of an earlier generation that servants were better adapted to climbing stairs than the gentry, the Thorbisher-Freeps' kitchen was in their basement. There, she located a middle-aged woman wearing a faded print cotton dress, a much darned worsted cardigan, and a silly white cap. The woman was setting out a tray for two people and looking none too pleased about it.

"Good morning," said Dittany. "You must be Norah. Are you the maid or the cook?"

"I'm both, along with everything else that's getting done around here now that poor Wilhedra's laid up." Norah measured a meager two teaspoonfuls of tea into the pot. "The mahster send you down?" She made a drawn-out mockery of the vowel. "What's the old blowhard want now?"

"Just his tea, as far as I know," Dittany told her. "I've got to do some errands and I wondered if there's anything you need in the way of groceries."

Norah snorted. "You might bring me back a couple of everything they've got in the store, long as you don't mind never getting paid back for 'em. I'm darned sick and tired of living on cheese parings and peanut butter sandwiches as I've told him to his face and I don't care who knows it. It it wasn't for Wilhedra needing me so bad, I'd be out of here like a bullet from a gun. Say, you're dressed pretty

183

fancy for a district nurse. How come you're not in uniform, eh?''

"Because I'm not the district nurse, just a friend of Wilhedra's who stopped in to see how she's getting along. My name's Dittany Monk."

"Monk, eh? Say, you're not that rich woman he's got on the string? Kind of young to be chasing around with an old goat like him, aren't you?"

"Perish the thought. You've got me mixed up with my husband's aunt. And if Jenson Thorbisher-Freep thinks he's got her on the string, he's got another think coming, but I'd as soon you didn't let him know just yet. Tell me, Norah, is it true Jenson's piddled away all his money in the stock market? I'm not asking just to be nosy. I'm worried about my husband's aunt and even more about Wilhedra. She's in a mighty tough spot, if you ask me."

"You don't need to tell me that. If any woman alive ever needed a helping hand, Wilhedra's the one. Here she is, eating her heart out for the man she loves, who's a decent soul for all his la-di-da ways, and there's old Jense trying to force her into marrying that Charlie Bledsoe who's not fit to clean her boots, in my humble opinion. The old fool's on his uppers all right, no doubt about that. He think Bledsoe's going to win the lawsuit and he'll use Wilhedra to get hold of her husband's money, now that he's thrown away his own trying to play the big millionaire. And Jense will win out, you wait and see. Wilhedra's scared stiff of her father and always has been. She'd never dare cross him. Oh, I could give you an earful."

An earful was just what Dittany wanted. "You couldn't for instance, tell me whether Jenson's bought any new cartridges for that old Smith & Wesson of his lately?"

"The one he carried when he played Jack Rance?" Norah snorted again. "I can't imagine what you want to know for, but as a matter of fact he did. He was mad as a hatter because he had to buy a whole box when he only needed one or two for the play. I heard him fuming to himself about it back there in the furnace room one day. He talks to himself a lot when he can't get anybody else to listen. And then it turned out he'd bought the wrong color and he had to paint the tops red. He spoiled a few, getting

them too bright at first, then having to tone down the color
with some old stain that was kicking around from the Lord
knows when. They had to be just like the old ones or the
play wouldn't go right, though how anybody could see
from the audience was beyond me. But that's him all over,
which I wish he was.''

"Did you see him painting the cartridges?"

"I sure did. I went to put the garbage out, eh, and I was
walking quiet so's he wouldn't hear me and start bending my ear. He's worse than the ten years' itch once he
backs you into a corner and starts jawing at you. Anyway,
I saw him fiddling around with those things and couldn't
figure out what he was up to, so I snuck behind the
furnace and watched him unbeknownst. I know that sounds
foolish, but there's darned little else in the way of enter-
tainment around here.''

"How long ago did this happen?"

"Seems to me it was a week ago Wednesday.''

"What did he do with the cartridges after he finished
painting the tops?"

"Put the one that suited him into a little box and carried
it upstairs. The rest he put back in the box they came in
and hid behind a beam back there where he'd been working. Ashamed for Wilhedra to find out he wasted good
money on that kind of foolishness when she has to keep
wearing those old suede boots of hers every time she goes
out any place because she hasn't got a whole pair of
stockings to her name and he won't buy her any.''

"You didn't tell Wilhedra about the cartridges?"

"Not me. No sense in making her feel any worse than
she did already, was the way I looked at it.''

"And how right you were. Did you tell anybody else?"

"When would I have got the chance? I don't set foot
out of this house from one week's end to the next, and old
Jense throws a fit if I use the phone.''

"I thought you had yesterday off to go to your great-
nephew's christening.''

"I was supposed to, but then Wilhedra fell on those
pesky stairs and hurt her ankle. He made me stay here to
take care of her so's he could go out and run the roads with
his rich lady friend, no offense to your husband's aunt.

How could she know? But I might as well be a slave with a chain around my leg for all the consideration I get from him.''

''You're not the only one,'' snapped Dittany. ''He told us he couldn't have Carolus Bledsoe here after coming out of the hospital because it would have made too much work for you and he was afraid you'd quit, so we got stuck with the job.''

''Huh! One excuse was as good as another, I suppose. All Jenson was afraid of was that he might not be able to hit Bledsoe up for the grocery money, or else he was scared Bledsoe would catch on to how broke he is and back out of the wedding. Though why Jense thinks Bledsoe's going to save his bacon is beyond me. That ex-wife's going to skin the pants off him before she's through. Of course there'll be the insurance eventually, but the way Wilhedra's been sliding downhill lately, poor soul, I shouldn't be surprised if Bledsoe turns out to be the one who collects instead of her.''

''Insurance?'' Dittany pounced on the word like a hawk on a mouse. ''Norah, are you saying Wilhedra and Carolus have insured their lives in each other's favor?''

''I'm saying old Jense did it for them. It's customary practice in a union of such unusual significance as this one. Those were his very words. You'd have thought they was royalty, the way he carried on about it. Made a big ceremony of them signing the policies with him and Bledsoe wearing their black dress suits, drinking champagne and eating them little fish eggs, and Wilhedra all decked out in her mother's diamonds. And the next morning Jense took and hocked the diamonds so's he could pay the premiums. Wilhedra bawled her eyes out, but a fat lot he cared. He'd got his own way and that's all he gives a hoot about.''

Dittany shook her head to settle her scrambled thoughts. ''Norah, would you happen to have a telephone down here? I've got to call my husband.''

''You go right ahead. It's around the corner in the scullery. I'm s'posed to take the calls when his majesty's out gallivanting in case it's the prime minister wanting him to take over running the government or something.''

''Thanks. Look, I'd better not keep you talking any

more. Why don't you take tea up for Wilhedra while you're about it, and a cup for yourself? She's got some cookies we brought her. Nice to talk with you, Norah.''

Dittany waited till the maid had clumped up the stairs with the tray then made her call. "Osbert, get Sergeant MacVicar and the Scottsbeck police with a search warrant and come straight to the Thorbisher-Freeps'. Quick, before Arethusa's perfume wears off. I've got to go.''

Jenson would smell a rat if she didn't get into her car and drive off. Osbert and the troops couldn't be here in much less than half an hour anyway. She made a quick trip to the nearest grocery store, then parked down the street from the mansion and waited.

She was eating an apple out of the grocery bag when the official Lobelia Falls police car drew up beside her. Osbert was at the wheel wearing his deputy badge on his parka, Sergeant MacVicar in uniform beside him wearing a grim and Scottish expression. Right on their tail was a delegation from the Scottsbeck police, the officer in charge waving a search warrant.

"Noo then, lass," said Sergeant MacVicar, "what's up?''

"Jenson Thorbisher-Freep's broke to the wide. He's pawned the family jewels to pay for a big insurance policy on Carolus Bledsoe's life, bought a new box of .38 cartridges the wrong color and repainted the wads to match the old ones. He set a tripline on the back stairs to take Wilhedra out of commission and lied to us about the maid so that we'd get stuck with Carolus instead of him. Good enough to go on?''

"Aye, good enough, Hoots awa', lads!''

"You'd better let me go in first," said Dittany. "I've got the groceries.''

"What's she talking about?" demanded the Scottsbeck officer in charge.

"I dinna ken," Sergeant MacVicar replied. "But dinna fash yoursel'. Lead on, Dittany.''

She was just in time. Jenson had Arethusa bent backward over a caseful of old theater programs and was panting words of passion straight out of Elinor Glyn at her.

Arethusa was panting back, "Unhand me, sirrah!" but

Jenson was obviously in no unhanding mood. Dittany had spied a handsome black umbrella with a heavy silver handle in the stand by the front door. She whizzed back and got it.

"Unhand her, sirrah!"

By way of emphasis, she brought the silver handle down as hard as she could on his flowing white mane. The mane came off.

"A wig, by my halidom! So, blackguard, even your hair is false." Even in the midst of trying to rearrange her woefully disheveled garments, Arethusa was right there with the mot juste.

"Madam, you wrong me."

Jenson began sidling toward a different case wherein lay a dagger that Sarah Siddons probably hadn't seen before her when she played Lady Macbeth. Dittany sprang between him and the dagger. She was using the umbrella tip like a rapier to fend him away when Osbert bounded into the room, followed by Sergeant MacVicar and about half the Scottsbeck police force.

"Aha!" cried Osbert. "We've got him on assault already."

"Attempted ravishment, ninny," his aunt corrected. "The caitiff cur was trying to work his scurvy will on me."

"She lured me on," Jenson shrieked.

Without that gorgeous white hair, he was no alluring figure. Arethusa on the other hand, flushed and disheveled in the accepted regency romance tradition, her jetty locks astream, her noble bosom aheave, and her lustrous orbs even more unfathomable than usual, was a knockout. The officer in charge, who'd up to now seemed more than a bit disconcerted at the prospect of having to pinch the neighborhood aristocrat, leaped gallantly to her side and faced the now wigless bigwig without so much as a nervous twitch.

"Jenson Thorbisher-Freep, I arrest you on a charge of attempted ravishment and I guess a lot of other stuff but we'll get to that later. We have a search warrant here and we're going to search, so why don't you just put your hair back on and go quietly out to the wagon with Officer

Knudsen here as soon as he gets the handcuffs untangled from his belt?''

The old actor recognized a cue when one was fed him. ''You'll never take me alive!'' he bellowed.

But they did, of course.

Chapter 22

"My stars and garters," Dittany remarked, "this has been quite a day."

They'd left Norah fixing a hearty late lunch out of groceries Dittany had bought. Wilhedra didn't need their company any longer. Leander Hellespont was with her, spouting Shakespeare by the ream and laying his modest but perfectly genuine fortune at her feet. They were going to get married as soon as Wilhedra's ankle was well enough so she could walk down the aisle without her crutch. Wilhedra didn't appear much bothered by the circumstance that her father wouldn't be free to give her away.

Carolus Bledsoe had been told the whole story. He was naturally relieved to learn he was no longer in danger of being shot, poisoned, or snakebitten; but it was finding out he'd been jilted by Wilhedra that had set off the fireworks. Antibiotics to the contrary notwithstanding, he'd raised such a ruckus about toasting the bride-to-be that Osbert had finally broken down and mixed him a stiff hot whiskey and lemon. After a brief but raucous period of celebration, Carolus had settled down to sleep it off.

Sergeant MacVicar was still in Scottsbeck, helping the police there wrap up the evidence. They'd found the insurance policies in Jenson's heavy old cast-iron safe, which they'd opened with a bent hairpin. With Norah's all too willing assistance, they'd located the box of wad-cutter bullets, several with their tops painted in various shades of red, behind the beam where she'd watched her employer stash them.

Behind another beam they'd found a couple of stink bombs like the ones that had rendered the old opera house unusable. Wilhedra had been able to cast some light on her father's motive for that outrage, though naturally she hadn't realized then what his random remarks had portended. He'd been concerned whether the Scottsbeck police might be clever enough to discover who'd rigged the so-called accident with the Smith & Wesson by which he'd expected to collect Carolus Bledsoe's life insurance. That comic-opera Scot (Jenson's very words) in Lobelia Falls, with his puny force of two young sprouts and one old coot, would surely present no threat to the success of his plan.

The comic-opera Scot had been the one to discover the venomous stuff Jenson had smeared on the rat trap, as well as the black wig and the mustache with curly ends he'd worn impersonating Andy McNaster when he stole the cobra. The Scottsbeck police got the credit for tracking down the messenger whom an elderly man wearing an obviously bogus black wig and curly mustache had hired to deliver a box of flowers to the Monk residence late Sunday morning. They'd made Jenson put on the wig and mustache and the messenger had unhesitatingly picked him out from among several other similarly wigged and mustached elderly men in a police lineup.

Wilhedra had even identified the florist's box. It was one Leander Hellespont had sent her on Valentine's Day, filled with calla lilies and stephanotis. Her father had snatched it away in a well-feigned rage, leaving fingerprints on the shiny cardboard that had somehow survived the subsequent mishandling. He'd claimed he was going to throw the flowers in the garbage. Instead, he'd wrapped them in red tissue paper left over from some earlier Christmas and carried them to Arethusa as an unsubtle hint of his matrimonial intentions.

More than the peanut butter sandwiches he'd made her eat while he was gorging with Arethusa on filet mignon, more than the fishline he'd tripped her with, more than the tarantula she now suspected him of having hidden in her mink muff until he saw his chance to put it on Carolus's

back, more than all his other rogueries put together, it was
this misappropriation of her beloved Leander's floral tribute that had impelled Jenson's daughter to testify so dam-
ningly against him. He was working up a King Lear act in
the hope of copping an insanity plea, but he wasn't fooling
Sergeant MacVicar any.

He hadn't fooled Deputy Monk to any significant degree, either. "I'd been thinking it must be either Jenson or
Hellespont," Osbert confessed, "because the shootout, the
cobra, and the poisoned rat trap, not to mention that
tarantula at the airport, reminded me so much of plots
from old melodramas."

"Not very good melodramas, i' faith," Arethusa scoffed.
"None of them worked."

"Yes, that's the factor the would-be murderer over-
looked." Osbert could have added that none of Arethusa's
plots would have worked, either, but he was feeling strangely
mellow and protective toward his aunt at the moment.

"Theoretically any of his tricks except the tarantula
might have done the job," he conceded, "but they required an element of luck he hadn't counted on and didn't
get. What confused me was that Hellespont's too skinny to
have impersonated Andy and I couldn't figure out what
Jenson's motive might be when he seemed so dad-blanged
set on Wilhedra's marrying Carolus."

"He probably would have waited till they were married," said Dittany, "if Carolus hadn't happened to sit
next to Arethusa on that airplane. Jenson could see Carolus
succumbing to her siren wiles and getting ready to ditch
Wilhedra, so he had to act while his story was still plausi-
ble. Besides, he was determined to get Arethusa for himself. And to think it all started over a packet of smoked
peanuts! I suppose until Carolus met you, Arethusa,
Wilhedra Thorbisher-Freep looked to him like a fairly
juicy proposition. Jenson must have had Carolus thoroughly convinced that he'd be getting his hands on the old
man's money just when Andy McNaster had practically
reformed him out of business and his ex-wife was in the
process of taking him to the cleaners."

"I expect it was Jenson's taking out that policy on
Wilhedra with Carolus as beneficiary that clinched the

deal,'' Osbert agreed. "Jenson must have planned on murder right from the beginning, knowing he could bully
Wilhedra into turning the insurance over to him, the old
brute! Still, I must say I'm a bit surprised a downy duck
like Carolus would be sucker enough to fall for his scheme.''

"Carolus may have had his own ideas about Wilhedra's
insurance,'' Dittany pointed out. "I wonder how long the
bride would have survived the honeymoon.''

"Alas, poor Wilhedra,'' sighed Arethusa. "She was
only a bird in a gilded cage. However all's well that ends
well, as Mr. Hellespont has no doubt reminded her by
now. Od's fish, whatever do you suppose has happened to
Archie and Daniel?''

"They went off some place with Andy,'' Osbert told
her. "Archie was pretty sore about going, though naturally
he couldn't say so. He'd planned to corner Daniel in my
office and wrestle a contract for Dangerous Dan out of
him, then drag you off to lunch at some secluded rendez-
vous and blow his commission on gourmet pizza and
imported beer.''

"And why not, forsooth? He still could,'' Arethusa said
notwithstanding the fact that she'd just polished off an
ample though somewhat eclectic meal here in the Monks'
kitchen and it was already getting on toward teatime because they'd been so late coming back from Scottsbeck.

"I suppose we ought to stir our stumps and clear the
table,'' Dittany observed with no great enthusiasm.

"And I should get back to work,'' said Osbert.

"Moi aussi," said Arethusa.

But none of them did anything. They were still sitting
around the table rehashing the events of the day when the
missing men drove up in Andy McNaster's baby-blue
Lincoln. Daniel was triumphant, Archie bemused. Andy
gave the impression of having recently swallowed a bolt of
lightning.

"What's up?'' was Archie's greeting.

"Jenson Thorbisher-Freep,'' Osbert told him. "He's up
on a charge of attempted murder.''

He, Dittany, and Arethusa all began explaining together
the startling events of the morning. The others listened
politely enough, but not even Andy appeared to be taking

in much of their narrative. Especially not even Andy. Dittany noticed first.

"What's the matter with you three? Did you all eat something bad for lunch?"

"It's me," Andy blurted.

"What about you?"

"He signed me."

"That's right," crowed Daniel. "I signed him."

"It's true," Archie confirmed. "We signed him."

"To what, forsooth?" demanded Arethusa.

"Are you kidding?" Daniel's little black eyes were gleaming like fireflies on a July night. "Doesn't it hit you like a ton of bricks? Doesn't it stick out like a sore thumb? I'm telling you, that man's a born villain."

"Huh," sniffed Dittany. "Everybody in Lobelia Falls has been saying that for years. Before he reformed, I mean. No offense, Andy."

"That's okay," he assured her. "I don't mind any more having my crummy past thrown up to me. It was a necessary phase in my development as an actor, Daniel says."

"And the result is worth every bit of skulduggery he ever pulled," cried the famous producer. "He's going to be the classiest rotter since George Sanders."

Andy turned pleading eyes toward Arethusa. "It's for you I'm doing it, eh. You do understand?"

"In a word," she replied, "no. Unless perchance by George Sanders you mean the late star of stage and screen signalized by his sneering and cynical portrayals of sophisticated scoundrels?"

"That's the guy. And I'm going to be another him, Daniel says. How's this for a sophisticated and cynical sneer?"

"Disgusting! Repellent! Unspeakably revolting! Andrew, you'll be magnificent. With a sneer like that, you'll have the world at your feet."

"And you, Arethusa? What to me the footlights, the spotlights, the plaudits of the crowd, the smear of the greasepaint, the adoration of the millions? When I sneer, my sneer shall be only for you."

"Why, thank you, Andrew. And I shall think of you sneering your way to stardom midst the plaudits of the crowd and the smearing of the greasepaint whilst I sit alone in my cozy office with my cat Rudolph snoring peacefully by my side. I'm already six weeks behind on *The Duchess and the Dastard* and can't wait to get back to it.''

"You won't be over at the inn playing footsies with Carolus Bledsoe?"

"La, sir, perish the thought. Carolus Bledsoe will be elsewhere.''

"Where elsewhere?"

"Somewhere east of Suez where the best is like the worst appears to be what he has on the agenda. He was making a good deal of noise about it shortly before he finished his toddy and dropped off to sleep. That was after he found out it was Jenson who'd been assassinating him off and on for the past month or so and that Wilhedra had bestowed her heart and hand upon another. Carolus mentioned Mandalay as his ultimate port of call, if memory serves me.''

"That's just about how far I'd have picked to send him myself," Andy grunted. Then a noble thought struck him and he soared above such petty jealousy, as a rising rotter should.

"Say, Dittany, how's about I drive Charlie over to the inn and let them take care of him till he's back on his feet, eh? He can have the room I use, being as how it looks as if I won't be wanting it for a while. I'll let him borrow Thusie for company and that waitress they call Petsy can bring him his meals and stuff. You know, the one with all the so forth.''

The lascivious leer that accompanied these last words sent Daniel into convulsions of ecstasy. "Look at that! Isn't he incredible? All my years in showbiz, I've never run across anybody with more different kinds of nasty looks in his repertoire. I've been watching him ever since I got here and so far I haven't seen him leer the same way twice.''

"So that's why you've been tagging after Andy like Ethel stalking a woodchuck?" said Dittany.

"Why else? He makes me feel like a prospector who went out to buy a hamburger and stumbled into a gold mine.

By the way,'' he murmured into Dittany's ear alone, ''I hope your aunt isn't too—er—what I mean is, Andy's going to see a lot of new faces, if you catch my drift.''

''Not to worry. Arethusa will adjust.''

She turned to the natural-born villain. ''Andy, you're an absolute angel, if you'll forgive the expression, for taking Carolus off our hands. But do you really think you can trust him with Thusie? I personally wouldn't want to see any cobra of mine at the mercy of a sidewinder like him.''

''What Dittany means,'' said Osbert firmly, ''is that Thusie ought to be in the snake house at the zoo, where she'll have a chance to socialize with congenial reptiles and enjoy the admiration of all beholders.''

''Gee, yeah,'' Andy had to agree. ''If I'm going to be a star, why should I begrudge Thusie her share of glory? But I'm going to miss her.''

''Ah, you'll meet lots of reptiles in showbiz,'' Daniel consoled him. ''Not to rush you, Andy, but shouldn't you get on with selling your construction company, subletting your apartment, and all that? We have to be at Stratford first thing tomorrow morning, and Archie ought to get back to his office so he can draw up your official contract.''

''And we still haven't settled the contract for *Dangerous Dan*,'' Archie reminded the producer. ''Osbert, you and I have to talk.''

What with holding conferences and unloading a drunken convalescent who'd have preferred to stay and recite ''Danny Deever'' to Arethusa while drinking a few more of Osbert's toddies, they had a busy time of it for quite a while. At last, however, the Monks were alone. Dittany had left all her groceries at Wilhedra's, as it would have seemed chintzy not to under the circumstances, so there was very little left to eat in the house. Still, the thought of going out to dinner didn't appeal to any of them.

''It'll have to be beans on toast, then, with bread and jam for dessert.''

''Wonderful, darling,'' said Osbert. ''I can't think of anything I'd like better.''

Dittany warmed up the beans, Arethusa reset the table. Osbert picked up the whiskey bottle and found just three fingers' worth in the bottom, as Carolus had refused to budge without a last toddy for the road. He shared out what was left into three tot glasses and passed it around as they sat down to their simple repast.

"Here's to us, and to heck with showbiz."

"I'll drink to that," said Arethusa, and did.

"Just think, Auntie dear," he said. "This is the first time since you got back from being crowned reigning queen of regency romance that you haven't got some goggle-eyed loon sprawled at your feet offering to stand you a pizza."

Arethusa's fathomless orbs grew lustrous with tears of joy. "My dearest nephew," she replied in a tone like that lost chord which linked all perplexed meanings into one perfect peace, "that is the most beautiful thing you've ever said to me. Now would you kindly quit hogging those mustard pickles, i' faith, and pass them along to the queen?"